To my dearest Karin
on the occassion of our
first Christmas in Australia

Much Love

Your

B.H.S

Elderslie, Camden NSW 1995

GW00630995

# THE GRASS SISTER

## GILLIAN MEARS

ALFRED A. KNOPF
SYDNEY 1995

# THE GRASS
# SISTER

An Alfred A. Knopf title
published by
Random House Australia Pty Ltd
20 Alfred Street, Milsons Point, NSW 2061

Sydney   New York   Toronto
London   Auckland   Johannesburg
and agencies throughout the world

First published in 1995
Copyright © Gillian Mears 1995

National Library of Australia
Cataloguing-in-Publication Data

Mears, Gillian.
  The grass sister.

  ISBN 0 09 183121 0.
  I. Title.
A823.3

Designed by Yolande Grey
Typeset by Midland Typesetters, Maryborough
Printed by Griffin Paperbacks, Adelaide
Production by Vantage Graphics, Sydney

For Peter and Sheila

I believe that always, or almost always, in all childhoods and in all the lives that follow them, the mother represents madness. Our mothers always remain the strangest, craziest people we've ever met. Lots of people say, 'My mother was insane— I say it and I mean it. Insane.'
People laugh a lot at the memory of their mothers. I suppose it is funny.

*PRACTICALITIES*
MARGUERITE DURAS

## ACKNOWLEDGEMENTS

This book was written with the assistance of
fellowships from the Literature Board of the Australia
Council and the NSW Ministry of the Arts. The
Marten Bequest Travelling Scholarship enabled me to
travel in Africa in 1990 and it was in the Keesing
Studio in Paris in 1992 that much of the first draft
was written. This support is gratefully acknowledged.

Two sections of the book appeared in early draft
form in *Scripsi* and *The Malahat Review*.

Material from *Practicalities* by Marguerite Duras
is reprinted with the permission of HarperCollins
Publishers Ltd; material from *Cry the Beloved Country*
is reprinted with permission of the Estate of the author
and Jonathan Cape.

I would like to thank the following people: Liz
Ashburn for allowing me three months at 'Cooroonya';
Sonya Giles for a corner for my caravan in her garden;
Karin Murphy and Susan Hampton for reading the early
drafts; and Jane Palfreyman of Random House.

My heartfelt thanks to Drusilla Modjeska for her
patience and editorial energy.

## CHAPTER ONE

'Hush your mouth,' says Lavinia, though I haven't been talking. 'Hush your mouth,' she murmurs and holds me close. I think for a moment about this expression Lavinia always uses in such a chiding, affectionate voice whenever it's time for me to get back to the farm. Quieten your mouth, I think, would be a so much harsher way of saying the same thing. Or silence your mouth. Shut your mouth. Shut up. But there is nothing harsh about Lavinia. She is the community nurse at Redclack. I can tell that she was never a horse rider. Her skin is too smooth, too unda-maged. No open-necked shirts ever let a hot day on the plateau burn spots and freckles onto this white skin.

It is an April afternoon and I'm afraid that in its cold light, Lavinia will be shocked by the way the skin is aging around my eyes, by what is happening to my throat immediately underneath my chin. I tuck my face into her neck. My toes are cold and arched away from Lavinia so they can't startle her own warm legs.

'I have to go,' I say, not wanting to. 'I said I'd help Ally with the tree house.' The other day, she was leaning out the car window saying, It smells of fresh air! It smells like the tops of trees. 'I'll never leave if you keep doing that Lavinia,' I whisper, tapping away her hand.

'Ssshh,' Lavinia takes my hands in hers and holding them cupped to her mouth, blows them warm with her breath. 'Tomorrow,' she says, 'I'll show you how to look after Iris Michaelhouse's feet.'

'Once I took my mother for a foot massage, when she was sick,' I feel my face go stiff with painful memories. 'She hated the experience. Do you really think old people like their feet being touched?' Already I am wishing I hadn't agreed to this idea. It will, I think, be worse than working in the library, requiring as much patience as the oldest borrower needing help to read her large print romance. Compared to Lavinia, I realise, I had no patience when I used to work at the Romance Library by the Sea. Tramps came into the toilets to pull at their beards in the mirror and I would herd them out as if they were cattle. Nor did I feel much tolerance for the aged borrowers with names now found mainly in cemeteries. There were women of all shapes and sizes who brought in badly-iced butter cakes or immaculate biscuits, depending on their skills, or the most beautiful roses from their gardens with heart-shaped petals and crimson and cold hips. Marguerite Rawlings, senior librarian, would have endless kindness for our borrowers. Whereas I'd view any request as an imposition on my time, and hide out in the office eating the treats they'd cooked for Marguerite, sketching like the wild artist I imagined I was becoming, Marguerite would be leading them on by their elbows to new authors they might like to try.

'Isn't it a bit invasive? Foot massages are so personal.'

'Not at all,' Lavinia says. 'Human touch is what they crave. And if they're bedridden, then it's essential. Otherwise the feet curl up. They become all soft and perished. As if, I sometimes think, it's possible in a lifetime to actually walk your feet away.'

'Will they smell?'

'Not Iris'. She still manages a bath for herself every morning. She's so excited that it's going to be you. I've been suggesting various volunteers for years. But she's very fussy. She always ends up asking them not to come back.' Lavinia waves her hands. 'I'm sure you'll find her feet are fine to work with. The main thing really with Iris is to keep her toenails short. They've been catching in the carpet. Tripping her up. She broke two toes last year.'

'No foot could be as smelly as a horse with seedy toe in its hoof,' I say, trying to persuade myself, trying to battle the sleepiness that comes from not sleeping all night, the warmth of Lavinia sliding over me, the rug falling off, my eyes shutting anyway.

When I wake up, Lavinia's moving around the kitchen, heating milk in the orange saucepan. One of the cats is sitting on the counter, watching the wooden spoon moving through the milk.

'You must've been dreaming,' she says.

'How long was I asleep?'

'Less than half an hour but you were twitching like a creature.'

'I think I did dream.'

'What?'

'Oh,' I wave my hand. 'Nothing. I'd better go.' I sit up on the couch.

'Feet tomorrow still?'

'Well, I'm not sure. It might be upsetting.' I bend down to pull on my boots. 'I haven't seen Iris since Ann-Clare's memorial service. My boots are work boots, ugly and old, with hand-stitched repairs from where the axe went through the left toe. I scuff at a patch of leather which has lost all semblance of polish. Ann-Clare was once caned by the headmaster of Lindley Central School for wearing boots not shoes to school. I heard my sister being marched towards the headmaster's office. I heard her green-hide soles on the verandah and looked out of my classroom window. There was no helping Ann-Clare. Mr May strapped Ann-Clare three times. When she came back past the classroom window I saw the red marks and that her boots were gone: in their place, a pair of gigantic black lace-ups from out of Lost Property. In Africa I think Ann-Clare must have remembered that headmaster. As she unlaced her walking boots and left them on the rock above the waterfall maybe it was of Mr May she was thinking, not me. Of Mr May lifting up the hem of her skirt. The freckles on his bald head as he flicked the cane.

'Except, Able . . . ' says Lavinia.

'Hmmm?'

'You'll have to dress up a little bit more than you do.'

'I'm not wearing a dress. As far as I remember Iris

was never interested in the heights of elegance. I'm quite clean.'

'I know that.' Lavinia sits next to me and examines the sunspots on my hands. 'Iris probably couldn't care less what you wear.'

'Yes,' I agree.

'Yes,' she says, laughing at the way my hair has tufted up on one side of my head. It is jaunty, she says, this bit of errant hair, like a little grass or emu wren's tail. 'Able?' Lavinia calls, bringing me back when I am halfway to the car.

'What?' I say, cavorting just a little for Lavinia, as I return to the garden gate.

Lavinia touches my cheek with her tongue. 'A lick and a promise,' she says, shooing me away then, saying 'Ally's tree house. Ally's tree house,' a small portion of the sunset seemingly trapped behind her tiny ears as a red-orange glow inside which I could warm my mouth.

A large herd of cows filling the road when I'm halfway home from Redclack means I must drive slowly. The young man in shorts who follows them is barefoot. He is fat and pallid but his bare feet are so fissured with black cracks they resemble a type of espadrille. Henrietta. All Cream. All Cream Two. I watch the swaying udders.

In my dream, my sister's face is blank. Each time she speaks, I check her face. But I can't read the meaning behind her stories. In this recurring dream I always wave my hands up and down, up and down, not a foot away from her face, trying to gain her attention and she never seems to notice. Ann-Clare, Ann-Clare?

The young man with the bad heel cracks raises his arm and grunts at me as I edge past. I grunt back. I am past all but a few of the front cows when I catch sight of the old cat woman of Redclack, moving down the laneway from the pink farmhouse on the left. Nine cats move behind her as if strung on a line. She moves without shame in the direction of her letterbox. One paddock has recently been ploughed, but the next one is bright with potatoes or weeds. This pattern is repeated and repeated as far as the eye can see, along and across the rolling hills, giving the effect that the land has been home-upholstered in warm red and virulent green stripes. Against the chill of the afternoon, the old lady holds a small blanket at her throat as a type of makeshift poncho. The letterbox has been blown by years of wind to lie almost parallel to the ground in the way of an alpine tree. She'll have to stoop to see if there is any mail. I drive slowly behind the last cow. The old lady becomes crafty. She begins to dawdle, pretending to survey the decrepit fence that wood-turners from other towns are always asking to buy because it was cut from red cedar over a hundred years ago. She picks an autumn leaf, hiding her face behind the trunk of the liquid-ambar. Some of the cats sit down and lick themselves. I think for a moment she's going to turn back altogether but as I move past the cow and accelerate, she too speeds up again, the cats resume their line, and before I have rounded the bend, I am able to see in my side mirror, the way she cautiously lifts up the

lid of her letterbox. The letterbox is empty. A finger
goes up to her mouth and I feel like weeping. It is
so sad, this lack of letters underneath the cold grey
sky, the cows moving past her, not as much comfort
in all the pendulous swing of their udders as there
would've been in a little fat envelope from an old
friend or a slender card of greeting from a sister who
has left the Lindley Plateau years before.

I also wait too hard for my letters.

I hide in the undergrowth, watching the road
through a gap in the foliage, for like the cat woman
of Redclack, I don't want my need to be so exposed.

Along one of the roads which run west from the
plateau, I sometimes see a lone woman who knows
no such restraint. She is young I think, no more than
twenty, and new to the district. She reads her mail as
she walks. She weaves on and off the gravelled track,
almost giving an impression of mid-morning inebri-
ation. Her feet, in very bright socks, slip across the
leather of the Grecian-type sandals she wears. Once
it seemed she'd almost fall over but the pages of the
letter fluttered her upright again as if they were small
wings grown from her hands. It seemed a shameful
thing somehow. I felt ashamed for the girl. She didn't
know her need was so naked in front of a stranger-
woman driving past. Or she didn't care.

I suspect my own eagerness on the track to the
mailbox tips my whole body forward so that my head
juts from my neck and my bottom pokes out in my
efforts to see in advance the box and what's in it: the
whole effect, I imagine, is incongruous, as if I'm

wearing an outlandish old dress with my boots and winter socks.

The mail holds the most tricks about a month before Christmas. My father tells Ally she can open the cards. There will always be a smattering of black nativity scenes with Africans as wise men on the cards sent by those supporting an institute of race relations, as well as the more usual kinds of images. My father barely seems to read the letters folded inside the cards. I really don't think he does any more. Each Christmas it seems to me that the way he glances over them becomes more and more cursory. In the time his gaze is on the page he couldn't possibly have read all the information being given. The envelopes covered in antelope or other animal stamps are, without fail, the early Christmas letters from Africa—full of news and chat about sons and daughters and grandchildren who mean nothing to me or whom I might've met in the blur of the time my father and I spent in Zimbabwe and South Africa. The handwriting is unknown. Yet each year I still cannot prevent the sudden feeling that I am holding in my hand a letter from my sister, or someone known to my sister, or who knows of my sister's whereabouts.

I think this, even with the knowledge of the certificate in a compartment of my mother's desk. Wherever the word death occurs a typist has run a row of five letter $x$'s in lower case. Because there was no body, it is a Certificate of Disappearance. It is of a fine, crisp paper, like decrepitating airmail paper when held lightly between two hands.

Someone, at some stage, has been smoking over it because there is a small cigarette burn in its lower left corner. The typist, I have always supposed, was the smoker. The typist who hit the space bar instead of the *s* when writing misadventure next to the apparent cause of my sister's absence. So it reads, Mi adventure. Although I have written in the missing *s* I cannot help thinking, My adventure in Africa, whenever I look at the certificate.

I imagine the typist was young and careless and much more intent upon looking attractive to Mrs Pluke than upon what he was typing. He would've been smoking and using only his left hand to type.

Mrs Pluke, not Mr Dilley, handed the certificate to my father. Her skin was as flawless as a fresh blackberry. I remembered Ann-Clare and the horses. Dark purple froth around their bits when we fed them the blackberries. 'I am so sorry to have to give you this,' Mrs Pluke was saying.

My father was also apologising.

'I'm terribly sorry,' said my father, wiping his face with a handkerchief. 'I'll be all right in a minute.'

The certificate has been folded about twenty times. I know this though I rarely look at it, because I watched my father doing so. In this way my father, in Africa, making the certificate smaller and smaller in his fingers as I counted the folds, unwittingly made it resemble some kind of game; a paper and pen game two sisters might force each other to play on a day so wet, going outside was impossible. My father tucked the certificate into his wallet and walked outside, saying again to me that he wished I'd worn something a little bit more respectable.

'Or a bit of makeup.'

'I don't have makeup.'

'You could've packed some of Alana's,' he said, referring to our mother.

'We threw out all of her lipsticks and powders. Ann-Clare and I decided to because neither of us would ever have worn them. I don't like makeup,' I repeated, my riding boots slipping on the parquet-floor corridor past some fumigated cockroaches. 'I don't think it matters. It shouldn't matter, Dad.' But he was crying again. When I looked sideways at him, I saw an old man, as sad looking as Mr Pearl who lost Mrs Pearl in my fourth year at the Romance Library and who in all his attempts to remember his wife had decided to read every book she had ever borrowed. My father's lips were shaking and the tears, which were little, weren't following any particular wrinkle down his face.

As far as I know my father only brought the certificate from Mutare out again to put it into the smallest compartment of Alana's desk when we were back in Australia. But by then it was too late. The creases that had formed like a grid over the typed details are set for good and won't be ironed out. The fragility of the whole document seems to be increasing. In places, the paper has even begun to tear along certain crease lines as if someone is surely in the frequent habit of unfolding and then refolding the certificate. Over and over again the unknown fingers must have been doing this for I'm sure the paper has deteriorated. Only occasionally do I open up the tiny drawer by its delicately-turned knob to look down on the certificate. When I showed Lavinia the other day, she said that in its little drawer, the paper looked like a tiny white and black blanket, waiting for its make-believe baby. I found I couldn't bring myself to disagree; that I couldn't voice aloud my belief that in fact the certificate lies waiting for the day when my sister decides, for reasons she will tell me in her own good time, that she has disappeared for long enough. Then I will lead Ann-Clare to the drawer, laughing. And my daughter, whom she has never met, will be holding onto her other hand, also laughing, as she sees how alike, as I've always promised, I really am to my little sister.

In the expectation of Ann-Clare's possible return from Africa, or at the very least, a long letter filling me in on years of news, I long resisted reading her correspondences or sifting through her possessions the way you do after someone has died. But now I sit each day at my mother's desk as I imagine a biographer would do. Only after seven years of not hearing a word have I begun to seek her in every memory, thinking that if the right one will float free, it might yield something important. That like a map or a chart, I'll sense her whereabouts by turning the memory around and around in my mind, looking out the window every now and then to compare its details to the landscape.

My father continues to disagree with trying to

read all the old mail in the house. In the evenings he pours wine and then recorks the bottle, as if this will encourage abstinence. 'My love,' he suggests, 'can anything really be gained?' And points out the effects alcohol, tiredness and bad handwriting may have during both the reading and the writing of the letters. 'Alana,' he says, 'wrote some very strange letters to me when she was tipsy.'

I reply that a drunken note may contain more truth than a constrained and sober letter.

He won't read any of the old letters I offer. For much longer than I've been reading letters, he has been thinking about the native grasses and soil types of cemeteries. At first he concentrated his thoughts on our farm's cemeteries but lately a series of journeys have taken him west over the ranges. He says that to dig your hand into the soil of a cemetery that has never been grazed is like digging your hand into Alana's vegetable garden when it was at its most productive. The soil is full of air and vegetable matter and worms. This, he insists, isn't because of the bodies but because the cemeteries have by and large been ungrazed and undisturbed by other farming practices. Using a hand lens, he studies the secretive flowers of grasses he finds tucked away behind headstones.

Into any small cemetery where stock have been allowed, he carries handfuls of dung beetles. He will elaborate at large upon the wild chocolate scent of lilies found next to the grave of a Miss Susan Apple as he bent to release a beetle.

How to publish the significance of undisturbed

native pastures occurring in small Australian bush cemeteries, is something my father occasionally thinks about. His jottings float around the house on notepads with tea stains, or are washed away in the pocket of his shirts or shorts.

My father has also taken up his painting again. He begins studies of grassy slopes and the lights over them, noting down the presence of Old World grasses and other variables that might change the colours of a slope. From his sketches it appears he has every intention of finishing what he has begun. However, within a few days, the picture has been abandoned, the foreground never detailed, and I'll almost certainly come across him in a paddock, beginning a new sketch onto a fresh watercolour block. He tries to finish his pictures at night, tempted by long stretches of sleeplessness, even though he knows that in the morning he will look with amazement at how considerable has been the damage inflicted. I in turn am amazed at the damage he wreaks on my paints which he borrows. He is lavish in the way he squeezes them out, and worse than Ally in putting the caps back without care, blue caps on red tubes of paint and vice versa.

When we came back from Africa, he said death was just like grass. I find I'm unable either to remember his explanation or to come up with my own. And if that analogy holds true, then is there one for disappearance and seven years' silence? I think about grass that grows like pale sticks through the slats of old floors, with which Ann-Clare fashioned her own bird nests. Or does my father mean grass that has died?: the long dead strands of kikuyu attached to the tails of the horses in winter? Or there is the kind of grass which grows on roofs, such as the one Ally was conceived under at Umli. I think maybe Ann-Clare was like that, blighted before grown.

I must ask my father again exactly what it was he meant about grass and death. During her illness our mother ironed handkerchiefs furiously, listening to something strident and punishing by Stenhammer, blocking the hallway with her ironing board. So that Ann-Clare who had come home to live, and I who had taken leave to help with the care of our mother, were forced into encountering her fury. But perhaps in the end, our mother's death was peaceful. If you leave a gate open by mistake while you watch the sunset, the cows file out behind you. When you turn around, the biggest impression is not of space but of silence. Alana's death was like that, I think. A whole paddock of grass, as if Alana had been waiting all along after all, for the open gate.

Whenever my father picks up any stalk of grass to chew he never fails to mention its name, scientific and common and some interesting information about the species. To open up any of the old *Agricultural Gazettes* bound in insect-eaten cloth or buckram, is to open up a kind of agricultural museum where sometimes my father is pictured, knee deep in pasture with an unfamiliar hat on his head or an unfamiliar head of black hair.

Though Ann-Clare and I grew up being told the difference between the blade shapes of paspalum and that of kikuyu, it was knowledge never fully gained. I know the difference if noticing the whole plant running amuck through an old garden bed, but just the grass tips—of course he knows I'm taking a wild guess when I say paspalum.

So that recently I've made a point of learning off by heart the scientific name of Natal Top Red grass. *Rhyncheletrum repens*—the roll of it off the tongue almost as lovely as it looks along an empty roadside, the late sun turning it silver. It's the feathery grass our father always added to arrangements of flowers he gathered from other people's gardens for our mother, in Africa. And it is the grass that likes to grow at the gates of Australian cemeteries.

Am I imagining that the language my father uses in his descriptions of grasses becomes increasingly the language of poetry rather than science? When I suggest this to him, he points out that many pasture and grass books are full of elaborate and prosy entries for this or for that grass and the soil where it likes to grow. The earliest grass scientists sent by the Plant Exploration Society to Africa and South America were poets, he says, concerned with capturing in a limited number of words, the most delicate curves or softest hairs. My father also tells me that it was the descriptive powers of certain novelists writing about Africa's grasses which made him want to work with soil and pastures.

One night, warning us that he might cry, a torn first edition of Alan Paton's *Cry the Beloved Country* is in his hands. Pages float free of their broken spine. Instead of finding what he's looking for though, he finds descriptions of the trains of his childhood and the magic of wattle estates just like the ones his father managed.

'The train passes through a world of fancy,' he reads, 'and you can look through the misty panes at green shadowy banks of grass and bracken. Here in their season grow the blue agapanthus, the wild watsonia, and the red-hot poker, and now and then it happens that one may glimpse an arum in a dell. And always behind them the dim wall of the wattles, like ghosts in the mist.'

'It's past Ally's bedtime.'

'Oh hang on, just one more minute,' my father flicks pages. He curls his toes up and down. My daughter sits in my lap, almost asleep but listening. 'The train gathered way, to creep along the ridges of the hills, to hang over steep valleys, to pass the bracken and the flowers, to enter the darkness of the wattle plantations, past Stainton, down into Ixopo.'

When my father stops reading, he doesn't seem to realise he hasn't mentioned grass. He is a beautiful reader. Up until the age of eight, he spoke more Zulu than English and there is a resonance of that language in his voice. He wipes his tears away using a much-crinkled serviette which he finds in a drawer of the sideboard, and it is Lavinia who goes over to my father, who puts an arm around him as comfort. It is Ally and Lavinia who hush him as I stand by, stiffly unable to do so. Because her grandfather is crying, Ally begins to cry too making me fear that Ann-Clare's ability to imagine patterns in anything will also be Ally's, who already sees pictures in the drop-pings left on an old dog-kennel roof by an evening kookaburra. And because Ally's skin is dark and gleams, I can see she tries even harder than we did, if that is possible, to not be noticed. I lift her high into the sky to make her laugh, and she does. She laughs and laughs but the moment the groan of the school bus is heard coming over the crest of the hill that impassive look I know so well settles over her face. And would she be happier somewhere else I wonder, would she feel the need to be invisible any less? What if we lived in Harare or Blantyre, where her father often is, who invites us every year?

What I most want to give little Alana is noisiness. I want her to be a talker, not a listener. I try to jolly my daughter. Ally, I will wave a toy, leaving the letters or the kitchen for a moment. I want her to grow up without wanting to be hurt.

'She's not a dog,' says Lavinia.

'That's right,' says my father, and tells my daugh-ter a funny story about Ann-Clare and me, but Ally's laugh is soft and she looks at me to make sure that she has my permission, that it is still indeed a funny story; this story that she has heard about her mother so many times already. And although Ally's never been hit, not once, not a smack, nor the flat of a wooden spoon, if I make a sudden movement softly and almost imperceptibly, she'll flinch away.

'Ally!' I said to her when she last did this. 'You rat. I never hit you.'

But I could tell that the people who had come to look at the last litter of puppies thought I was lying and looked quizzically at the scabs left on her from the pups biting and scratching. And even Grandma Patricia looked up at me from her glass of wine as if to indict.

My father tells little Ally that when we were seven year olds we were very, very naughty. He tells the story of the pixie raincoats we set off wearing one wet day, only to cut them up in pieces on a grave. These are stories so told they feel quite thinned, only the bare basics left of each story's structure so that they are more than ready to disintegrate forever.

When my father was my daughter's age, he tells, he couldn't read and he didn't know his own birthday! Nonetheless he went around with an air of great certainty. Old photos show this. He wanders around lush, large gardens, a teddy bear strapped to his back in imitation of his Zulu nanny, his mother behind him, her camera raised. He has the air of ease of any rich and only child in a warm colony where his parents had far greater wealth and status than they could've dreamt of having in their home country.

Over in England in the same year, Alana's face in any photo Grandma Patricia has ever shown me is a face full of tears.

It nearly breaks my heart that the expression on my mother's seven-year-old face is the same expression that dwells on my daughter's. Even though Ally will never be put in an orphanage as her namesake was, or chased around the kitchen by a bad uncle, all the pictures I've ever taken of my daughter capture an almost identical inner melancholy. Her lips look like they are trembling and afraid, as if I have, like Patricia, strapped silver tap shoes to my child's feet, and pulled the dress down off her unwilling shoulders, as if a seven year old could have breasts, and told her to smile. If I start thinking along these lines it is very distressing.

Ally knows the photo faces and all their names. She will stare at them without comment, standing on a chair in order to be closer to their height. She will startle me in her dress made of curtain material. Her entreaties for me to check the mailbox or to meet her over at the Abandoned House in ten minutes are as soft as the finger in my hair that has made me jump.

Some chance resemblances stir so many heavy-hearted memories as I walk down for the mail, that I forget to hide us from the postman. The postman is actually an old brother and sister who drive a smelly old brown sedan. I splash through the water on the track, haunted by a run of undesirable images and associated sensations. We reach the gate just as Cletus and Merle Morgan are pulling in. He is modern enough to know his name said fast could be mistaken as clitoris, and enjoys inflicting his jokes about this upon any woman.

If anything, the sister talks more than her brother. She holds her box of cigarettes to her breasts and begins, leaving me to looking despairingly at the pale and sparse bristles growing along the line of her throat. Lavinia says she's like a bitch coming on heat, facing her desire to be liked and wibblying (one of the Morgan's favourite words) her body. Cletus, says

Lavinia, is the kind who'd have warts on his breasts from hanging over the back fence.

Merle always looks at the mail she delivers. One day after my father and I were home from Africa, she was at the gate with an air of great excitement, with an envelope which she said held Ann-Clare's handwriting. She waited for me to tear it open. Even though I had no intention of doing this in front of her, how politely we stood there chatting, the light green envelope with a row of African stamps between my fingers; my baby kicking inside me and in no way concealed by the quite extraordinary maternity gown I had found in Redclack's Anglican Clothes Shop. The way Cletus and Merle Morgan looked at my size, saying nothing. Politeness, I decided that day, was a horrible inheritance. Yet I can see it goes too far back to be fought. Sometimes I think the only reason Ann-Clare married Mr Michaelhouse was out of that same awful politeness.

'Opened under the terms of the currency and exchange control regulations,' said a stamp on the outside of the letter, somehow raising my hopes. But the letter was only from a Harare policeman who had found my sister's address book and driver's licence she'd lost on her very first day in Africa. The policeman's letter said he had found these items on the floor of the Elizabeth Hotel but not, unfortunately, the thief who had stolen her purse. When looked at again, it was clear the writing on the envelope only faintly resembled my sister's small script.

Ally hangs back from Cletus and his sister. 'Ooh she's a pretty little picanin, isn't she?' Merle Morgan likes to say. 'D'you know. I've realised now. She's the spitting image of a little black dolly I had.' At the same time they assure me that the Morgan family isn't racist, pronouncing the first part of racist to rhyme with ratio and looking at Ally as if the gate wires are in a zoo. At this point I always remember that we are standing on the spot where my sister and I once killed a black snake using the jawbone of a dead beast. Or I choose to focus on the pictures I once painted on the letterbox which so infuriated our mother, which she tried to scrub off with metho. As Cletus raves on I can look at the ghosts of black horses and women through the grains of timber. I can look down at my boots and remember that Ann-Clare and I have the same kind of large feet that suit sturdy footware not sandals.

## CHAPTER TWO

I was fourteen years old and outside it was raining hard when Ann-Clare walked out of the Abandoned House and into the evening, wearing my yellow school raincoat and a section of old shower curtain folded into a triangle over her head. This is the clearest memory I have of being responsible for my sister disappearing. Over the years of our childhood it became such a habit that previous and subsequent disappearances aren't plain in my mind. I would only have to suggest a mildly upsetting plan or insinuate something horrible and my sister went into hiding. My sister was very thin. Her ankles weren't as thick as my wrists but she could outrun cattle dogs. If I gave chase I'd soon lose sight of her and have to stand bowed over for minutes waiting for the stitch in my middle to leave. By then she could be far away, behind me not in front, having looped cunningly around. Once I heard her crying in the blackberry bush cubby, but when I bent down to see her she'd anticipated my movements and vanished out the back door. Our mother used to say my sister was like an afraid creature, wanting to get away from the beast that had inflicted the injury.

Alana's voice clearly marked me as the beast. Later, Alana would accuse me of other things too: of long-standing inconsequentiality, and, on the Sunday before she died, of casting glare into her eyes from the glasses I was wearing in order to see the words she had asked me to read. As if all her life, up until its end, my mother could only see me as a tormentor. She was full of rushing angers which acted like tides in our lives.

Sometimes when I'm trying to think of my sister, I find I'm thinking of my mother instead. I think of taking Alana for the toe massage she didn't want. I think of a wilderness filled with angry and unpredictable sunsets and sunrises. Instead of looking down into a national park and seeing campers from the Naturalist Club in old circus-style family tents, Alana looked past them and imagined wilderness women: their backward vaults through the spray of the tallest waterfalls, the great splash of their muscled thighs entering the freezing pools below. Or they would be thin-tailed figures, flying over the valleys and into hidden green glades.

When I heard our mother banging the Boer War bell with a tablespoon, I knew my sister hadn't run through the rain from me into the safety of the New House. Even though we'd lived in the house for nearly six years, it continued to be known by that name, and still is, though its smell now is of old dogs, paper and people. In the cold weather especially, it smells like the Romance Library by the

Sea on a day when it was too wild to have the windows open.

I often lift a letter to my nose to smell its paper and usually I'm surprised. For it can be the oldest letter that still smells freshly of the lavender sprig or jasmine flower also enclosed, and the recent letter on cheap paper that is already musty enough to make you sneeze.

My mother hit the bell. It was suppertime. I held my breath. I wished my sister and I were already living in the Abandoned House, our plan to become artist sisters who ran a farm already in action. The room I was standing in smelt of the wild watermelons we'd carried up the front stairs, to observe and perhaps to eat, on a later day. Nettles had forced themselves up through the gaps in the floorboards. The nettles reminded my sister of the fairytale of the seven swans. In this story, the sister of her missing brothers had to weave seven nettle cloaks by hand in order to free them from the spell that had trapped them into the shape of birds.

I looked through the thick glass of the windows for any sign of my sister. No movement, so I sped, suddenly apprehensive, through the door of the old house and out into the rain, in time to the bell's insistent rhythm.

Our mother used to hit this bell as if she could bring out a fiercer sound than its narrow tinging range, or call up children other than her own from out of the valleys. If we were very far away, instead of hearing our actual names, we heard only the sound of her English voice between the noises of the bell and spoon. Then we felt sure she was calling for the six children she used to dream of when she was an unhappy child in an orphanage after the war. Or for the baby boy she'd miscarried in Africa following a bumpy tractor ride.

The bell had been looted by Tin, our father's grandfather, from a farmhouse one afternoon during the Boer War. Whenever our father picked it up, he would wonder aloud, with a degree of guilt in his voice, about the farm woman in Africa who must have once rung it. Did Trevor Irwin Nevitt take the woman prisoner? he'd ask into the air. Or was the farmhouse already emptied except for the bell, sitting to one side of a half-finished lunch?

Whenever we had South African visitors of Dutch extraction staying, the bell and all other suspicious brass objects would be put away. Our father said this was in case they might've belonged to the grandparents of our visitor.

'Oh you are corny,' Alana would say, oblivious to the bell's history. 'Please couldn't you just fix it, so it rings again?'

'Of course I will, darling,' our father always replied, only for it never to be mended.

'I'm afraid to say that little brass bell used to be used in our house to tell the cookboy that he could bring the next course.' Our father will still tell a total stranger, or Lavinia for about the fifth time, defensively, with embarrassment. 'Well, what can I say, that's the way it was. Ooh, I'm feeling awful, aren't I?'

Inside the New House I could tell immediately my sister wasn't home. On this particular night, my parents were happy. It might've been the cosy feelings rain can evoke, or that they were well into a bottle of wine. I could hear them laughing in the kitchen, making suppositions as to our whereabouts.

I squinted outside, using my bedroom window's factory-batch numbers, which I was meant to have washed off six years before, as small frames to the farm. It seemed to me that through the triangle of a number four, I saw my sister hunching off the side verandah of the Abandoned House, in the direction of the Stinging Tree Forest. The stinging trees were all that was left of original rainforest on the two-hundred-acre farm our father bought following the death of his mother, Betty.

I was named not only after this grandmother but my other one as well. Until Patricia went paragliding in Spain, there were never any photographs of the grandmothers about the house, only stories, which hung in the air around us as warnings. I could never understand why I'd been given the names of women so disliked. My father says it was because of guilt. By the time of my birth, not only had he completely abandoned his mother, but Alana had all but washed her hands of her own. Thus my name was, if I liked to understand it in a logical light, an awkward show of conscience. It would've been better to be born a boy, I used to think bitterly. To have been called after the grandfathers, Budge and Barney, whose photographs were obviously precious, sitting on our father and mother's desks respectively, would've been a fine thing and no cause for shame.

Alana displayed the paragliding photo for about a month. In this photo you can't see Grandma's face. It's turned away and her legs are in bandages from an operation designed to alleviate her intermittent claudication. She is about fifty feet above blue Marjorcan waters but nevertheless wears a jaunty kind of air.

It used to seem strange to Ann-Clare and me that although our grandmothers both enjoyed travelling, neither of them made the journey from England to Africa for our parents' wedding. Also, not only were they not friends, but they had never met. This point was first brought home to me when as a six year old, I tried to write to them for Christmas on the same card.

At the time of my birth, Elizabeth Mabel, our father's mother, but always known as Betty, was living in hotels around Europe. She was one of the Bones from Kent, our father said. If her funny maiden name was meant to help describe the nature of her illness, it did not. Her madness was always hinted at but never properly explained and we knew it hadn't stopped her from travelling alone in a quite bold and flamboyant style. We also knew that eventually she was dishing out such large tips and gifts as she made her way around Europe, that solicitors in Plymouth advised our father to restrict her access to the estate.

Even on the smaller income, Betty continued to move around England for another six years. Reaching the Cornish tip of England where our father had left her years before, she booked into the Blue Cap Hotel. Two weeks later she hung herself from an oak tree in its garden. Such was her will to die, she lifted her knees towards her face, the branch she'd chosen being too low for her considerable height. As is common with advanced schizophrenia, her handwriting had deteriorated so enormously, the letter she left for our father was never properly deciphered.

In order for Betty's belongings to be sold or shipped, and on the strength of our father's inheritance, we immediately went as a family to England. We were then able to meet our living grandma, Patricia Avis, an alcoholic Londoner of flirtatious disposition. After this reconciliation between Alana and her mother, Patricia came to Australia every few years. With each visit came a silver charm for our bracelets, a bottle of beer shampoo and frightening fights. If this was meant to be our normal grandmother, we used to ponder, what hope had we? My sister, taller even than our father, must've inherited her height from Betty, whereas I have Grandma's much smaller build. Therefore although my sister was two years younger than me, during our childhood people would always assume the opposite.

For years I was shy about giving the exact sequence of grandmother names that my mother had strung together. Who knows, I used to brood, my name may even have contributed to Betty cutting up the first baby photographs my father sent of me, before returning them to him bit by bit, inside English aerograms. As no extra postage was ever added for the enclosures, my parents had to keep on paying out fiddly amounts of money to Lindley's postmistress to make up the shortfall. Alana said it was as if Betty had murdered her first grand-daughter and was sending pieces of my dismembered body back in the mail.

This used to pang me. Also, that apart from being called Rent-a-Car at high school, no one ever found a nickname to save me from my real name. My sister had three nicknames—Nipsy Beetle, Gnat, Splinter. The last two arose from her thinness, the first from her affection for a local and drab-coloured insect with a double-jointed body. Sometimes, in my envy, I thought of one for myself and compelled Ann-Clare to use the nickname. But although she was very obliging, these names never settled or remained. My sister would use the nickname of the moment when discussing me, and Alana would say, 'Who on earth are you talking about darling?' The inability of my mother to ever call me by the nicknames, her insistence on my real one, seemed to make them fail faster.

As if to remedy the disaster of my Christian and middle names, my mother picked two short and easy ones for her next daughter and joined them with a hyphen. Not even an *e* on the end of the Ann. It had a lovely ring to it which I seemed set to envy forever.

As I stood at the window of my bedroom watching the dark shape of the forest, my mother came to stand by my side. 'Ann-Clare's gone out into the rain,' I said. I could smell wine on my mother's breath. The air was full of fine-winged cockroaches that made my mother moan. She thought the cockroaches were flying directly from the old farmhouse about two hundred feet away, into her narrow architect-designed house. I was hoping Ann-Clare hadn't put her hand into my raincoat pocket which I knew held at least five wishbones I'd excavated from dead wild birds and forgotten to put out for the ants to clean. I was interested in how dead things looked, whereas Ann-Clare was by far the best listener to the stories told about dead people.

'What did you do to her this time?' I thought Alana was going to hit me but she only took my wrist in her hand and held it hard. She made me look at her eyes which were as sharp grey as steel. We were never hit, only at most tapped lightly over the palm with a wooden spoon we were more often in the habit of licking.

Taking my torch, my mother slammed open the sliding screen door and went outside. I ate a pretzel sitting on a plate on my bedside table. I could hear my mother calling my sister, Ann-Clare, Ann-Clare, with the stress falling on the last, beautifully simple name. Long after the torch beam disappeared, I felt their progress was in a southeasterly direction, with my sister moving faster and always ahead of the weakening torch beam. I knew it would soon fail altogether, for earlier that day I'd been wasting its batteries, sitting in my mother's wardrobe in order to look at the glider aeroplanes I'd unwrapped before Christmas. As Ann-Clare's birthday fell on Boxing Day, her Christmas presents were always superior to mine and this year was no exception. It was not the glider my sister had hoped for but nonetheless, I felt Alana or Jack had chosen Ann-Clare an above-average plane, a much more beautiful balsa-wood plane than mine, the construction of which would require my considerable assistance.

The pretzels were stale. All their salt had fallen off. My father came into the bedroom. 'What's going on?' He wanted to know and pulled down the temporary bamboo blind which had become permanent. I gave an account that explained nothing. He said that if Ann-Clare and Alana didn't turn up soon, he'd also go outside. 'We'll just give them a few more minutes,' he said, as if we were playing some kind of hide and seek. Black margins of night lay at either edge of the blind. As I heard noises of my mother and sister coming towards us, I concentrated on the resemblance the blind had to pretzels. I didn't appreciate that at this moment Rosemary Kincaid, the girl visiting from Africa, came out from my sister's bedroom to smirk at me through the door.

'Oh, Rose,' said my father, 'you haven't happened to see Ann-Clare around have you?' As if Rosemary was likely to give a totally sane and rational reply.

Then Alana was bursting back through my bedroom door.

Suddenly I thought I could feel worms dying in my belly. I thought, *My mother has overwormed me and I'm dying too!* The rain must've been heavy for she was very wet.

'Shut up for a moment,' said Alana, though I

hadn't said a word. Or maybe she was talking to our father, who was making murmuring noises of general comfort and dismay. My sister had appeared. Even under the rain cap she'd improvised, the haircut was visible. It was an undercut, the style Ann-Clare had begged from me. She'd said she wanted it cut like the Baldwin boys' hair. I had followed her instructions and the shape of a haircut of a magazine child Ann-Clare periodically held up to the mirror. Nevertheless Alana moved towards Ann-Clare as if towards a small tragedy. I couldn't explain that it wasn't my fault Ann-Clare had inherited Alana's elephant ears or that the haircut was nothing to do with Ann-Clare's tears and flight out into the rain.

'Sheet, shame,' said Rosemary. Because she had been in and out of a number of mental institutions in South Africa, no one said a word, whatever four letter word she chose. 'Shame,' she said it again. She sucked and chewed at her stringy orange hair in a way that made me long to take the scissors to her also. Shame was a word all our white African visitors overused. Depending on the degree of upward inflection, it usually denoted a certain affectionate humour. Rosemary also used it as a withering, half-disgusted way of responding to something, without articulating it any further than that.

I went over to my sister, requiring her with a glare of my own to say that she'd asked me for a haircut, but she was still crying so hard she couldn't speak. The tears were coming not only from her eyes but from her neck as well, for when she was born, the gills that are meant to have closed over in human babies hadn't quite shut. And even to this day, I imagine, if something or some person is making Ann-Clare cry, the tears will be forcing themselves through the normally invisible holes.

Closer up I saw that what I'd thought were raindrops on her plastic rain triangle were actually little glistening insects, the size of lady beetles but without any patterns. I touched her wrist and she snatched it away. I wished she was younger. Then our father could piggyback her outside as he used to, to show her the stars, or the spiders in their webs at work for their supper.

I couldn't say, 'It's Rose's fault! Nothing to do with hair!' pointing to our visitor, without in some way implicating us all. I bent down instead to unlace the boots from the paws of the dog who had to wear them ever since he'd developed an allergy to the stinging leaves as a puppy. 'There you go Jasper,' I said, hugging him despite the smell of wet dog.

I don't remember any specific punishment but that in the ensuing fight (my mother accusing me, my father defending, my sister crying and crying in the bath until Alana said we'd have to take her to hospital if she didn't stop) no one remembered to bring the guinea pigs in out of the rain.

Ann-Clare's crying was really quite impressive, quite melodic, for all its softness, the new bathroom's acoustics holding the echo. I felt amazed at my power over her and watched for a while at the crack in the door.

I thought the tears were coming from Ann-Clare's sadness stream. Our mother said this stream runs through the body of girls and women, running alongside the various blood-carrying vessels. Sometimes it pushes itself up through your body, a small spring coming out of a hillside, which must leave not as fresh cool water but in hot tears. I feel Alana stole the metaphor from a novel without acknowledgement. But although in the years following her death I've read most of my mother's books shelved at the far end of the corridor, I've never yet found the reference.

'Here,' I said to Ann-Clare, standing next to the bath in her fourth hour of crying. 'Here. Have all my wishbones,' rattling them at her, a huge boxful, collected mainly from hundreds of roast chickens but interspersed with smaller or rarer types as well. 'Well at least wish on one?'

She didn't speak but I saw her poking around under her bud breasts in search of her own, which she said lay in humans just above the heart.

'That won't work,' I said. 'You have to break a piece of bone. There has to be a snap.' I upended my collection into the bath. They floated, and Ann-Clare was suddenly bathing in small fragile bones.

After she'd finally cried herself to sleep, wrapped around a large river rock Alana had warmed for her in the oven, I went to gather up my sodden trinkets. As far as I could gauge none of my wishbones were broken except that of a budgerigar I decided to pull and wish on myself.

That night I dreamt that my family's time at the

farm was over. Although the property next door was bright with winter ryes, in the dream, the grass around ours had turned pale and white like a winter lawn. Where had we gone? There was no way of knowing. The New House looked as derelict as the Abandoned one, which in the dream had fallen over. Somewhere just out of sight was the sound of horses eating the long stringy native grasses that grow in between the graves. The sky was becalmed, as if whatever action had taken us from home happpened a long time ago under long past bad weather.

Though Rosemary Kincaid clearly felt Ann-Clare was being too lenient, my sister and I became friends again in the morning when we found the guinea pigs drowned in a dip in the lawn. I cried, at the same time as feeling relieved, knowing that Alana's clean sheets wouldn't get into the guinea pig pellet poo under the washing line any more. Nor would their bright pink legs, keeled over in the heat of summer, anger her. Ann-Clare and I buried them in our separate cemeteries. My sister didn't cry. She was quite emotionless when it came to animals, though observant. A few weeks later she was able to point out the two bright circles of grass which began to grow over them. 'Wouldn't that have pleased the pigs?' she said. 'If only they were here to eat it.' She said I should try not to brood about my name any more. Suppose you'd been called Dorcas, she suggested.

'At least that means gazelle,' I said, looking it up in *Important People*.

But Ann-Clare said that dwelling on something

impossible to change just made me horrible to be around. Instead, I must think of Betty as the reason for our visit to England, the purchase of the farm and the building of the New House which had made Alana happy—even if we ourselves were not very keen on its appearance and all its accompanying chores.

The day our father bought the farm was at first without wind. Smoke hung in invisible seams of the morning's mist and slighter traces lay amongst the heart-shaped stinging leaves of the rainforest remnant behind the original house. The paddocks were full of cockatoos that Alana said looked like a bright white crop or bodies at prayer in an Asian field near rice.

The estate agent made an apologetic gesture towards the cemeteries and tried to get our parents to focus instead on the way the hills fell away from the garden's edge, the prettiness of surrounding farms and state forests, and the dark patch of original wilderness which had been a national park for nearly a century. Yet instead of the presence of gravestones making my family feel morbid, it was exhilarating. When the wind came up and began to cause small, soil-coloured waves in a trough, my mother was reminded of another time altogether: walking through an old square in Yorkshire, pushing Barney in a wheelchair, the wind spraying the water from a stone fountain at them in great gusts. Her father laughed though by then both his legs had been amputated.

If we'd seen fresh dirt or wreaths that had been in plastic for a fortnight, which might have made us uneasy, maybe the sale wouldn't have been made. At that time there were plenty of other spectacular holdings for sale just as cheap. Though the cemeteries took up less than five acres of the farm, the power of a burial can't be ignored. But burials on the farm were few and far between, most families choosing the larger cemetery on the other edge of Lindley. The land felt wild even though its last boundary connected to the houses at the end of North Lindley.

A brisk wind blew up and even the cattle began galloping in it, a movement of heavy Hereford red through the corner of our mother's eye. Were we girls or were we boys the real estate agent wanted to know as I chased Ann-Clare through the gravestones. The cemeteries held no one remotely known. Their stringy appearance, the lack of any tree heavy and dark was so different to English cemeteries our mother felt the levity of absence. It made her feel like singing, *It's a windy day today, the clouds are flying across the sky.* She always sang that song on windy days.

Our father imagined South African proteas might even grow well; the soil was almost unbearably rich along the top, poorer on the slopes; red-hot pokers would thrive; how Betty and Budge would've loved the birds. Plans spilled into him and out. For a moment he deceived himself that if he looked over his shoulder he would find his childhood home of beautiful South African stone, turtle doves cooing, the land running down to the Umzumkulu River, his father on the lawn enjoying the organisation of his Christmas sports day run along English lines for all his African employees.

My sister and I leapt from sun to shade. On guard, we yelled and killed each other again and again with the curved swords of cow ribs. Green cemetery bull ants bit us but we didn't cry. We spat and rubbed as our parents had taught us was the right response to pain. To our mother we seemed like wild children, and in a sudden non-recognition of us she walked past to see a strip of dark river moving in the valley far below into the frozen-looking whiteness of a small waterfall. Then beyond the valleys, hills and mildly pointed peaks. And the density of those hills. If you could live on colour alone, Alana said, then surely that blue would be the colour she would choose.

In one cemetery we saw blackbirds I'd soon know were white-winged choughs. Ann-Clare would never know their identifying names either scientific or common. She drifted along without needing to classify or to embroider the birds onto strips of cotton, every detail correct, for our mother's bookmarks. The choughs had red eyes and made a piped noise high up in the gum trees, and a noise more like a crow when they flew into invisible air against the deeper valley's blue. The way we were going to poke open cellophane wreaths to read the messages or to have jumping competitions over the gravestones on our horses with broken wreaths fastened around our necks to imitate wings, or to bake in winter sun on Emily Rose and her husband Henry's generously proportioned grave, wasn't considered. Then, and again and again over years, the fluidity of the land falling majestically away from the plateau arrested our play amongst the gravestones.

The estate agent averted his eyes from our parents who had to kiss each other to seal their decision. They hadn't even looked inside the weatherboard house which had once been painted red in an attempt to match the colour of the red basaltic soils of the Lindley Plateau. No one had occupied the house for over a year. Already, on the strength of Betty's money, our parents had decided that whatever farm they bought, they would build a fresh house. My father told my mother that after all her years of putting up with his debts, and the rented cottage attached to the Experimental Farm, this farm was his gift. And what about calling it 'Jocund Day', after that favourite line of *his* father's from *Romeo and Juliet*. Our father stood on his tiptoes and clenched the muscles in his legs and bottom, as is still his habit, and rocked from toe to heel to toe again, quoting. *Night's candles are burnt out, and jocund day stands tiptoe on the misty mountain tops.*

If ever Alana gave the farm's address over the phone, we would receive envelopes addressed to Jock and Day or even Jock and Dave, of the Lindley Plateau.

Hearing in advance that our parents were from Africa, the estate agent had prepared himself for black skin by borrowing his wife's sunglasses. Once he'd seen we were a white family, he'd pushed the sunglasses up over his hair. But when our mother, her lips still wet from excitement, or from the kiss, looked at him, the sunglasses came back down. Our mother didn't want him to hide his eyes. She wanted his enthusiasm. At that moment, even a racist audience would do, because he was the only one available. But highly embarrassed by our parents' lack of inhibition, the estate agent kept the glasses on and concentrated on telling them what he knew of the land. How a Frenchman had once had vineyards on the slopes, and of the subsequent residency of Arty Atwater, an ex-Anglican minister and his simple son Cecil. And that until very recently, the old wine bar itself had still been standing on the corner of the eastern boundary which ran along the road. Local Aborigines, he said, using another word, were thought to have burnt it down, last cold winter. Our mother told him that in the event of her children ever using that word or any others like it, we'd be punished severely. Eenie meeney minie moe, catch a monkey by the toe, we knew to say.

In the Catholic cemetery I was telling Ann-Clare to look towards a rhinoceros we'd know later as the coffin-shaped grave of the original Mr Michaelhouse, Iris' husband, struck dead by lightning on his fiftieth birthday. I ordered my little sister to squint up her eyes and to look through a telescope of curled-up fingers. I said it wasn't a rare white rhino such as we had seen in the London zoo but an old and motley and ill one inside a poor rusty Australian enclosure. And later, in very hot summers, if we really stretched our minds, the sweating stockhorse could be an okapi, tilting backwards and raising her long neck to reach the leaves of a camphor laurel tree.

Whenever our father pretended to be an African animal, it was always a rhinoceros. He made terrifying noises in imitation of the first rhino he ever saw, which was Budge pretending to be one, with two hands pressed into a horn above his head. I'd leap onto our father's back, to be an amazing African child who could ride rhinoceros, or attach rose thorns to my nose using spit, to be the rhino child. But Ann-Clare would burst into tears, attracting the attention of our mother who would put down the book she was reading and end the game.

Warning us to watch out for snakes, the estate agent ushered us into the old house. It smelled abandoned. The ceilings held the triangular shapes of huge, dark-winged moths that changed position when we moved. And though it was a rule from the first that we were not to play inside there, we were in love from the first hesitant steps we made into its gloominess. We were to grow up in opposition to Alana's fussiness, with none of her qualms about other people's renovation attempts and smells.

'Oh look girls,' our father's voice promised something rare. We followed him into a bedroom to find him staring with delight at an iron bed, its two single mattresses latched together with laces into a double one, sprouting grass. 'Oh Alana, look at this. *Erogrosta curvula* growing in the mattress!'

'Darling,' said our mother and held his hand at the same time as wrinkling her nose against the dust.

'What? What's so special about it?' we wanted to know.

'African love grass,' said our parents at once, laughing.

'Someone,' said our father, 'some farmer or his wife, or a travelling hobo must have last lain here with grass seeds in their socks.'

The empty bedroom, with its floor that tipped our feet slightly downward so that in future we'd walk in it always barefoot in order to grip with our toes, was the beginning of our addiction to the abandoned. At the end of the house was even a wood-panelled room shaped in a curve like a ship's chapel. A whole host of romantic and melancholic possibilities set seed in us. We lingered at every age by the big St Anthony's Cross spiders in their webs and never tired of shifting the loose plank of the lid off the well, this way or that, to find the forbidden cool smell. We dreamt of living amongst the semi-disintegration of an old farmhouse, instead of Alana's one already on architect's paper and quickly built, with its children's end of the house and the end for grownups. Or the dream might only have become clear a little later, when Ann-Clare found a welcome swallow sitting in the ashes of the old bedroom's potbelly. It must have flown down the flue and died straightaway, for there were no ashes on its feathers. We kept this dead bird, with its neatly folded wings along with other fossilised treasures, china relics or leather remnants from harnesses on the table in the kitchen. The swallow stayed there, always remembered as the beginning of the collection, until one day some unknown creature plucked it from the teacup we had rested it on and chewed every bit up apart from its small head, which we found under a chair in another room altogether.

## CHAPTER THREE

Lavinia has skin like silk and I've become her lover more effortlessly than I've ever become anyone's.

'I'm like a cat in bed,' I began to warn the first time we went away together. 'People get hay fever.' But there wasn't time for any conversation. There were only the tips of her breasts, glowing at me like blood plums I should bite. She kissed my face and said she owned five cats. Her fingers found my lips and pressed them shut. Her tongue darted in and out, in and out of the tiny hole she had formed.

Until I met Lavinia I used to feel edgy at night. Frightening music being played on the radio could make me unsettled. Or a strong wind and a door behind me would open, as if my sister had returned. Or the wind was just too high in the stinging trees and sounded like a slow-moving car.

'When are you going to come to live at Redclack with me, darling?' pleads Lavinia. 'Able?'

Only now, after I'm forty, a nickname at last.

I was in the garden smashing bottles when Lavinia first called at our farm to attend an ulcer on Grandma's leg. Patricia rarely agreed to come into town

44

with either my father or me, saying that the Australian angle of parking was totally disorienting. She had phoned for Lavinia herself, first rubbing spit into her sore to make it appear more infected. Even after Lavinia's arrival I continued to hurl the ugliest household pottery at a wall to release tension.

By the time Lavinia had finished talking to Grandma, it was nearly dark and I'd become self-conscious about the noise. When I came inside Grandma cast me a baleful look and said thank goodness, a bit of peace and quiet at last.

'Have you been smoking, Grandma?'

'Just a puff from this lovely nurse.'

Lavinia was slipping her tobacco into the pocket of her uniform which I noticed was covered in small glutinous lumps.

'She was told in London she'd lose her legs, if she kept smoking. What's on your uniform?'

'Unsuccessful starch job. I was striving for that lovely bustle and creak. What are you going to do now?' asked Lavinia, referring to the buckets of shards in either hand. 'You've cut one of your fingers.'

'Read letters,' I replied, as rudely as Alana might've, years ago. 'You couldn't post some mail for me, could you?' And without waiting for Lavinia's reply, put down a bucket and handed her the three letters on the counter.

'Okay.' She paused, taken by surprise but noticing immediately my initials on the back of an envelope. 'The climate's really beautiful and good for lunatics,' she said.

So against my will, I laughed out loud and looked at Lavinia's face.

'Snap,' Lavinia said, not laughing. 'Jane Bowles. I'm reading letters too. That one was from about 1938. I've forgotten who she was writing to. She never dated her letters so they've had to scrounge approximate years and months from the date stamps.' Then she turned her attention back to Patricia, with last-minute instructions about sponge bathing for a while until her ankle had healed.

'Be careful, won't you,' she said, looking at me.

'Sorry?'

'Not to cut yourself again. On the broken glass.'

'The glass is for glazes,' I said, making it up on the spur of the moment. 'If you fire crushed glass you get a beautiful cracked kind of effect.'

'I have a patient who'd pay you if anything you're smashing is old. Old Iris Michaelhouse.'

'My goodness, is she still alive?' said my grandmother.

'We once knew Iris.'

'I'm afraid,' said Patricia, 'I once made Iris rather drunk.'

'Well,' said Lavinia, 'she's still going for it. She collects bottles for her grandson. He's very sweet.'

Without explaining my sister had once been married to the grandson, I snorted my difference of opinion.

'He comes to see her quite often. Never loses his temper.'

'Anyway . . . ' I turned away.

'Whose letters are you reading?'

'Ahh. A mix. Old family ones.'

'Pff. Letters,' said Grandma. 'All she does with her days. I wish I had an attentive grandson. Anyone would think she was a remedial reader not a librarian.'

'I used to work in a library for a while. After high school. To pay for art supplies. A kind of a joke really,' I looked at Lavinia. 'Not ever my real occupation.'

'You worked for years didn't you?' Patricia waved her hands. 'In that one by the sea. I remember you writing me letters from there. The way you'd describe it always made me think of a nursing home. And even when you were in London. At a library.'

A mouse popping its head out of the stove stopped the horrible rejoinder on my lips, and Lavinia left. But since that first day, when she must've seen my initials on the envelopes, my nickname has been Abe, now turning into Able. I write it, still with a degree of shyness, at the bottom of the notes I sometimes leave for Lavinia at the hospital.

It was shyness, Lavinia says, that turned her from a singing career to nursing.

'You don't seem at all shy,' I protest.

'My legacy of a country town childhood,' she explains. 'All the years of having to perform for the Operatic Dancing Society. At first the adjudicators felt I had this tremendous promise. But the older I became, the more precarious I felt, and gradually a kind of nervous advice crept into the judging reports. They began to say I must enter the stage more boldly.

At the same time they felt that my mother, who sewed all of my costumes, was making my headdresses far too tall, as if this alone could cover up my hesitations.'

In the end it was Lavinia's left foot in the ballet sections of eisteddfods which brought to a halt her singing career. She has shown me some of the old reports.

'Strive not to sickle your left foot, darling.'

'Pet, your ankles and feet need work. You sickle your feet quite badly.'

'It is good to watch you point your foot Lavinia, because I can see your beautiful arch.'

It seemed all that the judges could see were her feet.

By the time Lavinia was seventeen, she was so self-conscious about them, she crept across the stage as The Little Matchstick Girl, staring at the floor, thinking of herself as a lavatory (her school nickname) on legs. But even so, her feet would betray her. A shoe would fall off in the middle of the routine or her foot seized up like a puppet with tangled strings. Eventually an adjudicator of kindly disposition suggested that she didn't really have the temperament any more for this kind of section. Lavinia's mother, still hopeful of a musical career for her daughter, enrolled her in an academy in Melbourne, thinking that the change of state might make all the difference.

'But it was no use,' says Lavinia, waggling her left toes at me. 'My body couldn't forget its early humiliations. And I left to do nursing instead.' She puts a toe in my mouth. 'It was the fault of my feet!'

Now it's as if I've always had women lovers though
the truth is that only once before, after the book
launch of her sixth romance, was I hauled into bed
by Marguerite Rawlings, the senior librarian. 'As far
as in me lies,' she said. 'I will love you tonight Avis
Betty.' She was so passionately drunk she hadn't
removed her cardboard and elastic party hat. All I
really remember is the morning: my flattened and
star-spangled cone resting between Marguerite's
breasts and her own hat, its elastic strap broken, on
the pillow beside us. And that when I saw Marguerite's shaven legs, I charged into the bathroom to do
my own. Still a little drunk, I shaved an entire strip
of skin off my calf bone.

Whether or not my father and grandmother know
about Lavinia is open to conjecture. One morning
when Lavinia stayed overnight, it was rather absent-
mindedly, I felt, that my father mentioned in the
kitchen at the kettle that my fingers were covered in
dry blood. 'There's a dab on your cheek too,' he said
before swirling the ancestral teapot that is the shape
of an elegant oil can and asking us if we'd like a cup.

My daughter Ally is much more forthright. 'Hmm,'
she says, examining the loveship card I painted
Lavinia for her birthday. 'And I believe these are love
hearts,' counting out loud the number of tiny pink
and green hearts along the riggings.

Whatever Grandma thinks, she continues to lap up
Lavinia's attentions. Now that her ulcer has totally
healed she scans her own long-distant nursing past,

thinking up other half-dramatic complaints that will bring Lavinia round to see her, not me. She asks Lavinia can she foxtrot, explaining that it was a matron in the TB hospital in Sussex who first showed her the steps.

Each morning Grandma drinks first one litre of warm water followed by one litre of cold. Then she eats six small green pellets she calls her pearls of garlic and won't touch tea or coffee. At half past eleven she pours her first riesling, expressing surprise that Australia produces its own wine. She spreads three crackers with butter.

Sometimes my dislike is nothing more than the way the facelifts have drawn the skin away and out from her old skull and then collapsed again. Or the feeling that she is endlessly performing to some shadowy audience of men she imagines must be watching. Or it is simply that she is here.

I beg Lavinia to drop hints to Grandma. Talk to her about her parlour palm and leopard lily, I say. Suggest they may be languishing. I'm afraid that in the high heels my grandmother totters around in, she'll break a hip and be here forever.

'Able,' says Lavinia. 'Stop panicking. Here. Have a heart not a star,' proffering me a plate full of short-bread biscuits. 'The hearts are better than the stars.' Crumbling my determination to get out of her bed by kissing me in a horizontal line between my shoulder-blades.

Whereas at the farm we must act like forbidden schoolgirls, at Lavinia's we always end up in her huge, high, hand-built bed. More and more frequently, I find myself there, watching the luteous whisky grasses on the hill outside her bedroom, their awns ablaze in the late afternoon light, the sky which I think of as Lindley blue, rushing down to meet the land. On Sunday mornings we lie listening to classical requests on the radio. The most frequent is for Max Bruch's violin concerto no. 1, in G minor, and always the request comes from a woman far away, in Western Australia or Tasmania, asking for this particular piece for her dear friend, Isobel Somebody or Other or Marion Somebody Else, leading Lavinia to the firm conclusion that these women are, unlike us, practically dying of a romantic, unconsummated love they are only able to truly convey in the passionate Allegro energico with which the concerto ends.

I can't pinpoint the year when the New House, designed with the lean, modern lines and large sheets of glass Alana so desired, began to seem older. Over recent years there has been a steady inward drift of objects from second-hand shops, or the clearances of deceased estates, or even up into our fingers from the unruly stuffings of old furniture. From time to time my hand or the hand of my daughter, lover, father or visiting grandmother will slip into the torn lining of the chair and pull out a plastic piglet or a mother pig, its snout or its teats the sharpness I felt in my idly searching fingers. Or a black horse will appear after week has followed week since the last discovery. It's as if the plastic animals are living in the furniture at different levels, or roam from one depth to another.

Usually only farm animals rise into our fingers, not being as precious or as hoarded as the African animals. There has been one giraffe. My father made a floating motion with one hand above the other to denote the length and grace of a giraffe's neck gliding through the canopies. '*Hlula miti*,' he said. 'Isn't that lovely? It means passing through trees. Now whatever did happen to your Little Animal Gardens, Avis?'

'I don't know. They'd be somewhere. *Hlula miti*. Can you say that Ally?'

'*Hlula miti*,' says my daughter in her Australian accent.

'Surely they haven't all fallen in the settee?' My father begins to poke ineffectually into the cushions.

'I really don't know,' I say, though this isn't true. They're in three paper bags, the stiff tall ones family groceries used to come in from Persimmon's Store. I put my Little Animal Gardens, the African animals collected through childhood, into the bags and into a box at the bottom of the blanket chest years ago. I have enough animals to set up a game park.

'Well, Ally would like to play with them, I'm sure.'

Suddenly, I am worried about my mouth which, like Ally's, twitches on a fib. I gather my daughter into my lap. If only she wasn't so rough on her toys. They would only get ruined, left out for the dogs to chew. I begin to read from *Just So Stories* so she'll stop craning around to look at my face.

Most recently, Ally's begun to ferry over to the so-called New House treasures from the Abandoned.

Thus on every window ledge of the house now seem to march sharp pieces of ivory I'd mistake for chips of shell if I didn't know they were from a long line of half-feral farm kittens and cats. There are Aboriginal scraping and skinning tools too, thick with household dust. My own or my sister's initials scored with nails into the back of them seem shameful now and preclude a decision on whether to return the tools to the land or to give them to a local group or museum. Lizards rustle in the boxes of letters stacked in the corner to the left of my mother's desk and millipede bodies appear from nowhere. I know I've trodden on one in the dark corridor lined with books, by the confectionery-like crunch of their shells underfoot. After Africa, after not finding Ann-Clare, I never went back to the Romance Library. Unable to break the habits of work I spent a long time cataloguing every book that had ever come into my family's keeping. I repaired any damaged book and sorted every title, keeping each individual family member's books separate from one another so that in effect the bookshelves are like five little libraries within the one house. I began to type the numbers out when Ally was a sleeping baby, but by the time I stuck the last label onto the spine of the last book, she was a four year old, with hair down to her collarbones. The bookshelves stay regimented and precise though dust hangs off them in threads. Sometimes, when selecting a book from the Budge and Betty library, I'll find the light leg of a dead spider placed like the bookmark of an invisible reader.

Lavinia's books are kept in no such order. Nursing

textbooks are next to the letters of Virginia Woolf, or both might be balanced on top of many others, all precariously at rest on a thin paperback of T.S. Eliot cat verse.

My father continues his habit of hanging the mail rubber bands from the knobs of doors. These can feel odd in the dark if your hand, expecting brass, squeezes old rubber. Ally likes to put them into her mouth to chew and I worry, as Alana did with us, that a tragedy will occur from this habit. Some bands are so perished, they fall apart in my fingers.

If the afternoon sun unexpectedly lights up a ceiling corner and if there is wind, an array of insect wings in high cobwebs begin to dance. Then I'll become as stunned by them as if I'm in a city gallery, and they, and the arcs of dust closer down, are all part of some whimsical and ephemeral installation Lavinia and I have left Lindley to see. My father, or one of the dogs snoring on a chair, is the sleepy sound the invisible artist chose to accompany her piece.

At the farm, the emerging plastic farm animals in the settee remind me that things can stay hidden for a long time. Sitting at my mother's desk, the scientific name of the African kikuyu grass our father spent thirty years trialling for the Lindley Experimental Farm comes to mind; *Pennisetum clandestinum*—so named for its surreptitious journeys through soil or the air behind old weatherboards. When I was working at the Romance Library, a mechanic found a red-belly black snake living under the back seat of my car. He said it could've been there for years and that I might've picked it up in Lindley and been driving it round ever since.

For some reason I'm reminded of the extensive bridge repair presently going on within the shire following the summer floods. My car slides over this smooth new cement work. Yet all the while I know underneath is the older, truer type of bridge that used to go rickety-racket, rickety-racket, very loudly, making Ann-Clare cry when she was a small girl. Or I think of the ingenious hiding places Alana found for Betty's silver. My father still likes to burst into a room, waving his arms or the previously lost duelling pistols around fondly; exclaiming over where Alana chose to hide the long, ornamental weapons. The bundle of fish forks Lavinia pulls out from under my mattress makes me call her the Princess and the pea. 'I've been sleeping on them for seven years,' I say. 'And never felt a prong.' The silver is still silver, Alana wrapped it so carefully in tissue paper before putting the forks under my mattress.

At the Romance Library certain borrowers went to extreme lengths to hide books. Mr Roper, a cantankerous man with little belief in the reservations system, adopted a system of his own. Behind a normal row of books he would place ones he wanted to borrow in the weeks ahead. Other borrowers more covert than Mr Roper must also have existed because every three or four weeks, Marguerite or I would go through the shelves, returning as many as fifty hidden books to their places.

Found photographs; they can abound in revelations or mysteries. The secret natures of middle-aged men. Mr Michaelhouse, Iris' grandson, who courted my sister with cooking and letters and gingernut biscuits in the post could also be capable of darker actions. His biscuits would arrive wrapped like bridal bouquets, with silver paper and ribbons wrapped around early Australiana biscuit tins. The biscuits were made to Iris' own recipe and were like rounds of solid gold with none of the normal cracks a gingernut can be expected to have. Although Mr Michaelhouse was a turkey farmer, he was quite romantic, even selling turkey feathers in the turkey farm's shop as strummers for the musical instrument known as the dulcimer. Mr Michaelhouse also used to draw a musical score over any mistake he might make in a letter, with a treble clef commencing, so that Ann-Clare might imagine not a word but a bar of music.

When I look at photos from the seventh Christmas in the New House, the smile of Ann-Clare is the most secretive and shy, as if even then she knew she was going to disappear. I am fourteen and my sister twelve years, 364 days old. Our hair is so short we look like chimpanzees. It's darker too, all the bleached top bits missing after the haircuts. Having failed in my quest to convince Alana that the haircut had been at Ann-Clare's request, I asked my sister to give me a short cut too. Not because I was interested in an undercut like a Baldwin boy but as proof of our goodwill and affection.

In this photo, its edges curling in my fingers, Rosemary Kincaid sits between us, a more exotic simian, an orangey longer-haired monkey, with accordingly stranger features. 'Sometimes I think of cutting her out of it,' I confess to Lavinia.

'Able.'

'Well I do. She was peculiar as a child and peculiar in Africa.'

'But what would the point be? What good would it do? To massacre a photograph? It's babyish Able.'

'My mad grandmother used to.'

'It's no reason. Think of the stress Rosemary Kincaid must've been under in Zimbabwe. Being the last person who was with your sister. From what you've said she went to every length possible to be helpful.'

'I still feel like doing it sometimes. Particularly when I remember her as a child.'

'But as an adult she wasn't peculiar.'

'Oh, I wish I had a photo from the Chimanimanis to show you. There was something about her face. She looked like Debussy. Only her hair had turned a sort of vicious gingery-yellow colour. Her face looked like a swollen ankle.'

'What in the hell's that meant to mean?'

'Featureless.'


Photographs and letters. They seem to go together or are often used in conjunction with one another, the last page of a letter having been folded as a kind of wrapping paper around a photograph. Or the letter is full of descriptions that elaborate on what is pictured.

I look into photo faces from long ago, from when we were children on our mother's passport, as if many tears might begin to flow down from the grey and deep-set eyes of our mother and from the black deep-set eyes, from the long brown throat of Ann-Clare, and so release them from the sadness that more than any other thing linked them and excluded us. My father says, oh no, our darling Alana wasn't sad, but he chooses to remember her like that, as I choose to recollect the shadows. Now I see some kind of sorrow passing between my mother and sister forever: an endless transference in their absence, via their old letters and my memories, which the letters sometimes revive or alter so that I feel with each day of reading old mail, my own past has been subtly and irrevocably affected.

For some photographs, there are no explanations. Some fall out of their hiding places and are without captions or dates. In one such photograph, Mr Michaelhouse's hands are near my sister's throat, as if about to strangle her. I think it is one of Mr Michaelhouse's famous self-timer shots. He was never without his camera, a heavy Canon F1. He carried it around his neck in a beige-coloured padded protective cover which had the effect of pulling his head even further forward. His desire to photograph every occasion quickly became a family joke, as well as that he also had to be in the photos. I remember the tiny, frantic whirr of the self-timer button; his camera perched on a fencepost or car bonnet or screwed into his travelling tripod; the smiles settling too soon over my family's face so that by the time Mr Michaelhouse had postioned himself behind us and the shutter release was clicking down, our smiles were invariably, with a number of different grimaces, already in the process of leaving our faces.

This photograph holds a repellent quality. Through the holes in his singlet, I see Mr Michaelhouse's nipples. They are the colour of early summer ticks or of a pale cat's paw pads. My sister's face is blurred, her lips out of focus. She seems to be looking up at the small grey money spiders in their frail webs that lived on the canvas blinds of Mr Michaelhouse's verandahs. The photo holds such a vivid quality the fat is almost trembling in his belly as he forms his long fingers into a circle about to close.

'There are many men,' says Lavinia, turning the photo away from us, 'who like to circle their hands around a woman or a girl's neck.'

'Do you really think so?'

'Really. In fact there's nothing unusual about it. My bloody brothers did it when I was growing up. Even now, they still do it as a kind of joke,' she says. 'And only the other day old Mr Lee put both his hands around my neck.'

'You didn't tell me.'

'I was dressing the wound under his wife's knee when he said something that so shocked me, I cut short the visit.'

'What?' I ask. 'What on earth did he say?'

'He said, "I could kill you like this." He's about eighty-six,' Lavinia says, picking up the photo of Ann-Clare and Mr Michaelhouse again. 'He used to clear land around Lindley. Ringbarking and burning trees. That's what it felt like. That he had the sudden urge to ringbark me.'

'Lavinia. That's awful. What a revolting old man.'

'She has such sad eyes, your sister.'

'Yes,' I say, seeing in Ann-Clare's photo eyes the same kind of sadness found in the eyes of old people in homes, or the oldest and loneliest of ladies who'd only borrow from the comedy and biography shelves. 'The kind of eyes,' I add, 'that an animal liberationist group would take photos of to woo public money and support.'

When Ann-Clare married Mr Michaelhouse and went to live with him in his house next to his turkey farm west of Sydney, she'd write to me listening to the slow roll of cars through the avenue of weeping figs as if to music. Snoopers, she wrote, were trying to catch a glimpse of Mr Michaelhouse's house at the end of his avenue of trees. Owing to the dilapidation of the garden and the quality of stillness emanating from shut louvres and slatted timber blinds along one wing of the house, there were frequent and loud deliberations as to whether the house was for sale. People assumed it was, or was soon to be, a deceased estate. My sister wrote to me of plans she'd overhear, the snoopers' renovation ideas, which were fancifully endless rather than practical. She'd listen to how they intended to repaint the witches'-cap roofline with stars and moons, or turn the whole place into a restaurant. Some of them, grown bolder by the continuing silence of the house came through the front gate to poke around under the cabbage tree palms and old mangoes. They stole rusting garden implements, flower cuttings and whatever fruit was in season. Ann-Clare never stopped them because of her belief that the garden's extraordinary and ramshackle beauty should be shared by everyone, or that the unfortunate whiff from the turkey farm's killing sheds, or of laying mash and sour guano, was making the strangers make haste anyway. Or they would beep their horn as the sign suggested, indicating that they'd like to buy some fresh turkey. My sister was showing them a line of deep freezes, explaining the different cuts. She was telling them no, they could not go to look any further than the baby birds in the first pen closest to the house. They were holding their noses, she wrote, or dipping them into a magnolia flower taken from a tree. They were driving away, she wrote to me, always posting her letters to the Romance Library by the Sea.

'To make the library seem less dreary,' she would write, 'I have enclosed a lollipop.' I wrote back to my sister at work, hiding the letter in progress beneath a variety of pretend library activities. In this manner, unable to bear telephones, we wrote to each other over years, even though we never lived more than a two-hour train trip apart and might have seen each other a week or so before at my place or at Mr Michaelhouse's.

'Have you found any more photos?' Lavinia asks.

'No,' I say. 'No.' I pull a face. Not mentioning to Lavinia the three yellow slide boxes at the back of one of Ann-Clare's filing cabinets. Not yet. Not ready to undo the packing tape my sister has wrapped so fiercely around and around, to keep the lids down tight on whatever it was she felt had to be so secret. Needing to read letters first. Needing the reassurance of the written word. The letters, for instance, that my sister wrote to me from school when I had first left home—I find I have kept them all, stuffed into shoe boxes or in the lid flaps of suitcases or the bullet boxes I bought in haste at a clearance—but never thrown away. And I find in Ann-Clare's things almost every letter she must have ever received and carbons of her own replies—a habit of Alana's which became Ann-Clare's.

The comforting prattle of the early letters:

*Dear Avis,*
*Am writing this in secret, between the pages of my history folder. Am also sucking on an SOS cough sweet, also in secret. Freezing cold! I can see Mrs Vole's legs have mottled blue underneath her white stockings. Three chilblains are lumping up under where I hold my pen. Great you got the job in the library to help pay for some of your paint and paper. Funny it should be a job in a library. Hee, hee, hee!!! It is nice that all the old ladies call you the New Child. When Mr Michaelhouse drives me to Sydney at Easter I will come to visit your Romance Library by the Sea.*

These letters even smell to me of an old classroom. At this stage, Ann-Clare's handwriting is a neat, averagely-sized school print. Easy to read the in-sister banalities that can have only me and no one else grinning down at the torn-in-two foolscap paper on which she used to write, the jokes as fresh as if I've only just opened the envelope. But also, the paradoxical distance imposed by old mail, as if I am reading the letters to someone now dead; to the young person I once was, from my young sister, also therefore dead, who writes to me no more.

'You and Ally could move into my place tomorrow. You know that Able.' My lover hovers over my shoulder, anxious for me.

'When I have finished reading the letters, Lavinia. When the letters are read.' I think I have snapped at Lavinia for the first time. 'Oh dear,' I look down at my boots, at my large woollen red socks rolled down over them. 'I'm sorry. The thing is I can't read them any faster. There's only so many letters you can read in a day. You'd be surprised how tedious it is.' I am reading all Ann-Clare's letters, the outwards and inwards files. The repetitions are steady as she wrote not only to me but to all her correspondents about the same books read and characters encountered at the turkey farm. Marguerite Rawlings and me and many of the Romance Library borrowers also appear as characters of a kind in my sister's letters.

'Able,' Lavinia curves around me to hug me from behind.

I see the hurt in my lover's eye when I involuntarily cup my hand over the page I'm reading as if I'm fourteen not forty. I read bits of the letter out loud to compensate but they are not so very funny. The words are too naked in the autumn air so I put the letter down. I place it carefully back with its other pages. At that moment, the tiniest, lemon-green caterpillar drops from Lavinia's hair onto the page. We exclaim together. At its back is a frail black mast, the size and width of a hair pulled from my belly.

63

Yesterday I drew circles around where the hairs grow near my navel then joined them all up. No pattern really emerged. I wish I didn't have these hairs. Another unwanted inheritance from my mother. No amount of chemicals for her cancer could affect Alana's belly or toe hairs, though every other hair fell out.

Lavinia carries my sister's letter outside and I tap the caterpillar onto the grass. I see how careful she is to make me see she isn't reading any of the words on the page. I hug my thanks. We say goodbye. I watch Lavinia move towards her car. She moves with such huge grace, even the ridges look thinner in the background of her presence. Farewell, Majestic Artichoke. I raise my hand. I haven't told her this name. She waves back. My Majestic Artichoke slams her small truck into first and as it bounds away down the road, I can feel there are tears in behind my eyes. I can't cry. This is another thing I haven't yet told Lavinia. I can't go to the local library. And I'm reading all Ann-Clare's letters, I cannot say, to see if her continuing absence in Africa, her possible death, could in any way, be my fault after all.

## CHAPTER FOUR

Is it significant that Ann-Clare first saw Rosemary Kincaid and then, a few years later Mr Michaelhouse, as strangers through the lenses of average but certainly not high-powered binoculars? Two kinds of strangers visited our farm on an infrequent basis and Ann-Clare was fond of watching their movements. The first kind were relations of people in the cemeteries or amateur historians, and Mr Michaelhouse was that kind of stranger. No matter how many times I used to point out to Ann-Clare that there were other visitors far more interesting than the Moondaisy, Alana's name for Mr Michaelhouse long before we'd ever met him, Ann-Clare's interest didn't wane.

The Bereaved Man, I'd say, was very fascinating; the Bereaved Man who came to the farm for no other apparent purpose than to read. He'd drive his car into a kind of amphitheatre formed by graves of my cemetery. He'd read for two or more hours, sitting in the car that was the shape and colour of a little cockroach, his arm out the window and upright, the fingers lightly holding the top of the window. There was much family conjecture about his presence. He must be watching someone, thought Ann-Clare. But who? There was only us. No, no, we agreed. His wife or mother must be buried here. He always wore a black hat. Never once in all the time that he came did we see him alight from his car and nor did he ever make eye contact.

Three women Alana nicknamed the Miss Marshmallows because of their soft immensity also came to the cemeteries. If ever Lavinia goes for a wander through the graves as she is quite fond of doing, I can be startled into thinking she is one of the Marshmallow Sisters. These sisters didn't seem to be visiting any grave in particular but at the end of their walk would without fail sit on Albert Mason's and share a bottle of beer. After drying their enamel cups with the hem of their dresses, they always left the empty bottle sitting on the straining post. The label would turn generic in the sun and a spider might drown inside the glass after rain, but we resented the bottles far less than the things people from Africa, the second group of strangers at the farm, left behind. The worst thing a visitor from Africa could leave was a coil of *boerewors* sausage which sat in the fridge like a great cold snake. The moment the visitors had gone, Alana would order us into the garden to bury it deep enough that the dogs wouldn't dig it up.

Rosemary Kincaid's visit was arranged in the way most of the white visitors from Africa chose. About half a year before they were due to travel, they'd send our parents a chatty letter, mentioning their Australian itinerary and intention to visit our farm for this or for that week. They almost always came in the winter months, looking for affirmation that to move from Africa to Australia was the right thing to be thinking of doing. Or they sent their children or even friends of children, totally unknown to our father, let alone Alana. Though we left the Australian cemetery visitors well alone, respecting their presence as valid, we conducted, in imitation of our mother, a kind of campaign against the visitors from Africa. One of Alana's favourite ploys was to call them Africans, which they found shocking because they were white. Ours was to trick them into thinking our father had died. So that when they first arrived and asked in their strange, thin, white-African voices, with just a hint of patronage: was our father in the paddock? ('Bloody hell,' Alana would say, 'what they mean is, instead of in a swimming pool while the African labourers weed the paddocks with hoes'), we'd drop our faces to say we were afraid not, he could be found in the C of E cemetery. We even had a particular headstone picked out, a tall, once white one, fire-scarred with charcoal. We would insist that they knew which one we meant, no not that one, that one, to the left. So that even now when I notice that particular headstone, I momentarily think I'm passing that of our father, Jack Alan Peter in advance of his death and buried true to his school faith and not next to our mother who at the last minute resumed her Catholicism.

Although our mother seemed to dislike all the visitors from Africa, this wouldn't prevent her from a cleaning frenzy before their arrival. She'd say, 'We don't put on the dog for anyone', before proceeding to do so. Guest soaps in the shapes of lemons, special towels and flower arrangements all appeared. In

return the visitors stained the best sheets and servi-
ettes, and within the first two days made our mother
feel like screaming. They took afternoon naps which
they called zizzes, at moments inconvenient to Alana,
drifting off before anything was cleared away.

Our father, on the other hand, was easier going
altogether, even seeming to enjoy the company of
men with whom he might have been at school or
university. After lunch, as Ann-Clare, Alana and I
cleared up, and the wife went to fix her face, the
husband and my father would stand in front of the
school photographs on the wall, holding their glasses
of beer. We'd hear them running through the names,
trying to give one to each face in every line. Or
laughing at the winged kind of collar that they'd all
had to wear. Many had belonged to the Michaelhouse
Health and Strength Club, and our father in the presence of the visitor became just like a boy again, sand-
wiching his muscles out to make them appear bigger.
Or they might reminisce about university high jinks.
How one year our father and Douglas Kincaid
climbed to the top of Pietermaritzburg's town hall to
leave a potty and a bra on its spire.

If the afternoon passed with a steady consumption
of beer followed by wine with dinner, the visitors
might have the urge to take down the variety of
African ceremonial dance spears hung high on the
New House's brick walls as decorations. Then they
would stomp their feet and sing war cries and end up
doing one dangerous thing after another with the
spears. As an argument broke out between Alana and
the visiting wife, our father would intervene saying,

'Oh! Come and have a look at this,' pointing to an arrangement of shadows and light on the floor. Explaining how the house had been placed on the land in such a way that everything lined up. That the shadows were lineal at a certain time of the year to the sun. Everything aligning itself. Shadows. Light. On the equinox. Like Stonehenge. Only, our father would confess ruefully, his calculations had been slightly out, by about twenty-one days. So the parallels are not quite straight.

One night we were woken up by the sound of our father and Douglas Kincaid singing on one of the water tanks. We watched their backs. Our father's singing sounded quite sad, but I think this was more to do with the sadness that hearing a language you can't understand brings, than the song itself. Or some kind of prefigurement of sadness to come. Or our father singing like this because he had abandoned his mother and she had killed herself; imagining putting a rope around our own necks and lifting up our knees in our nighties. And when the song ended, all we could hear was the sound of the river in the valley, rushing into our ears and along and away.

The departure of Rhodesians and South Africans from the house left us feeling sure that though we weren't and could never be proper Australians, we were certainly not Rhodesians or white Africans of any kind.They had no heroic deeds to tell us of apart from pranks our father might have played in ovals and colleges thirty years before. The women invariably wore apricot-brown foundation creams and surrounded their eyes with coloured shadows. When they kissed us goodbye it was always a quite garish shade of pink lipstick we had to wipe off. If they'd brought Zulu beads as presents they warned us not to let them dangle between our own legs lest they had already dangled between the legs of black women. In my memory, Ann-Clare and I dancing after they'd gone, the blue and green beads a tickly delight as we watched ourselves in the mirror.

I was alone in the garden the morning that Fairy and Douglas Kincaid arrived with their daughter. Though not remotely interested in birds, Ann-Clare had gone with our parents on their weekend bird-watch walk. I was clipping the wings of my ducklings when I heard the roll of car wheels. As was often the case with visitors from Rhodesia, they had muddled up their day of arrival and were a day early. No sooner was I about to launch into the trick about our father (with less enthusiasm due to Ann-Clare's absence) than the woman and man laughed at me and said they'd been warned to expect this, from Chester and Rosalind Lewis, the last visitors. 'You must take after Jacko,' said the woman, introducing herself as Fairy. 'He loved a good joke.' I did not like the way she added the *o* to the end of our father's name.

Rosemary, their daughter, didn't immediately get out of the car but I could see her, pressed into the futherest corner of the back seat behind a suitcase.

'Rosemary, Rose, come on girl.' Fairy Kincaid opened up a door, bent to her knees and patted them encouragingly. 'She can be a bit shy.' She turned back to me. 'You must be Jacko's eldest?'

70

I nodded, appreciating the woman's tact in not mentioning my name aloud.

'Rose is fifteen, which I think is between your age and Ann-Clare's?'

Without correcting her, I too bent towards the car to look in at the girl. Her skin looked green and this strange pallor set off to alarming effect the girl's orange, anchorless eyes. When she at last began to move, it was down on all fours.

'She suffers terrible motion illness,' the mother explained, which was self-evident as before the girl could make it around to the other side of the car, she had begun to sick up. 'Heavens,' said the mother, pronouncing it hivens. Despite the sincere and rapid blinkings of Mrs Kincaid's eyes, I didn't feel I could believe a word she said. And from the moment Rose stood up mid-vomit, so that it streamed all over her clothes, I knew that here stood the most incapable visitor we had yet encountered, worse than Simon Lewis who tried to grope us in the river, or his sister who'd thought washing up involved giving every individual piece of cutlery its own squirt of detergent.

As Rosemary was being undressed by her mother, my sister, approaching the house from the direction of the cemeteries, asked Alana could she have a go with the binoculars. She saw me standing as far as was polite from the new visitors and that I had on my face a terrible, unhidden look of dismay and judgement. When she changed the point of focus to Rosemary, she saw a skinny, half-naked, orange-haired girl with orange eyes, and more fully-developed breasts than our own. Later, when I said to my sister that from that distance she couldn't possibly have seen the colour of the visitor's eyes, a look of bafflement came over Ann-Clare. She knew this, she said. However it was as if the binoculars suddenly had become much stronger and that as she'd twiddled Rosemary Kincaid's face into focus, the mad girl from Africa's eyes had lifted to look straight into her own.

As a child Ann-Clare only ever pretended her desire for Africa. Yet it was she who copied Alana, calling the Australian hills we could see from the verandah, the Chimanimanis. And it was Ann-Clare I heard, pointing out our mother's Chimanimanis to Rosemary almost immediately after they'd met, even though Ann-Clare's interest in Africa had always been an ill-defined, half-hearted kind of thing in comparison to the intensity I felt. She never read or looked at nature books or *National Geographic*s or books about other countries. She didn't read *Just So Stories*. But in her childhood imagination my sister wanted to believe that Rhodesia held those same shadows of blue as a New South Wales ridge in afternoon light. She wanted to believe this not because of any particular longing for Africa, but in order to please our parents. More specifically, she wanted to please our mother.

Sometimes Alana and Ann-Clare called the mountains just by the first, prettiest syllables—the Chimanis—which made them sound more breakable: the fragile name of a landscape in the eastern highlands of Rhodesia where our Londoner mother had finally said yes to our father's third proposal of marriage.

Rather than agreeing with my mother that the colours of Africa could be seen in the Australian hills our house partially faced, my most intricate knowledge of African animals and landscapes came from books. These were the books with Budge or Betty's name on the inside flyleaf. Next to the Shuter & Shooter bookseller's stamp which depicts an owl perched on books next to a quill and ink, I'd establish a new ownership over the book with my signature. Looking at these earliest signatures, in baby running writing, progressing through to a signature that resembles my one of today, I can acknowledge that this appropriation of my father's books was significant to me for a great many years.

Alana's buried in Ann-Clare's cemetery. Mine was the other one, the Church of England paddock of graves. We were as territorial of our graveyards as of our feelings about Africa, or as the nesting plovers that dive-bombed our faces each spring, whose calls made us feel like crying. With only two years parting us, we had to own everything, even graves, even parents.

After rain, Ann-Clare used to say that the broken headstones looked like old grey ponies who'd fallen to their knees for a roll in the mud. Rain darkened the colours of the graves as well as altering in some subtle sense the way we used to perceive their shapes. The headstones became stubbier and far less likely to turn into the lean, geometric and white ghosts we imagined stalking away down the hills under star-blown nights.

Ann-Clare told Rosemary that another way of seeing the graves was as a higgledy-piggledy chess game, too many tall kings and queens moving stiffly into checkmate and stalemate. The dark pawns at the front were the baby graves who'd never proceeded past the middle of the board before they were taken. Headstones of children from the 1930s were in the shape of arrows pointing skywards. Their details were lost or perhaps never recorded. But although this was so, we used to think we could see in the mottles of cement or marble the faces of the ghost children. There was an eye. There was a mouth. We could run our warm tongues over their cold ones.

The type of grave popular in the sixties is history— the geometric, bathroom-like patterns, the colours of pale greens and whites or mucky yellows. Alana said it was a wonder the dead didn't come industriously out of their graves with Ajax and toothbrushes to clean the grouting. She'd quote some relevant Walt Whitman. Walking around the graves with the Kincaids on their first afternoon, Alana painfully embarrassed us, lowering her breast towards an empty flower arranger on the oldest baby grave, saying it was milk the poor baby needed not stalks.

I often speculate to Lavinia that if I walked through the doors of the Lindley Library, to the back section where fairytales used to be shelved, and if I pulled out the right hard-cover volume, I might somehow understand far more about my sister than anything an old letter can show. As if the secret about Ann-Clare's final movements in Africa may suddenly be revealed. From the cement structure of Lindley Library, painted white to imitate stone or marble, the books Ann-Clare most liked to borrow were fairy stories of the world. There were collections from many different countries and she'd read these over and over again. The Lindley Library's fairytale books were covered with plastic so old I'd hear it shattering when Ann-Clare began to read a long unopened volume.

Ann-Clare's favourite fairytale was *The Juniper Tree*. According to my memory, in this story two children are looking in the oak chest for windfall apples to eat. They're very hungry because the wicked lady her father has remarried will not feed them. As the little sister leans in to reach for a small, shrivelled apple, the stepmother slams the oaken lid of the chest down onto her neck. The sister turns into a bird in a juniper tree which sings a song of the sad thing that has happened. I pictured the bird would be an eastern yellow robin, with a fine, dark beak.

Ann-Clare would mention this story to me when we were nearly out of chaff which meant we were leaning deep into the horse-feed bins. She was always seeing disasters. She told Rosemary Kincaid she could see our heads lying in the oaten chaff and the looks on the face of our mother and father when they found us; the darkness of our blood; the sad sweetening sounds we'd make in the native trees outside our parents' bedroom.

Other books in the library, although as poorly covered as the fairytales, were surprisingly distinctive, reflecting the eclectic tastes of librarians before

Mrs Watts who is still the librarian there today. It was a mutual agreement between Ann-Clare and myself, that to borrow certain books long out of print, without leaving behind a record of our borrowing, was the only way we could own such books for ourselves.

This we did with great success until the afternoon Rosemary accompanied us. Because of Rosemary's sickness, and because of our father's memories of how wholeheartedly Douglas' large family had embraced him as an only child into its company, Fairy and Douglas Kincaid had prevailed upon our parents to look after their daughter during the three weeks they would be away. When our mother expressed surprise that they would spend Christmas apart from their only daughter, Fairy said that Rosemary was used to that. They were going further north to look at the farms of ex-Rhodesians who'd settled in Queensland. It was not only the carsickness to which the Kincaids were referring. Since the age of ten Rosemary had been in and out of South African mental hospitals, with nervous complaints the doctors found impossible to track. She greatly disconcerted our father, standing in front of the pictures of Michaelhouse School and saying that yes, the uniform was really still quite similar.

'Oh,' said our father, walking into her trap. 'Are some of your cousins there?'

'No,' said Rosemary. 'But my father remembered the nuthouse next door and arranged a visit for me.'

Her symptoms had included semi-ferocious attacks, usually using her teeth, upon her parents. It was after she'd nicked her mother Fairy's wrist with Douglas' hunting knife that she was first sent south into hospital care.

We had seen the scar, when Fairy Kincaid, during talk of the troubled times looming for Rhodesia, had put her wrist into the air and said : 'I am a Rhodesian. I'll fight to the death!' in a way that so repelled Alana she had had to go for a walk. Until then, although Fairy Kincaid had told our parents of Rosemary's attack, she was careful to keep the scar partially obscured either by wearing long-sleeved blouses or by holding the scarred wrist in her other hand. The scar did not look like a nick but as though Rosemary had tried her best to lop off her mother's hand. Rather than query the safety of leaving Rosemary in our company, our father seemed convinced the normal behaviour of his girls could only have a positive bearing on Rosemary's. He told us we must on no account ostracise Rosemary from any of our activities. Reluctantly therefore, but obediently, on the very next Friday, I allowed Rosemary to accompany us on our rare book acquisitions scheme, even persuading myself that her presence might be an asset.

Mrs Watts might've been younger then than I am now. Although her perm was greying, under her arms grew great clumps of red hair. Ann-Clare and I always made sure that we worked our acquisitions scheme on pensioner afternoon when the library could be expected to be busy. At four o'clock, when Mrs Watts would sit down to eat a half-slab of butter cake with banana icing with her tea, Miss Philpots, a younger woman, with vaguer ways, would stamp out the books. On the odd occasion when Mrs Watts left her afternoon tea to survey the behaviour of borrowers, the strength of her perspiration would alert us to her presence long before she reached the bookshelf where we were standing. I felt dubious about bringing Rosemary into the library but Ann-Clare, who'd taken such a shine to Rosemary, assured me that the girl's presence in the library could only assist in our removal of old books from the shelves. Rosemary was to keep guard near the bookshelves near the small office that doubled as the library's kitchen and if Mrs Watts looked like being nosey, immediately come to warn us.

We were apprehended by Mrs Watts at a point of true concentration as Ann-Clare, less vigilant than usual, tried to push a big volume of *Australian Women's Showjumping* underneath the back of my bra strap. Rosemary Kincaid, we noted as we were marched into the office, seemed to be masturbating unnoticed where she stood. Our downfall had come about due to a stroke of bad luck. Instead of keeping guard as ordered, it was apparent what had happened. Rose had moved to stare wild-eyed at some books from the small sex bookshelf, which Mrs Watts had arranged to be in sight of where she sat having her afternoon tea.

Even though the records clearly showed that Lesley May's *Showjumping* hadn't been borrowed for fifteen years, there was an immediate library ban. Mrs Watts hand wrote the sign that told everyone who passed through the doors what we had done, and as if we were criminals, had cut our photos out of the school magazine and stuck our faces next to the warning. Alana cried and said we had spoilt everything for her too; that she felt unable to face Mrs Watts who would look at her thinking here is the woman who bred two book thieves; that one of our mother's only town pleasures had finished forever.

Trying to explain to Alana that we only ever took books about to be cancelled, that had been so long neglected we were doing the books a true favour, was useless. Or that it was not me but Ann-Clare who had dreamt up our daring method of smuggling out the books.

'You're overreacting, darling,' our father said to Alana. He reassured us with stories of his own childhood loneliness which had also driven him to do dangerous things. As an only child he'd read Rudyard Kipling and Rider Haggard to his dogs and to the black mamba he imagined lived in the furtherest corners of Black Rat Hollow, his cubbyhouse under the earth.

Sometimes, in the ensuing, libraryless years, we'd give our father complicated instructions about books we would like him to borrow on our behalf. We'd draw maps of the upstairs children's sections. We thought we remembered our favourites' covers, and their whereabouts on the shelves and that even if we couldn't remember their exact titles or the names of the people who wrote them, this should be enough information for our father. But it soon became clear he wasn't very good at following our instructions or that our instructions were hopelessly awry. Although he was responsible for bringing home reading delights previously unencountered, he never seemed able to locate the books we pined in our hearts to read again. Whenever I've come across these in second-hand bookshops, or in reprinted versions minus their original and whimsical covers, I am terribly disappointed. The span of grownup years has lamed the power those particular words telling that particular story once held. In the process of a moral lesson, Mrs Watts stole something from us now irretrievable.

Mrs Watts' sign stayed up on the library door for two years. Our library cards soon fell sideways off the door and were thrown out, but even after the sun had completely faded the words of the warning against us, that piece of paper stayed stuck to the glass. We would go to look at it sometimes, on Sundays so empty it was possible for us to ride our horses into town and right down the middle of the street. I was always checking my growing shape in the windows whereas Ann-Clare sat shyly on her horse, one shoulder always forward, hiding and protective.

Our horses often seemed to lift their tails as we walked them up the library ramp. I would say to Ann-Clare, just leave it there, leave it, let Mrs Watts step in it! But my sister would hop off her horse in order to carry the still steaming manure off the path in her hands. Ann-Clare liked to leave no traces. She was so self-effacing she'd never check her change in case the shop assistant would think Ann-Clare didn't trust her appearance.

My sister had an immediate affinity with Iris Michaelhouse, who can still coyly hide her face behind one hand. On trips through strange towns when our father asked Ann-Clare to lean out of the window to ask directions from the side of the road, my sister's voice came out so softly he had to lean across the car to yell out the direction sought. She said she'd probably choose to die if she got into difficulties on slippery sea-fishing rocks, rather than do something idiotic in front of any stranger. She said she could easily imagine herself disappearing in the last silver curve of a wave. As long as the wave didn't break, she didn't die, but soon she watched it crash down onto the high-tide rocks. Even before the wave had turned into a pretty water-fall running towards the sea pool, she'd imagined herself vanished.

Although Ann-Clare loved to receive letters I had clattered out on the Romance Library's Remington and although she too could type, she wouldn't because of the noise. Because Mr Michaelhouse at some other position in the house would know at exactly what point she was pausing and for how long she was pausing and would lift his head to listen and wonder what it was his young wife was writing to some man or woman who wasn't her husband or mother.

Once, when she was nineteen and already Mrs Michaelhouse, my sister went into a hairdresser's, wearing a note pinned to her clothes. The note explained that she had been deaf and dumb since childhood and that she'd like her hair cut short. This pretence allowed her to remain impassive as the two hairdressers moved around the otherwise empty salon.

Ann-Clare never forgot the comments one of the hairdressers made. The hairdresser had said that she could have made Ann-Clare's face look like a pensioner's. That something old was already laid down in my little sister's face. Yet also something so childlike it could be the hair of a silent seven year old the hairdresser was cutting.

## CHAPTER FIVE

Iris' feet pop out from a rug crocheted for her years ago by Ann-Clare. I smile when she flutters her long toes at me. I have massaged her feet about half a dozen times and take this bold and friendly display of toe as a sign that I have won her trust.

'How's that Lavinia?' she wants to know, as I unfold a clean washer from my basket and test the temperature of the water in the basin.

'Oh, she's fine,' I say. 'And how about you? How are you?'

'Not too bad,' she lowers her voice. 'He's in a bit of a mood today, though,' she says.

'Who?'

'Him,' she points over to the photo portrait of her dead husband. 'Let's turn him round the other way. Let's.' She arches her shoulders up into a childlike and plaintive plead. 'Could you do that for me darling?'

I reach up behind the picture frame and lift her husband off the hook. The place where he has been hanging is a different colour from the rest of the wall.

She ducks her head. 'Ooah, I don't think he likes

me very much today.' As she flares her nostrils in a kind of fear and defiance, I see how her autumn cold has plastered the hairs in her nose back onto the skin in a way that looks painful. The skin around her nose is chafed from blowing and I will suggest some Vitamin E oil.

He glares at me as I prop him against the wall.

'That's better!' says Iris triumphantly. 'Don't need Gus watching us.'

'Why keep him hanging up at all Iris?'

'Oh. You know. History. He's dead and I'm alive. He was an angry man. Ann-Clare and I used to throw darts at him.'

My visits to Iris make me remember that my sister's affinity for old people began long before she met Iris. For Ann-Clare, the highlight of any visit to farms of the district with our father was always to sit with the farmer's wife and the elderly sister if there was one, who always wanted us to talk to the hot budgie in a wire cage or to say hello to the ancient cockatoo tethered to a post. If the farmer's wife or her shrivelled sister made noises at their birds, a particular kind of tchh, tch, tch with a little suck at the end, I'd laugh across at Ann-Clare who'd frown at me not to hurt their feelings.

When we were too old to go with our father to farms, Ann-Clare began to make volunteer visits to the old people's home. For at least a week of the summer holidays I'd join her, feeling a fervour of care for the charges assigned to us for conversational entertainment. We didn't have to talk much, only to listen. Knowing that these were women whose

Australian families could no longer be bothered with them used to make our hearts burst with love. It was incredible too, to see how beautiful they had been in the photos next to their bed, and to shift your gaze from photo to old face and back again, trying to find the resemblance. But then the rooms full of beds would heat up unbearably. No air shifted the curtains or the hair of our ladies, fallen asleep in wicker chairs. Little old lady pee seemed to get on our own clothes and as well, the horrible smell of turnip being boiled. It usually took less than a week for my ardour to dim in favour of the delights of the river that, even in summer, ran with freezing coolness over our bare bodies. Ann-Clare's care was more determined.

The foot in my hands is ninety-six years old. It is surprisingly weighty and I find that I like to hold it for a moment, neither rubbing cream in or moving my hands. In places the veins have pushed almost beyond the skin and only the finest membranes of the vein wall itself seem to be stopping the perse-coloured blood from flowing into my hands. Over the years of wearing shoes, each sole has flattened, the edges becoming almost square, as if the foot has been poured into a mould too rigid for the delicate nature of a foot.

'Oh my ugly, ugly feet,' says Iris and curls her toes up.

'No, Iris,' I say. 'Not at all. These are feet of character. Imagine! If we could work out how many miles they've walked for you.' Her ancient feet carry for me a strange kind of beauty that is a mixture of fragility and strength. 'Apparently our feet, on average, carry us four times round the world in a lifetime. Yours have probably gone six or seven.'

She gives her laugh. 'I've never left Lindley.'

'Never? Are you serious, Iris?'

'No. This town has always been home.'

'Do you mean you've never been to Sydney?'

'Not once. Grace has. She goes for her eyes.'

'That's incredible.'

'Never been on a bus or a plane. Or over the sea. Olive tried once to get me to go on a cruise but it wasn't in me to leave Lindley.'

'What about to see your grandson?'

'Well the fact of it is Johnny likes to come to Lindley. Didn't like it so much when he was a boy but once he became interested in the old bottles,' Iris titters. She shakes her head and I see against the light from the window that the hairs on her chin are like a foal's beard. 'Oh dear,' she says, looking over to the wedding picture of Mr Michaelhouse and Ann-Clare. 'I'll never understand.'

Underneath the magazine table a pair of slippers are pushed together. They're embroidered in cheap, unravelling gold thread that seems to depict in Japanese style a scene of an ornate rooster about to rape a cowering flock of hens. Has Iris ever looked down to notice the poultry crisis being played out on her feet, I wonder, and hope not.

I can imagine from the size of the bunions on Iris' feet, that at one time she used to wear pointed blue or cream shoes with a sensible heel. I can tell this too

from the way the calf muscles of her legs are so con-
tracted. Yet there must also have been times in her
life when she wore sandals or no shoes at all for
patches of skin on the top of her foot resemble a kind
of very fine, speckled leather.

'You just relax,' I say. But her eyes, which are the
colour of faded leaves, always stay on my face. She
likes, she says, to watch my eyes. 'They're just like
Ann-Clare's aren't they?' Whenever my sister's name
comes up between us there is a slight awkwardness
and I concentrate more on the foot in my hands. I
move my thumbs fast across the section of big toe
that is meant to be the section for memory.

Iris says, 'Ohhh, I still don't understand why she
had to go to Africa. I tried to find that country she
went to on a map but it wasn't there.'

'After she was no longer married, Iris, after our
mother died. She wanted to do something entirely
different.'

'I miss her so much,' says Iris. 'I miss her more
than anyone else in the world. She was my daughter
and my grand-daughter.'

'You were a favourite of Ann-Clare's too, you
know.'

'We kept up with our little letters. Right to the
end.'

'I know. I know that, Iris. When our mother was
sick it used to be Ann-Clare's break. To go and write
her letter to you looking over the valley.' In fact, it
was a chore Ann-Clare refused to relinquish.

'Is that right?' says Iris.

'She'd sit writing to you in the late afternoon.'

'She could write a beautiful description of a sunset,' says Iris. 'And then I'd write her one back. The sunset from my back garden. Not that you can see it any more. Those rotten vines. The sun in Africa was bigger apparently. Redder.'

'The dust,' I say and change the subject back to feet. 'Do you know,' I say, 'that our heels are the equivalent of a horse's hock? We run on our hocks. That's why we don't run very fast.'

'Well for goodness sakes,' says Iris. 'He,' she says dismissively to the back of the portrait of her husband, 'had hammertoe.'

'Hammertoe?'

'Kind of a clubfooted condition. It afflicted him all his life. He was the barber.'

'That's right.'

'He was in a mill as a young man. Then he lost half the fingers on his left hand.'

'How could he cut hair without his fingers?'

'Oh, he had enough to do the job. After a fashion.'

But immediately I am picturing Lindley nearly fifty years ago, the streets peopled by men with peculiar haircuts until a lucky stroke of lightning put the town's barber into the ground.

Nor can I stop myself imagining the delicate bones underneath the skin I stroke; how when this foot is no longer alive, the body will release the phalanges of the toes first. How fast the little bones will fill with soil, how fast they will disperse; finding their way out of the coffin through the splintering that might occur if the bearers jolt the coffin into the grave.

Little toes look obsolete on most feet. Lavinia can

barely move hers and when she manages to do so, they appear like blind fat caterpillars with nothing whatsoever to do with a human body, let alone my Majestic Artichoke's. And when Lavinia once cut my nails, she found that my little toenails had completely vanished. However Iris' little toes are long and well formed with nails as tough as yellow leather. I hold a little toe by its pad and rotate the joint, three times clockwise, three times anticlockwise; then up and back. I watch the way the five toe tendons splay like a paper fan that begins at her ankles.

Iris falls asleep and I look at her face cautiously, seeing that she has put on lipstick. I want to lean up and brush my fingers through the long fluffy hairs that in a foal would moult at about six months. Outside the bedroom window are ledges of light in the afternoon cloud over the plateau, and the same silver light seems to rest in Iris's hair too. Her hair has never been permed and is not mauve in the way of many of the old ladies of Lindley. It is so fine the scalp shows through as pink and delicate looking as something newly born. I stroke and stroke the skin of Iris' feet, thinking that I know much more about the shape of them than probably anybody else in the world. Her mother, when she was a baby or a young girl, might have spent a little time drying her toes but then the skin of Iris would've been without blemish. Or a sister might've once helped dig a splinter out of a toe. Iris has three sisters left alive, and though they are scattered throughout the state, they all ring around each evening. Beginning at six o'clock, Olive phones Grace, who then phones Gwendoline Pearl, who waits until six-thirty to phone Iris who will have usually finished her dinner by that time. Olive the eldest, is unfortunately losing her memory, which sometimes means she forgets the hour. Then panic breaks out and the phones are engaged as Grace, Gwenny and Iris try to find out what disaster has befallen what sister.

As Iris is sleeping, I take her hand and begin to massage the fingers. They are Australian hands, much weathered by years in the garden, by ninety-six winters and summers. The hand I am not massaging rests on her middle like a little claw about to play the piano and bears as little resemblance to something human as a lank rainforest skeleton to a lizard.

Alana's hands were fine English hands, only slightly mottled by the Australian sun and I was never allowed to hold them. I need to address this issue as well as the smaller things she did such as dressing me in brown clothes when I was a small girl. Why did you choose to dress me in rust? Why, when I was turning from a girl into a woman, did you call me Peanut Bottomed? Or Pygmy Bottom? Even now, I can't look at a peanut in a shell, without wondering if what Alana meant was a double curve or if the expression held an older, English meaning. I didn't know what a peanut bottom was but it sounded like a sin far exceeding the usual figurely ones.

When we had to pour Alana's morphine and our father suggested a few extra mils, she'd bare her teeth at him too, and threaten to drink the whole bloody lot. In one photograph taken a month before she died, she has hidden the swelling in her hands with mittens. She is walking between us, holding

Ann-Clare's hand in her right. Her left hand, only an inch from my right, is clenched into a fist. This is a photo I wish I'd never looked into so closely. The last two topsy-turvy smiles Alana ever gave were sent across the bed to my sister. They went past my father and me and landed on Ann-Clare, the effect of them heightened by the crooked top of the hat Alana had on her head.

I have made Grandma cry several times, telling her about the last few days, and feel no remorse. Alana wanted Grandma to visit before she died but Patricia chose to send five one-hundred English pound notes instead, folded in two, inside a get well card illustrated with a kitten playing with a ball of wool.

I watched the tears falling from Patricia's eyes with a curiosity I could barely disguise. I fetched a box of tissues only in order to watch her crying more closely. There is something strange about my grandmother's eyes, as if someone has cut channels into their corners so that tears stream rather than drip. They find the runnels in her skin all the facelifts in the world could not forestay.

In the light of Patricia, it is easy to understand why Ann-Clare loved Iris so dearly. According to Alana, Patricia was a wicked mother who once tried to pop a mole near Alana's eye with a key. Alana was twelve years old. Patricia was drunk. Uncle Richard, who had come back from the war, was also drunk. Every few weeks Uncle Richard was allowed to go into the bathroom with Alana because he said the vein running along the back of her neck was a tidemark he was going to scrub off. A meal couldn't pass at our table without Alana saying how Uncle Dick used to make her and her brother Edward sit with their hands made into fists above the table until eventually he was taken away in a straitjacket.

I try to remember Alana and it is hard. The sickness memories have such a weight. They are like floodwater, eroding all that was before. But if I can remember she was scared of storms, I can also remember that she was scared of me. 'You have a forehead just like Uncle Dick,' she'd say, with such a tone in her voice, I would've changed the high dome into something low and hairy if that was possible.

I used to pray to the Jesus birds that lived on the first dam. I used to pray to them to make my mother love me while Ann-Clare might mutter, in Jesus Christ Bird's name, please don't let Alana make me go red in public. But our prayers went ignored.

One Saturday morning after shopping Alana noticed the closing down signs on Lasting Styles. Everything was to be sold. Ann-Clare and I followed Alana inside, expecting that she would need our opinions on dresses or skirts. Instead she asked Mrs Claudia if the mannequins were for sale.

'Oh,' said Mrs Claudia. 'Are you here for the museum? Of course. Someone phoned the other day. For historical costumes.'

'No,' said Alana. 'I only want one. She's beautiful,' she said, reaching out to touch the fingers of a brunette dressed in a tweed suit.

'She wouldn't be for sale,' said Mrs Claudia. 'She'll come with us to the next shop. Go upstairs and have a look what's up there. I'll send Mr Claudia up to assist you in a moment.'

'Not dummies,' Alana said, in the room full of faded and undressed dummies. 'I hate that word. It makes them sound stupid when really they have such a sadness, don't you think, girls? Which one would you choose? Ann-Clare?'

Ann-Clare obediently made an attempt to enter into the spirit of the purchasing. Then the buyer for the museum came up the stairs too with Mr Claudia. The buyer was of such colossal ugliness I took two steps back. He immediately wanted to purchase the one Alana had most liked. Alana stepped forward to begin to haggle.

'Oh yes,' enthused Mr Claudia, who at first had seemed relatively normal. 'She was one of our very first. She's been in countless, really, I couldn't say how many front window displays. Look, look at the lovely line of her jaw. And compare her breasts to those who came later.'

Even as he was talking, Alana was walking dramatically from dummy to dummy, pulling off eyebrows, staring into plastic eyes. 'Oh let him have her. There are plenty of other beauties.' There was nowhere we could hide except by moving behind shop dummies too. I could hear the painful hmming noises Ann-Clare commonly made in other such situations.

As if on purpose, as if for street theatre, Alana had parked the car blocks away from the main street. I carried the top half of the dummy. Ann-Clare held her naked legs and bottom. Even in half, Lotho (the name of the manufacturer printed inside when Mr Claudia swivelled her apart at the hips, which Alana said could be the dummy's name) was heavier than anticipated. Occasionally Alana helped us steer her purchase past the faces of Saturday morning shoppers before hopping off the path to walk in the ditch that ran between the footpath and the front fences of houses.

'What are you doing?' I asked.

'Lindley is so clean compared to London,' said our mother. 'In London, in the mornings, all the lost clothes from the night before lie in the gutters like small deceased babies.'

Lotho's legs bumped along behind Ann-Clare. I grimaced at my sister whose ankles were so skinny I could wrap my fingers in a circle around them and still find air between them and her skin. But Ann-Clare was siding with no one. She'd fixed her gaze on the bonnet of the turquoise car far in the distance and walked towards that point with a steadiness I couldn't muster.

'Hang on a minute, girls,' said Alana. 'The butcher's,' and left us outside on the street. I saw that beads of nervous sweat and exertion had grown underneath Ann-Clare's nose. We stood facing the window, watching the meat in its dark blood puddles. The young butcher boy serving seemed frightened of our mother. She was ordering him around with such a quiet voice he had to keep asking what she was saying. I understood how he felt.

'Oh no,' said Ann-Clare in a low voice.

'What?'

'The Baldwin boys.'

Leaving Lotho's breasts resting against the glass shopfront, I went into the butcher's shop to tell Alana to hurry.

'Oh don't fash me!' she said, the tone in her voice making the butcher boy freeze over the legs of lamb. I could see the Baldwin boys moving closer, already laughing. I shrugged my shoulders at Ann-Clare who was bowing her head. I could see the furious colour of her blush and how in the end it reached even into the crooked line of her parting.

Alana often used the don't fash me phrase. Or was it gnash me? As if that was all I had been born for, to be my mother's fasher or gnasher. The story had been drummed into me of how as a baby fresh from Africa, I would resist her every hug. A monster baby, I would struggle out of her arms and then out of the bunny rug where I had been so lovingly swaddled.

When I accidentally on purpose shot two Jesus birds with my stinkwood bow and arrows, our father told me that the blue we could see in the wing feathers was not pigment at all but a trick of light being scattered in minute air-filled cavities within the wing. For the death of the birds we had to stand at either end of the playroom cupboards, thinking about our actions. The sorrow began in Ann-Clare first. Tears ran silently off her face and down her neck. Why had we done such a needless thing, our parents wanted to know, as my loud crying commenced. And there was no way of conveying to them that Alana's behaviour was at least in part responsible.

If my mother was still alive I'd like to tell her I now appreciate more fully her tendency to match up

95

landscapes that were before us, with landscapes of her past. Lindley with London. Africa with the farm that faces in one direction towards the fake African hills and in another, the two small cemeteries. And that I realise how little it matters if there exists only the remotest resemblance. I would like to hold her hand to say these things. How natural, I'd say, stroking Iris' fingers instead.

In the picture of my sister as a bride, which Iris always puts out on foot massage Tuesdays, my sister is standing tentatively in a pair of white wedding shoes. She preferred boots. She wanted to be married in boots, so small and white they could've illustrated *The Elves and the Shoemaker* in a precious edition with red-pebbled cloth binding and the title stamped in gold. 'But Mr Michaelhouse. Mr Michaelhouse, Avis,' said my sister. 'He wouldn't approve of boots,' putting down the dainty white pair we'd finally found and selecting a more conventional pair of wedding shoes after all.

At the Mutare magistrate's office, my sister's walking boots were on a table. The bows were neatly laced yet they were arranged so that if I'd've slipped them on in that position, the boots would've been on the wrong feet. Other things were on the table too, that Rosemary Kincaid had brought down from the mountains. My sister's books, her pack, a map, but it was the boots that held my attention.

They were Italian hiking boots with green and red laces. We had chosen them together. They'd had a glossy maroon finish to them and I had paid half their exorbitant price. We'd hopped into the Romance Library to see Marguerite, wearing one boot each. I sat opposite Ann-Clare in the office overlooking the sea, our buttocks unbalanced in the chairs due to the uneven height of our feet, Marguerite bringing farewell chocolates and cakes and all the library's solo women traveller books for Ann-Clare to read.

I picked the left boot up from the Mutare magistrate's table and looked inside. My sister had chosen to leave behind my present. One of the laces was burnt. Grass seeds had dried in patterns along the tongue of one boot but not the other.

'Have you read these?' I asked the young attendant in the corner, indicating the clippings from newspapers.

The man nodded slowly but took them from me again to reread, his lips mouthing the words. The most macabre clipping said the body of the Australian woman had not been found at all because of the drought-affected baboons. The story was written in the style of a children's cautionary tale, with four exclamation marks at the end, the moral being not to go wandering in a strange landscape without your boots on. As if the absence of boots, as in a fairytale from Africa, had rendered my sister immediately invisible.

Another article, in a more archaic prose, said that if guerillas in Mozambique had taken the missing woman, then of course there would be no traces. The melancholy that can arrive with the mist in the Chimanimanis had most probably prompted the young Australian wife, so far from her husband, home and family, to go wandering too close to the border. Perhaps she had even thought to end her life at the waterfall. The poor body may be discovered years from hence, he suggested, with bullet holes or some other method of execution evident in the remains.

'Is it true,' asked the man handing back the clippings, 'that in Australia there are washing machines in every house?'

Through the window outside I saw Ben Jussab, leaning against a wall, his shoulders stooping over as he smoked a cigarette. I felt this desire, remote yet clear, to straighten him up; to touch the muscles running between his neck and shoulders. I thought about touching them with my mouth and pushed the thought away. At the time of my sister's disappearance he had been miles away. Even though the plan for him to walk in the Chimanis had fallen through, he'd fully expected that after Ann-Clare's time with Rosemary, she'd resume renting the spare room in his house in Harare. A chicken ran past his feet. He kicked at it almost absent-mindedly, the cigarette dangling loosely in his fingers. The impact of his shoe against feathers made the bird give a squawk of outrage before it disappeared back onto the street where it had come from and Ben Jussab put the cigarette back up to his mouth.

I stopped watching Ben Jussab when an anxious and earnestly hopeful Mr Dilley came into the room with my father and Mrs Pluke. It was very unfortunate, he said, but the pest control unit had arrived and we would have to go now.

'I'm terribly sorry,' said my father, who began to cry. 'I'll be all right in a minute.'

'Oh dear, oh dear,' said our official, radiating courtesy and despair. If only everything wasn't happening today. We had been expected yesterday, this was the trouble, he said, ushering us down a corridor that already held the smell of vaporous cockroach killer.

'Was there any tooth found?' I wanted to ask Mrs Pluke. 'Was there an earring that had been made from a tooth? And what about travelling barefoot? Could Ann-Clare's feet hold up? Or would she, in memory of ancient horseshoeing techniques mentioned in one of our horse books, fashion for herself two foot pads made out of tough grass and manure daub? Would she remember to do this, or would her feet, as when she was a child, grow so tough she'd run without shoes and without pain along red gravel roads or climb barefoot up the roughest kind of rocks? Would her nails grow so long she'd have to file them with blady grass? Couldn't messages be left for her in the mountains, I wanted someone to suggest. Canned food and her boots returned to the cave where she'd camped with Rosemary, a new lace replacing the burnt one. A new green and red lace whose stripiness would remind her of the colours of the paddocks of Lindley and of her sister waiting.

'Ann-Clare,' says Iris opening her eyes, 'was a great one for letters.'

'I'm reading all her letters,' I say.

'Is that right?'

'Yes. She kept them all and copies of so many of her replies. She belonged to that letter-writing group if you remember. The Faraway Group. She'd keep copies of her own so as not to repeat news.'

'She wrote a lovely letter.'

'Yes.'

'I have all her little letters. I keep her last one in my pillow. You'll think I'm silly.'

'Did she write to you when she was in Africa?'

'Oh yes. Almost every fortnight until the end. Until the last goodbye. I could show them to you. You can read them for yourself then. I've never shown her letters. Not to anyone. Not even Johnny, though he's asked. Would you like a chocolate?'

The magnificently boxed peppermint creams from Lloyds of London are ancient—a gift from Olive the traveller who hasn't been on a trip for years. In their prime, the chocolates would've been plump, larger than normal creams, but as it is, fifteen years or more expired, the peppermint has shunken away from the chocolate and tastes of toothpaste hardened on the outside of a tube. The chocolate itself has a white bloom of age.

'No thank you, dear,' she says when I offer the box back to her again, 'I've had an elegant sufficiency.'

I feel the tedium of the room. Although Iris hardly cooks, preferring to live on sandwiches, chocolates, jubes and sweet cakes, the house smells of pensioner recipes, pills for making the bowels move and the musty, swirling brown carpet Mr Michaelhouse once organised for her living room. 'I'd better go now,' I say.

Her eyes search the room, seeking to detain me. 'What about one little letter for today?' she says, clasping her hands in front of herself. 'You could read it out.'

'Oh, not yet, Iris. I'm trying to go through the letters systematically.' But even as I'm saying this I think how on some days I do the exact opposite. I take any letter from any box or envelope. I read letters as Ann-Clare used to read fairytale collections—at random.

'Sarah couldn't write at all, I don't expect,' says Iris.

'Iris, I've really got to go now.'

'Do you remember when all those poor horses had to be burnt?'

I nod. I must've been about ten when the Mutts child, with slightly mongoloid features, had opened the gates of the show ring full of buckjumpers. The horses galloped down the range until road founder felled them to the tarmac. Every single horse had to be shot. For two days the road was blocked while the shire considered what should be done with the carcasses. Eventually they were pushed over a cliff and incinerated. The episode held a ghostly resonance for Lindley's oldest inhabitants who could remember the drives of local Aborigines over similarly steep gullies. I'm in such a hurry to make my getaway, I take no care going past Iris' spindly flower arrangement. My arm knocks it over and it in turn spills water over the dresser and then over onto the carpet in a sour-smelling cascade.

'Don't worry too much about it,' says Iris, putting a toe into the spilt water. 'I'll fix it, but I suppose you'd better put Him back up.'

'I'll just mop up the mess I've made.' I find a cloth hanging on a hook at the back door and stand looking into the derangement of Iris' garden. Branches and trunks have broken under the weight of vines which having conquered trees are crawling along the ground towards the flowerbeds next to the house. More than half the picket fence is gone as if sucked down into the valley which falls away steeply at this part of the plateau. Iris comes to stand by my elbow. 'The garden,' she says and shakes her head. Without shoes on she is tiny.

I put the flowers back into the vase, recognising them as coming from the vines. Then I pick up the picture. 'Are you sure?' I notice for the first time that the portrait's face is indeed scarred with the small marks of darts.

Iris nods. 'My word. Would you take a look at the face on it.'

I feel for the wire at the back of the picture. It always takes several goes to get the wire over the hook. Then Iris chuckles at me, as if I am in some secret collusion with her against the dead man who was her husband. 'Poor Sarah, Poor Sarah,' she says as if repeating the noise of a rainforest bird.

'Sarah?' I say, thinking she has forgotten my name.

'Who lived in one of the huts behind the wine shanty. Poor Sarah. Poor Sarah,' and strokes the soft skin underneath my forearm with one of her knobbly fingers, leading me out through the front door in this way, to the front gate where she leans. 'A crying shame,' she says, waving me goodbye with both her arms up in the air, a weed stalk about to flower dangling from her mouth.

## CHAPTER SIX

As I read letters from the past miscellaneous details of letter writers other than my sister keep coming to mind.

Our secretive Uncle Edward in Africa, Alana's brother, used to be a wonderful correspondent, until one day it occurred to him that even the sight of his own handwriting on a page of white paper was an exposure of sorts. To counteract this he commenced a correspondence course from England aimed at totally transforming his rather messy handwriting into copperplate. Yet sometimes his copperplate lapsed into the old scrawl by page two, only to reassert itself on page three. Our father said it was a sign of emotional disturbance, but Alana said it was a symptom of secrecy; the same as the big bushranger beard her little brother had grown to hide his face.

It was secrecy that eventually persuaded Uncle Edward not to write letters at all and for years he didn't. Only Alana's illness made him take up his pen again.

I think of the letters my father receives from other grass scientists around the world. Sometimes the scientists have failed to seal in sufficiently the seeds that accompany their letters. So that in the bottom of the envelopes my father finds a cocktail of them, their colours harmonious, as if specially mixed. Whereas once he would've sown them with care and made positive species identification as they grew, now I see him tipping the envelopes upside down, tapping free the seeds from the envelope's seam, as we walk back from the mail and he reads the accompanying note. The requests for reprints of his old papers sift from his desk to the floor or I see them poking from the pages of other books, to mark his place.

Many of my correspondents seemed to take the time to prepare the statistics of musicians and artists who also died young before daring to make contact. Instead of writing about Ann-Clare, Marguerite Rawlings wrote about European boy musicians who'd died long ago in cold cities. She told me such things as if the mere existence of these facts, which as far as I could tell had nothing to do with my sister not coming home from a hot country in Africa, could subdue the panic bursting out like wreath wings from behind my back.

Ally's father, Ben Jussab, writes quite a good letter, though never reliable letters. They are letters such as I used to send Great Aunt Noel or other obscure relations in England, when I was about ten: many meandering stories and a boastful air. Certain pieces of information in one letter contradict what he has said in a letter of a few months before. The effect of this is dizzying. I am always having to steady myself in readiness for the next version of his life. For example quite recently he was going to go to

Mozambique to build boats. But then his next letter is from Malawi after all, from Blantyre. There is some kind of festival and the roundabout in the middle of town is strung with neon lights around which the dangerously rusted traffic whizzes. Cars going round and round for the thrill.

I have less and less to say in return. The stamps of Malawi are very beautiful, I write, telling him how Ally steams them off the envelopes and keeps them in a box next to her bed. I always send my letters to his Harare house and he always receives them eventually. Once, he said, he came home to find no less than five letters from me, waiting on the table in the hallway. So that I felt a kind of guilt. As if I had been excessive in my correspondence. That must have been years ago, the year my father and I first returned from Africa because these days I wouldn't write him two letters in a year. I can barely write to him at all now that Lavinia is in my life. It seems traitorous somehow. I can hardly bear it if Lavinia happens to bring the mail up to the house and there is my name on an envelope from Ben Jussab. At first Lavinia tries not to care. She makes a valiant effort to distract herself, pouring a wine to have with Patricia or tipping out a puzzle to put together with Ally. But I can feel her waiting for the envelope to be opened. If I leave it sitting on the kitchen counter and join Lavinia in a drink or down on the floor with Ally, it can't be forgotten. Apart from the stamps, the envelope is always so slight and unadorned, practically invisible, yet it radiates a powerful unease. To take it into another room, however, would immediately invest the letter with emotional significance.

After the letter is opened, after I have read his scanty bit of news or long, stoned meditations, I try to approach Lavinia and she turns away. 'That's the second letter in a month, isn't it?' She can't keep the accusation out of her voice. 'How is your boyfriend?'

'Lavinia. He's not my boyfriend. You know that.'

'Well why do you keep writing to him?'

'He's Ally's father. She writes to her father and he writes back. She might want to meet him one day.' The letter dangles from my fingers. Then I might wave it at Lavinia. Telling her to read the words for herself. Saying to burn it for all I care. It is my misfortune that she selects the letter from Ben Jussab with a description of his latest lover's nipples.

'Christ, Able. What is this? A porn page? Do you write to tell him the colour of mine? Able! He's barely literate.'

'He's a mathematician.'

It is so silent sitting at a desk. Lavinia is right. His letters are inappropriate. They make me feel a kind of shame, as if, even though this isn't the case, I must've been writing similar kinds of things to Ben Jussab. As if it's a correspondence based on smut.

I wish I could make the sun that floods onto my shoulder at mid-morning arrive early and stay there long after it is gone. I wish it wasn't true that I cherish the appearance of his letters not because he's Ally's father or that his letters are sometimes interesting but because he was the last person except for Rosemary to spend time with Ann-Clare.

Ben Jussab's so good at drawing it's often his pictures rather than his words that give to me the clearest image. His pictures often begin as a way of covering up a word or sentence he no longer wants read. Then I am compelled to hold the letter up to the light to try to see behind the dense ink what on earth he has thought must be hidden. This makes me wonder why Ann-Clare and I have always been so much more addicted to the not revealed. To the not known. Why try to wheedle out of paper what I am not meant to see?

In Ben Jussab's last letter, the one with the unfortunate mention of nipples, I notice that in between the words are tantalisingly visible traces of the letter he must've been writing on the pad before he wrote to me. Using a lead pencil, I shade over the indentations. But this technique works only as far down the page as he'd been pressing fairly hard. By the third paragraph the remains of the old letter have totally dried out, the last illicitly read word being Ann. It seems to me he has been talking to some other correspondent about my sister. Upon assuming this I feel a fierce, brief sensation of hope and hold the letter up at every conceivable angle, to various different light sources trying to read beyond where the ghost letter ended.

Love letters. Now they are usually a different kind of correspondence altogether, stored somewhere special, or tied with thonging or a chain of old clover and hidden for years after the affair is over. I think of the first love letter I ever received. A Rhodesian boy, having stayed at the farm and deciding that he liked me, opted to copy out an old English love verse. He substituted my name wherever the name of the poem's heroine occurred. The effect was so mortifying, Avis instead of Miranda, not even the right number of syllables, that I ripped the poem into tiny pieces.

Our father's love letters to Alana include small cartoons of himself as a little green man and our mother as a little red woman with gappy teeth. In one such card he has drawn two question marks with his paintbrush. The green question mark lies underneath a hasty depiction of Africa; the red under a more carefully rendered shape of Australia. Our father's signature is always a quick sketch of the green man standing on his horse swinging a bunch of fading flowers instead of a polocrosse stick. Or a wild line of kisses. His watercolour kisses bound off lines in a way Ann-Clare and I emulated in our own love letters of the future. We fought so much about who should own them that Alana said they were still her letters to keep, and stashed them away in a place so safe they have never been found.

It makes me realise that there has long existed in our family not only the habit of writing letters but of reading old letters too. And of being influenced by them. My sister for instance, after she was married, read all her husband's letters and all the copies he kept filed of his replies and, though horror-struck at their contents, felt little guilt.

Budge and Betty only married because of letters. And when our father abandoned Betty, though they never saw each other again, letters passed between them frequently until her death nearly twenty years later.

Betty's supposed madness never matched the cards she sent our father. Alana seemed madder, dancing naked with Lotho one night on fresh lawn under a full moon, in order to illustrate the moon shadows of an alive and a dead woman waltzing.

Letters written in pencil. I think about those. As if the writer wanted to rub them out again. I think about how Lavinia is the first lover to whom I have never, apart from small notes, written to, or received a letter from, and wonder if this is what is making all the difference.

Famous letter writers. Rilke's 'Letters to a Young Poet'. Vita's to Virginia. Always out on loan, these correspondences published long after the writers are dead, being pored over by living readers, seeking an echo. Love letters between women who had to keep their love forever hidden. Jan Vermeer's *The Love Letter*. The secretive appearance of the woman in the painting receiving the letter from her maid. Harold Cazneaux's photo of mail time at the central post office in Sydney. Letters not written—revenge as silence, as no letters in the box. Eggs sent by post. The postmistress of Hahndorf, in sending turkey eggs to Hans Heysen that later hatched, provided the inspiration for the artist's vivid watercolours of turkeys.

My sister's letters could make people fall in love. Some of her letters made certain normally level-headed country people race out of their houses into town to arrange secret post office boxes. I remember how I wanted her to write to my correspondents too, so that she could tell them stories of me. In this way I used to try to enlist Ann-Clare's words—as if they might well make my correspondents like me more. Reading my sister's letters and their replies leads me to believe that people became addicted to her writerly self or to the notion of a paper romance. If for some reason my sister didn't write to them for a while, their letters would grow maudlin and pathetic and they would cast around for ways to entice her letters to resume. My sister's handwriting is weedy and secretive. She is a good speller. Except for the words pigeon and occasionally, which she consistently gets wrong all through her letter-writing life, I notice no other errors. Though I know my sister owned about ten letter knives, the envelopes she received and kept invariably show how she ripped them open. When addressing her envelopes she never put the person's surname, only their christian one, often in fanciful script.

Thoughts of letters haunt my days and stop me sleeping. I think of the letters people have put into coffins next to the bodies of their dead. When Alana died, our father took a pen and an Experimental Farm workpad down to the river that is the furthermost boundary of the farm, and even though she would never read it, wrote my mother a fifteen-page letter.

Mr Pearl who lost Mrs Pearl in my last year at the Romance Library began to read every book his wife had ever borrowed as a way of saying goodbye. I thought his resolve about this would be short-lived, that his enthusiasm would slip, that he'd be quite unable to resist the temptations of a new sea adventure over *Jessie Come Barking*, by Mrs Pearl's favourite author. But he began to read all the books his wife had ever borrowed with a kind of piety and strict regime, sitting each Saturday morning in the chair by the window to begin the first of four he was borrowing. On Saturday morning shifts, the librarian on duty had only to look after the counter, and usually I'd sit in a chair in the sun reading the newspapers. But after Mrs Pearl's death, I'd find myself watching Mr Pearl reading his wife's historical romances. Sometimes some small relic indicating his wife's presence would bring his tears; an Anglican gift shop bookmark he felt sure was one of hers or the spidery writing in the margins, and he would totter over to show me as he mopped his tears up with large white handkerchiefs, his teeth chattering with grief, no Mrs Pearl by his side to take him by the elbow and down the rather steep steps onto the street for the icecream on the jetty they always used to share.

In the absence of Alana and Ann-Clare I continue to find I can no longer cry. The last time I cried was at Umli, in the presence of Ben Jussab. I began to cry and the comfort offered was sexual.

I know Lavinia is right. It would be for the best, she suggests, if I wrote a letter to my sister soon. Though I have no address, it can still be sent, via soil or fire or floating away from me in a boat made of twigs or wishbones. I'll write it by hand not typewriter, and I'll write it in one go. I know from past efforts that I can't begin a letter towards the end of February and then return to it in March and expect the letter to proceed fluently. No matter how many times I reread its beginning, the words feel too abandoned, too removed in time, to pretend that there hasn't been a gap of days. Also I find the old words usually have taken on an acutely awkward air. As if they don't really mean any more what they began with such fervour. And I mistrust my own correspondents, Ben Jussab for instance, who can make a letter span a month or more, so that it resembles a series of short diary entries.

I confess to Lavinia that such has been the power of reading certain old letters, it's almost as if I was once the young wife of the turkey farmer too, with the surname of a South African school, who kept his birds west of Sydney. A certain kind of light glancing through the trees along the mail track can make me recall something. Or music on afternoon radio coming from the old red wireless next to the fridge that hasn't been switched over to the afternoon's rural report. A soprano singing the madness scene from Donizetti's *Lucia di Lammermoor*. Seeing the bloom of skin cancer across an old man's face. I can feel Ann-Clare's reluctance. I can feel Mr Michaelhouse's control. I have a memory of my sister standing totally still in the middle of a turkey pen. The young meat birds surrounded her in pink and white bobbing waves. Mr Michaelhouse said: Don't breathe. He clicked his camera, wondering if my sister in a pink and white dress surrounded by turkeys could be some kind of poster in the turkey farm's shop. He wondered could she be bare-breasted. From almost the first day he was taking photos. There are photo albums full but there are some things I haven't been able to open. The boxes of slides. Mr Michaelhouse's pictures, says my sister's handwriting.

'For you, Able,' says my father.

I look up.

'A letter. From Zimbabwe,' says my father, 'for you.' And although obviously curious, leaves the room. I feel a sensation of wet, dark wings.

The envelope is handmade and a decorative border surrounds my name and address, its vines looping through Australia. Rosemary Kincaid's letter is written in a spiral. I have to turn and turn the page and feel a kind of motion sickness. It is easy to skip bits, like a needle jumping a song track. She is writing, she says, after all this time, to say how sorry she is for how things worked out between us in the Chimanimanis. Sorry that any real communication seemed, at that time, an impossiblity. That there were things she wanted to tell if only the old hostilities of childhood hadn't immediately risen between us.

*There are things I should've told you Avis. It was wrong of me but in the Chimanimanis you were so unapproachable. I think that's a fair comment. But I should've persisted. Instead I said nothing.*

*Did Ann-Clare ever say to you too, that she wanted Africa to alter her so she never resembled a wife again? That she felt time so far away from him could neutralise all the defilements? But then she found them all over again with Ben Jussab. And drinking. That was their link.*

So says the miniature script.

I imagine the impossible; what a crying photo would look like. I imagine photo tears—pale blue and perfectly circular and falling at an even pace.

On the wall to the left of my mother's desk is the picture of the Chimanimani Mountains that has hung there ever since the New House was built and which hung in my father's home when he was a boy. It shows a section of Long Gully on a fine but windy-looking day. Smoke-coloured clouds are rising like signals or plumes behind hills which are gently portrayed. On the other side of the wall I have taped a topographical map of the Chimanimanis. I can see all the threads of rivers and rapids and little grey lines denoting waterfalls like veins in a leaf. Yet at the same time there's something medicinal about the look of a map; it suggests secret cures and information. My father says it's just his old map of the mountains.

*There are things, no matter what, that I should've mentioned*, says Rose's letter.

*There was a letter. Ann-Clare put it with my own to be posted before she began the walk to the waterfall. At first, after she disappeared, I didn't follow her wishes. I forgot about the letter. For all the days I was with the search party, I didn't once think about unposted mail. Then I was going to give the letter to you. Not to your father, because I had a feeling that it wasn't a letter written for a father. But after you called me a mad bitch, I resolved not to say anything. I was furious with you. We walked back out of the Chimanimanis with Ben Jussab and your father and I posted Ann-Clare's letter the next day. I nearly opened it. I began to unpeel the glue. Coffee had somehow spilt all through my pack and stained the envelope. That was going to be my excuse. To put it in a fresh envelope. But at the last moment I felt that wasn't right. That it wasn't my letter.*

*I can't remember the name of the woman now. I have no memory for names. But possibly it contained something about Ann-Clare's intentions? I remember her writing it. Taking her time. Then giving it to me, to put with my pile of postcards.*

*I thought now you might know who the letter was for and be able to retrieve it? That even after this much time has gone by, it would be worth a go.*

'It's a letter from Rosemary Kincaid,' I tell my father who has come back into the room. 'Look, she's sent a photo of Ann-Clare.'

'Ohh,' says my father wistfully, looking. 'She looks so young.'

'This was the very last photograph.'

My father takes the photo and reads the back before looking at my sister in a blue raincoat with white vapour hanging in a puff near her hands, making her seem to have just made something disappear. Her nose pokes out, long and thin, from the raincoat's hood.

'I'll have to send Rosemary some pictures of Ally,' I say. 'She doesn't even know about Ally.'

'How would she? Unless she'd decided to get back in touch with Fairy and Douglas, and as far as I can remember she was pretty determined never to do that. Is she still in the eastern highlands?'

'I think so.' I look up to a photo of Ally I have stickytaped near Alana's desk. Her hair as a baby was tall and spiky and in the supermarket old people came up to touch it. Ohhh, they'd exclaim, bending over the basket at the top of the shopping trolley, I'll have ten tickets in this raffle.

I'll send Rosemary Kincaid some photos. I'll send my favourite: Ally with her face pressed up against the old dog's who is wearing a crown made out of chocolate wrappers. I'll write to Rosemary. 'You see,' I'll say, 'how can I regret your silence, or my anger with you that made me behave so badly, that stopped you talking? For here is Ally. This is my daughter. Ben Jussab is her father.'

'She says there was a letter,' I say to my father. 'That Ann-Clare wrote someone a letter just before she vanished.'

'For heaven's sake. Why has it taken Rosemary this long to tell us that? Is it enclosed?'

'No. Oh no. She posted it to the person a long time ago.'

'I wonder who she would've written to if not to us?'

'To Mary Shore? That was my first thought. Her letter-writing friend, remember? Who came to stay when Alana was sick.'

'No. I don't remember that name.'

'Remember? We'd gone to the coast to look for driftwood. For Alana. For the grave. She sent us. And then this woman came to stay. Ann-Clare wrote to her for years. She was the original convenor of that letter-writing group Ann-Clare belonged to. The Faraway Group. Ann-Clare used to visit her a lot when things began to go wrong with her marriage. Mary Shore had moved to Sydney. Ann-Clare used to borrow more books from her than from the library. She was quite wealthy I think.'

'Now, that's right. We passed her, didn't we, as she was leaving the farm? She was in an old Mercedes.'

'Well, she was probably Ann-Clare's closest friend.'

'You'd better write to her.'

'I'm going to.'

Did you ever receive a last letter from my sister? I will write to Mary Shore. I will have to look for an address. I will begin to read the letters that passed between Mary Shore and my sister, neatly kept letters in a shoe box file, looking for any kind of clue explaining why Ann-Clare would've chosen to write to Mary Shore instead of to me, her sister.

Did you have any idea about Ben Jussab? asks Rosemary's letter, which I glance at only once more before tucking it back into the pretty envelope.

'Did you, darling?' Lavinia asks. 'Did you have a . . . Did you come—when he did it to you? African sun going down. And all that.'

'Lavinia,' I say. She is close to tears. 'My love . . .'

'Well, Able. I need to know. You're so mysterious when it comes to Mr Jussab. So bloody vague.'

'No, Lavinia. No, the answer is no. Lavinia?' I am watching with amazement the tears coursing down my lover's cheeks. I am thinking with shame of other things kept hidden; of plastic African animals I should give to my daughter, and liaisons with men whose names are best unpicked from the mind. Memories I try to hide from myself.

Lavinia's tears seem to fall not just from the corners of her eyes but from along the middle edges of the eye as well and immediately her eyewhites are streaked with tiny pink trails. Even though I'm sitting in the town park with the community nurse from Redclack, I push my face into hers, wanting to tell her that when she is crying, she smells like a little wild rabbit. I remember that the last time I cried, my tears ran along my face and into my left ear, making me slightly deaf to the noises Ben Jussab was making behind me.

'It is hard to explain,' I say. 'I've never even explained it to myself. It was an inexplicable thing. It was after we'd been to the Chimanimanis, on our way back to Harare. I let it happen because of what had happened to Ann-Clare.'

'You didn't know what had happened to your sister.'

'That's right. And I thought it might help.'

'To be fucked by a stranger.'

'Not exactly a stranger. Because of Ann-Clare's

letters. She'd portrayed him to be like our brother.'

'So you let your brother in Africa fuck you, hoping for some clues about your sister?'

'Lavinia! Careful.' There were two little old ladies watching us.

'Well?'

'Well, he is Indian anyway. His father had a restaurant in Harare.'

For a while, after conversations such as this, we don't talk. Then I will venture that whatever the nature of the history, there is Ally. 'Little Alana Clare, Lavinia.' So that the reality of my daughter erases to a point the uncertainties of the past. And as if on cue, if we are at the farm or at Lavinia's, Ally might even come into the room, moving with hesitation towards us, pulling short the conversation that didn't know where to go next, anyway, making us rush to reassure her as if she might have accidentally on purpose been listening behind the door.

My father looks baffled when he begins to read Rosemary's letter and hands it back quickly. 'Too avant-garde for me, I'm afraid,' he says, referring to its spiral shape. He bends down to pat a dog boisterously on the head and never asks for the letter again. I too find I'm extremely reluctant to decipher every squashed word Rosemary has written.

Even though I should read Rose's letter properly, it's almost as if all letters have become irrelevant and another story is being told, not by me at all, but by a stranger in Africa. I find I can be massaging Iris' feet, or watching Ally do her homework, at the same time as listening carefully. My bewilderment at how thoughts of Africa creep into even the most intimate moments with Lavinia; street scenes that have nothing to do with kissing Lavinia's neck. Sleazy magazines laid out on corners, their pages curling in the sun, or a clump of bananas for sale.

The storyteller stranger is possibly Ann-Clare. Under the jacarandas at Ben Jussab's, whose place isn't far from Enterprise Road, it's a hot and shadowy day. I find myself holding unlabelled brown beer bottles up to the light, checking for floating moulds. He makes a joke about Australians and their alcoholic capacities. He calls my sister Australia in a way I find disturbing.

Ann-Clare's fingernails in Africa have become creamy and ridged. She tells me her name is now Hansel and that though she's been travelling for months through Mozambique forests on a filthy monkey-infested raft, it's a beer of local rather than western type that has kept her in good condition. I don't point out how bad she looks, bloated rather than well—like a boy not a girl, or an old gnome sitting in a back lane with its hat knocked off.

Ben Jussab has a beautiful mouth. I can see teeth marks at the side of his throat have turned purple and wonder are they my sister's? My questions are trapped like chalk dust in my throat.

When she left the boots behind, Ann-Clare explains, the entire sole of both feet filled with blister fluid. 'For days after the waterfall, I had to walk on tiptoes.'

I want to ask Ann-Clare why she left behind the

boots I helped her buy. I want to tell her how for years after she disappeared, our father and I have lived for the mail. I want to tell her of the heaviness in my heart as we make our way back to the farmhouse and how our father gamely begins to talk about new weeds beginning to take hold on the farm. Does she know I have a seven year old? To Ben Jussab? Ann-Clare?

But Ann-Clare and I were never at Ben Jussab's house at the same time, and the stories that have left me living as a grass sister, on my father's farm, are imprecise and incestuous. In the absence of any other history, the old letters begin to apply secrets to my days with the precision of small shocks.

If someone were to ask me what am I, I would reply, I am a grass sister. I've even written it on forms, under the spot where you put your occupation: a woman whose sister has been absent for a period. And if they then asked about Ann-Clare, I'd reply, she was a letter writer. Not because she didn't have other talents, or because of her long association with the Faraway Group for Rural Women but because her correspondence was more important to her than anything else. An example of her obsession with mail occurred when I came back from my year in London. Although I was there before her, and she was quite pleased to see me, she seemed more excited by the thought of the final mail I'd preceded, arriving into her letterbox in later weeks. And if I sometimes refer to Ann-Clare in the past tense, this isn't so much because I've accepted she's dead, but because she no longer writes letters. Her last letter to me, written from Harare, gives no indication of her intentions, apart from her desire to get to the eastern highlands soon. A miniature map of the Chimanis had been sketched for me, and some of her last-minute words crossed into its contours.

## CHAPTER SEVEN

Although Ann-Clare took the precaution of travelling with one of Alana's teeth to Africa, a charm preferred above any pretend wedding ring the women-travelling-alone books from the Romance Library by the Sea recommended, she didn't have good luck. My sister thought she'd be home after about six months. But like Lancelot Fricker James, a boy our father was at school with, only with a pen, not a medallion in her hand, Ann-Clare apparently walked away from Rosemary Kincaid and the cave where they were camping, reached the edge of a waterfall, took off her boots and disappeared.

'I really regret telling her that story,' my father says. We are swimming in the dam rather than taking the half-hour walk down to the river, and the dam is marginally warmer as well.

'What story?'

'When Ann-Clare was still married, I had a dream about Lancelot Fricker James, not actually about his death, but it was a dream about one of my old school's Sunday picnics. And I happened to phone up Ann-Clare that day from work and I was telling her the dream but for a moment I couldn't remember the name of the boy. Straightaway Ann-Clare was able to say Lancelot Fricker James. Don't you think this means she placed unreasonable meaning into the story in the first place? You know Alana always did fear one of you girls would end up in Africa. That us having left would mean one of you would go back and never come home. If only I'd given Ann-Clare more addresses of people to stay with in Glendale.'

'She didn't want those, Dad. She wanted to travel in Africa without all those connections.'

'And then she had to meet up with the Kincaid girl.'

'But in fact Rose was really quite sane, wasn't she? I wish I'd been nicer to her.' I wish I hadn't told her she was like a bit of old rattle weed, shaking with self-importance.

'Lancelot Fricker James,' says my father.

'Ann-Clare only remembered the name of that diving boy because it's so peculiar.' But imagine being taunted to your death, I am thinking. Think of poor Lancelot Fricker James, champion diver of the whole of the Natal province, being urged to the very edge of Howick Falls and then urged to show exactly how good a diver he was. Imagine the noise and all the colours you'd suddenly become aware of in the waters and the rocks. Imagine tensing your buttock muscles and then stretching your hands down and down, so that even your neck feels ready. Then testing the rock under your bare eighteen-year-old feet for spring. Discovering that rock can have a bit of give. Taking the diving medallion off from around your throat to see how it fares through the air. The fear glinting. The other boys drilling it into your back so that you can't turn around. So that there is only one way to go and that is over, in a plain and swooping dive.

I understand my father's desire to assume responsibility. I have to stop making similarly unlikely assumptions. Of course Ann-Clare didn't decide to not come out of the Chimanimani Mountains because I persecuted her steadily throughout our childhood. Or I will wake from sleep and see all the cruciferous landmarks visible from the house as if noticing them for the first time. With an air of blame, I notice not only all the obvious crosses in the cemeteries but also the shadow cast from the timber washing line, or that a faraway line of telegraph poles at dawn looks like a row of crucifixes waiting for bodies. Of course this doesn't have anything to do with Ann-Clare disappearing near a waterfall in Africa but sometimes my reassurances fail me completely and I know my sister has gone, in whatever way—the way doesn't really matter, because of the power of her childhood over her. Although following Alana's death, Ann-Clare wanted to leave her family behind, once in Africa it seemed she was unable to stop looking for resonances of us in strangers.

Her early letters from Harare are full of family wonderings. Would her twenty-eight-year-old self, alone in Harare, have liked to meet our mother as a twenty-four-year-old secretary? Did I believe a girl from Lindley could've had anything at all in common with Alana thirty years beforehand, a Londoner in

Africa, who always wore makeup, high heels and classy dresses? My sister said she loved the city best of all for its sense of being left behind—old-fashioned packaging in half-empty supermarkets, for example, which gave her a feeling of moving through the time of our parents when they were young. Bottles of sarsaparilla in tall, old-fashioned glass bottles Mr Michaelhouse would've loved for his collection. The way she had to jump on and off local buses when they were still moving because if they stopped they might stall and not start up again.

In Ann-Clare's letters, her visibility in being a white person on a local bus was something to which she never adjusted. She'd taken to dressing in black and walking in the dark she said, so that she couldn't be seen. On some nights she walked through Harare until the buses and trucks began to arrive with workers from Chitungwiza. She walked past night-watchmen in front of small fires and sometimes they answered her hello and sometimes they didn't but never once did she feel out of place in Africa at night; to be invisible, worth any risk. And never once, she wrote, did she ever feel the sense of danger or dismay that could easily overwhelm her in the daytime. She walked and walked, wearing black, until the turtle doves began to coo; their song, she said, just as our father had promised, so much fatter, more lush, more mauve-tinted than any Australian dove.

What has struck me upon rereading Ann-Clare's early letters from Africa is the innocence of her quest. It doesn't surprise me at all that on her first day in the city, as she sat eating her Qantas cheese crackers against a palm tree in what used to be Cecil Square, someone stole her jumper. Or that still on this first day, in the late afternoon haze, her wallet was slipped from her pocket as she waited, the only white person in the queue, for a bus in Rezende Street.

These early letters are all written from her bunk in the youth hostel, before she met Ben Jussab. I can so easily imagine her, hiding from the other travellers in the concentration of a letter, her knees up inside her regulation cotton inner-sheet. I see her shy terror of the other people, and how when she finally does fall asleep, her elbows splayed out like wings from her ears and no pillow, her sleep is so sound no snorer or sleep-talker can disturb her.

From the first, I felt that Ann-Clare was failing me in her descriptions of Africa. Although I longed to receive letters full of descriptions of landscape and wildlife, that isn't what my sister chose to describe. And when she did eventually describe Hwanke Park, where she went briefly with Ben Jussab and his brother who was over from England, I was reminded of nothing so much as an African safari novel by the American children's writer Willard Price.

'What I've never been able to understand,' I say to my swimming father, 'is why Ann-Clare wanted to walk to a waterfall in the first place. She hated heights. From a certain age she developed terrible vertigo. So to leave her boots right on the edge?'

My father doesn't seem to hear. He strokes on ahead in the water, his hair half-wet now.

There came a time when I had to push Ann-Clare

into the part of the river which swept us over a small waterfall and into Lindley's best swimming hole. What I made myself do I always made sure my sister followed. One day I said let's jump our horses down the stormwater drain and she didn't ever seem to hold it against me that one of her insect-sized ankles snapped when her horse misjudged the leap. No children from school approached my sister in order to fill her plaster cast with colourful graffiti or names. The blankness of Ann-Clare's leg plaster emphasised our isolation. By the end of the first week, unable to bear it and unable to explain to our parents why it was that Ann-Clare should be allowed not to go to school, we decided to fill in the plaster ourselves. We got so carried away we believed we'd created the impression that a rowdy party of Australian families had converged at our house on the weekend and descended on my sister's leg.

Staring up the length of a tall dead gum tree against a blue sky on a hill can conjure up the kind of sick elation you would feel if you were going to jump over a waterfall. The dizziness of blue moving so fast towards you. Or the first symptoms of a serious disease. Grandma's young husband Barney, Alana's father, who developed multiple sclerosis—telling her how he felt, as if he was walking about a foot off the ground but that the texture of the air kept thickening then thinning and keeping him off balance. Betty buying a length of rope. Our mother saying how at first cancer felt like dancing when tiddly on a platform afloat in water. A kind of recklessness. Followed by a kind of shame.

During my sister's memorial service in Lindley, people came sneaking in late, out of curiosity, the way six farmers had come years ago to our father's talk in the Fairy Hill Hall about tobacco production in Rhodesia. I was sitting next to Iris who was weeping into hankies too small to hold her grief, who seemed to be talking to herself rather than to her grandson. I was back from Africa and couldn't cry. I wanted to take Iris by the hand. I wanted to tell her that I hadn't given up hope and that none of us should. Mr Michaelhouse, I felt like calling out in a whisper, leaning across Iris to reassure him too, to stop his own snorting kind of crying; to offer my own large and dry handkerchiefs. But the smell of the geraniums in the arrangements for the memorial service brought on a morning sickness so severe I had to rush past Iris and Mr Michaelhouse, through the side door and behind the plumbago hedge.

Each day, before I sit at Alana's desk, my father and I swim underneath the early morning mist. In the dam my father always moves faster than I do towards the broken boundary fence that limps through the water. 'This is just like the cold plunges at school,' he says, a glee in his voice. When his hair gets wet, it's like some kind of grey, waterborne tussock. At times he buys swimming caps from the North Lindley store and the laughter bubbles up in me. With a cap on, he looks like a woman of indeterminate age trying to swim off the small rolls of fat growing underneath her ribs.

'Is it appropriate,' Lavinia asks, 'to swim without anything on?'

'I don't know, darling. I'm not sure,' I reply adding, 'Wouldn't it be just as inappropriate now to suddenly don swimmers, after years of never having worn any?' But I know I haven't convinced her and I know what she means. I reassure Lavinia that these early morning swims will soon be a thing of the past anyway. That it will soon be too cold; that in Redclack Lavinia will swim with Ally and me in the small memorial baths there, teaching Ally how to dive and eating lollipops afterwards and that perhaps, occasionally, my father might join us on a Saturday or we might come back to the farm for the day.

'Do you remember,' says my father, 'when I said to the old boys' master at Michaelhouse about my delighted memories of naked swimming at the school and how embarrassed he was? "Ooh," he said, "the boarders don't do that any more." And I said, "All the boys' balls jangling".' My father likes to talk about his school years, which were happy years, he says. He quite often reminisces about them or about our visit there following our time in Zimbabwe. He lists the outlandish names, Christopher Wetherstone Clark, Lancelot Fricker James, Alistair Shipston Evans, Michael Basil Blyde, it seems to me for no other reason than to enjoy their quaintness aloud.

After a swim my father's hair lies down past his shoulder-blades. I wonder would Ann-Clare recognise him? I imagine telling my sister how he increasingly resembles our nameless seventeenth-century ancestor hanging on a wall in the sitting room. The one Alana dubbed Sir John Who's Gone.

If my father had some kind of seizure when swimming, I'd have to ferry him ashore, my arm around his shoulders. I'd wish then that he was wearing swimmers or that I could remember school lifesaving procedures; the correct ratio of cardiac massage to mouth-to-mouth, which Lavinia keeps reminding me of but which I continue to forget. I could grab him by his hair and sidestroke. Or there's the position I remember where the drowning person hangs onto the saver's neck. As the saver breaststrokes, the drowner is meant to float along underneath.

'Oh but I'm just an old man going to hair, aren't I?' he likes to say to Patricia as she unwinds her own hair from clips each morning. People he used to know quite well don't even nod to him now let alone ask him onto their farms to give advice. Is this because of hair, or is it because of disaster?

At first the feelings of estrangement from people who had never been his friends, but who'd certainly been friendly, caused my father considerable sorrow. He'd return from a trip into Lindley and shake his head over so and so or so and so, who hadn't said hello as they passed on the crossing or as he'd stood next to them in the bank.

From time to time, someone who has lived at Lindley, some old coworker from the Experimental Station who has been in China for ten years, or a farmer moved to another district who never reads the papers or who must've missed the news at the time of Ann-Clare's disappearance, will ring up and think I am my mother. 'Alana,' he or she will say, with genuine pleasure, asking after the girls.

Once, instead of the dreary explanations that my mother had died and that Ann-Clare was also gone, I couldn't restrain myself from pretending to be Alana and giving happy answers. All the time as I spoke as my mother to Heather Langley, I also longed to speak as myself; to tell her how much her presence had, at the back of my mind, influenced my life. How though I thought she meant nothing to me when I was growing up, I still carried an image of the shorts and boots she wore as she strode with our father through flowering Australian grasslands when we were children; and how even as an anonymous traveller in Africa, Ann-Clare could think of Heather Langley, our family's lesbian friend, at the most unexpected moments; that two of Ann-Clare's letters had made mention of Heather Langley.

In the very first letter from Ann-Clare in Africa, she exhorts me to remember the light of Alana's last Christmas for it is a little like the African light.

According to my sister, when she stepped off the plane, the heat came bowling into her, not like weather at all but like a badly-trained dog. The sweat prickled in beneath her skin so much that she thought her scalp was moving in the way I used to be able to move mine.

The light of the Christmas before Alana died was red and dry and in it all our noses looked long and strange. 'It's a dying light, girls,' our mother said.

'Don't be macabre.' I offered her a piece of cake. But there had never been such an evening. The hills rolled with red lights and in the stinging trees too the light was very heavy and red. 'The light's certainly weird, but not without life. Listen,' I commanded, 'to all the crackle going on. And there's a wind coming up.'

'A dying wind,' said Alana. 'And a dying light.'

The sunset caught at the swaying tooth in Ann-Clare's ear. Where the jeweller's drill had entered the tooth, some of the gold had crazed slightly. I was feeling resentful that my sister was going to get to Africa before me and that nothing I could say would persuade her to wait until I also had the necessary funds. It was too painful to acknowledge that no one would be travelling anywhere until Alana had died so we were all talking as if Ann-Clare would be setting off any day.

'I suppose my tongue must've once licked that tooth,' Alana said next. 'Would you mind cutting me another piece of cake with mainly just marzipan and icing.'

Our skins were dark, our teeth very white. I imagined I was looking quite handsome and put my camera into my sister's hands. I wanted her to take photos of me jumping a fallen tree with my dog. I can hardly believe this now. I was about thirty-three years old. Our mother was dying, I wanted to hold my mother's hand, yet I still required my sister to be taking pictures of me I could later pore over, looking for myself in feats that belonged to childhood. The childhood horse albums are full of me when now I'd like to look at Ann-Clare.

Even my letters written from the Romance Library

to Ann-Clare at Mr Michaelhouse's were aimed at making her pause and watch my life. Her letters, in contrast, avoided herself as far as possible, focusing upon the quirks of Mr Michaelhouse, the rambling garden, her duties at the turkey farm, logos she'd come up with for Michaelhouse Turkeys, such as, 'Frozen without feet, Basted for magnificent meat,' the books she was reading, her incredulity, that this author or that had replied to her note of thanks about a novel she'd read.

At dusk, our father began to set up the table outside for dinner. We knew it was likely our mother would be dead before the next Christmas but no one talked about this. We spoke as if she would be well in no time at all and that as soon as this happened, Ann-Clare would commence her holiday. The fairy lights couldn't be found so our father brought a standard lamp from the sitting room out into the garden instead. For such an interior object to be placed so suddenly against a big cloud-festooned sky made us laugh. The darker it grew the stranger it looked. Not even the moon coming up over the cemeteries could seem so spectacular. Under the lamp, my family looked longer. 'Like Modiglianis,' said Ann-Clare.

'Crazier. Soutines,' Alana suggested.

'Oh that's a bit extravagant, isn't it? Why haven't you ever pruned these trees?' I said next. 'What's the point of having a view,' and leant out of the light to touch the foliage. The smallest criticism had always been enough to make our mother cry. I remember our mother was crying at the table, the tears rolling out from underneath her reading glasses, which had at that time a five-way crack through the left lens.

When I offered her a box of tissues from my car glovebox, Alana said, 'You know I never use trees,' and took one of the handkerchiefs Ann-Clare was able to offer because she had a summer cold.

In deference to Ann-Clare and her recent separation from Mr Michaelhouse, there was no poultry for Christmas dinner. Our father tried to jolly the meal up by telling us about Christmas days in South Africa. 'Betty and Budge would've organised a big lunch on trestles underneath a big gum tree. In the gum tree,' said our father, 'there were the nests of the weaver birds hanging down like little Christmas stockings woven from spider webs and grass. So that all through lunch if you looked up, you could see the birds going in and out through the sock part of the nest.'

'Was there anything special for the Africans?' Ann-Clare asked.

'Yes! Darling, thank you very much for reminding me. Budge used to organise things like a public school sports day. With egg-and-spoon races, tug-of-war, three-legged races or eating small cakes tied with string to a tree. One of the favourite things was a tub of water with coins in the bottom and my father would always do this first with his hands tied behind his back. Trying to pick up coins with his mouth. There were sticky buns and it really was a happy day. You know, it was my dad's day.'

Leaving Ann-Clare sitting with our parents, I drifted away from the table to read the Christmas cards hanging on rows of string in front of the mantelpiece and the Christmas circulars from Africa and England that Alana always left in a ceramic bowl, ready for her replies.

I grimaced at Ann-Clare who'd followed me inside.

'What?'

'Have you read Alana's circular?'

Ann-Clare also pulled a face, squirming as she began to read.

Each September, as well as making Christmas cakes, Alana would begin to construct her Christmas circular. She'd type three carbons at a time. The circulars ran to about five pages. As she had an extensive correspondence, she would type out the letter again and again. The old circulars were full of glowing reports about girls who in no way resembled her daughters. A listing of our annual achievements was never followed by our disgraces. The circulars wanted their reader to feel admiration not only for Alana but for Alana's landscapes and stories, dogs, horses and children. If this meant diverting from the truth, my mother always acquiesced to the necessary lie.

The voice of these letters is not Alana's but of the woman in Australia Alana imagined the recipients imagined. They were very gushy. Although it was Alana who always put together the letters, they were written as if simultaneously, by our mother and our father. This technique of narrative helped the circular carry an additional burden of phoniness.

In the circulars we could read a sanitised version of our family, wherein Alana or Alana masquerading as our father, sought always to gain the invisible approval of invisible people and to highlight Australian words or out of the ordinary events by putting them in inverted commas.

According to Alana's last circular, I was back from London and working at the Romance Library again, with little romance and not a suitor in sight. And although Alana would have known she was ill, not one mention of this.

'Here's one from the Kincaids,' said Ann-Clare. 'In all this news, not one mention of Rose. Nothing. As if she no longer exists now they can no longer bung her into hospitals.'

'Do you *still* write to her?' I couldn't keep the old derision out of my voice but Ann-Clare, appearing not to notice, told me that Rosemary was living in a self-sufficient community near the Chimanimanis, a cheese-producing community, writing poems about local women who'd survived the Independence War.

'Listen to this,' said my sister. 'This is Fairy Kincaid: "I have been busy doing up houses and keeping seven black ladies busy making thousands of Christmas decorations out of wheat and maize husks ... little ol' white me has had to trim and finish off each one ... if I tie another tartan bow I will go scatty. 'Tis all great fun." '

'As bad as Alana. You're not going to stay with them are you?'

'No, but with Rosemary, yes. We're going to go walking in the Chimanimanis. Look at this,' she said and isolated her left eye in a frame of fingers. 'What do you see?'

'Your eye.'

'But doesn't it remind you of anything?' Ann-Clare framed her sleepy eye for me with her fingers but I still couldn't see at what she was hinting. I think I will find out many things when I attend to the slides. In their flimsy yellow boxes they sit in a drawer of Alana's desk, waiting for my gaze.

There are so many letters but recollections of the night Ann-Clare stayed out in the rain often distract me from my task. Then I must go back a few pages in the letter at hand to see if I've blotted out what is before me with the power of my memory. I picture my sister's running legs. They have the fragility of a firetail finch and the knees are always reddened, bringing to mind Cinderella, down on her hands and knees, scrubbing the floors as her sisters have ordered.

I will never forget the quiver and tickle of my sister's hands, holding me by my fringe, as she ran the clippers up the back of my neck the day before Christmas. Whenever she paused to check the level of hair over each ear, my eyes met hers in the mirror. My sister's eyes were a dark shade of brown. Above her sleepier eye, her eyebrow used to sprout for a moment in the wrong direction, before resuming an even flow of hair.

Rose Kincaid stood watching Ann-Clare cutting my hair, standing against a blue hydrangea whose flowers had sprung through a missing plank in the wall. We told Rosemary how we were going to mend the shattered glass windows and fix up the rotting floorboards. One day too, said Ann-Clare, we'd install an old tin fan to spin cooler air into the room on hot January days, onto our arms still sweaty from a day in the paddock.

In all the minutes I sat having my hair cut, not one reference was made to Ann-Clare's haircut and subsequent crying fit of a few days before.

As Ann-Clare snipped and organised my hair, I too felt friendly towards Rosemary, suggesting that if she ever wished to emigrate later on in her life, she would be more than welcome to come for a holiday to our house, which would maintain a certain dilapidated air because that was what we liked.

In this same friendly spirit, Rosemary showed us two small round rugs of hair on the back of her thighs and said though she used to borrow her father's razor to shave it off, she now rather liked their hairiness.

The tanneries were boiling down blood and bone and I said I rather enjoyed its smell. Ann-Clare said she smelt the beginning of despair and held her breath.

'A terrible, sad smell,' said Ann-Clare.

'It signifies endless transformations and possibilities,' I said adding that Ann-Clare was morbid.

'I think actually that it smells like a *braai*,' said Rosemary Kincaid.' Anyone else hungry?' From her pocket she took out a piece of the biltong her parents had left for her to chew. 'Bil,' she said, meant buttock in Afrikaans. And she waggled her bottom. Tong was tongue. The meat was cut from the buttock of a beast but looked like a tongue. 'Want some?'

Rather gingerly my sister took a piece of the meat.

I went outside with my finished haircut, to catch sight of it in a window and to feed a horse handfuls of blackberries. The saliva frothed up. As the horse moved his head he dabbed the purple froth on my shoulder. I looked over to see the shade as dark and cold as a sheet of glass, cut deep across the hills.

Rosemary's hair looked more yellow than orange in the crinkle lines left from plaits.

The land began to curve in the late light. The wind whistled through my legs and skirt. It rustled the fallen gum leaves.

'Hey,' I called out to the Abandoned House. 'Let's show Rosemary the tumbling trick.' This trick, taught to us by our father, involved gripping each other's arms, holding our breaths and somersaulting between each other's legs. Once in motion we couldn't stop. Our limbs were locked into a continuous, caterpillaring somersault. Grass seeds clung to our sweat.

Rosemary's eyes grew glisteny with excitement. She said she would like to have a go at it with Ann-Clare, who was more her size. Their attempts looked like the mating ceremony that a strange African insect might adopt but I tried not to pay the thought much attention.

'Come on Ann-Clare,' I said. 'We should go home.' I was stung by the look of eagerness in my sister's face.

'You don't have to go with her,' said Rose. 'You're not her slave.'

'I think I will stay for a while,' said my sister, not looking at me. Sweating from her exertions.

'We'll be back by six,' said Rosemary, her accent making it sound like sex.

I shrugged my shoulders. Rosemary Kincaid made me think of thin blades, slicing off our nipples in the night. She'd already told us how she'd tried to slice off her own but that they were too tough, like old field mushrooms.

In the middle of Rosemary's wild-coloured eyes lay her maddestmost point. I found I couldn't tell Ann-Clare or anyone that the girl's madness might be contagious or that her proximity would draw out our own grandmother-inherited but hitherto hidden madness. I couldn't say to Alana that Ann-Clare's haircut was nothing to do with the tears she had cried for five hours.

It wasn't the haircut I gave Ann-Clare that made her disappear into the rain crying. The haircut had been an act of free will. She'd been happy as I draped her shoulders with a piece of shower curtain and whirled the old typing chair on which she sat. 'With stupendous style, the girl barber will give her sister an undercut.' I spun the sewing scissors near my sister's ears. I cut off Ann-Clare's bunches first. They had never hidden her ears, only emphasised them. By the end of a school day, I could always recognise Ann-Clare in the bus line by the way the light shone through them, lighting up the veins. I remember the frizz of broken hairs around the rubber bands Ann-Clare used to keep her bunches in place. I remember the snip of the scissors but not at what exact point in the haircut that I mentioned the incident that prompted Ann-Clare's tears. Something shifted in the dry rot of the windows so that I expected to look up and see a face framed by orange hair. My sister's tears were to do with Rosemary Kincaid. I said to my sister that I had seen her with Rosemary down near Jesus Bird dam beyond the graves. I had seen them I said.

'So,' said my sister, but even as I held her head to tidy up the hair around her ears, I was aware of the possibility of tears. The back of her neck, so skinny and exposed, went red.

'And I saw you,' I said, 'with the kittens. Near the chimney.'

What could she have been thinking of, I wanted to know, showing Rosemary that? For I had actually seen my sister demonstrate to our visitor how the black kittens mistakenly believed that the piece of skin between the legs of girls was the mother cat's teats. After Rosemary and my sister came back to the house, they went into the kitchen. I was there ahead of them, drinking the last of the red cordial.

'You know,' Alana said to Ann-Clare, 'we've got to find a home for your little charges soon.'

'Yes,' said my sister, holding a a kitten's face up to her own. As if she was totally innocent.

I don't know why I bothered to mention the incident with the kittens as I snipped and trimmed. I don't know if I knew the word lesbian then. It is possible. I think it's possible I even said my sister had been a lesbian with Rosemary Kincaid as the tears began to drip from her eyes and she said she couldn't wait for me to finish tidying up the haircut I'd begun. Even now it is a strange, sliding word in my mouth, with its inappropriate man's name contained in the first syllable.

'Come on,' I said to Ann-Clare, who had taken the scissors from me and was cutting out a piece of the shower curtain. Under the noise of the increasing rain on the roof, my voice bounced off all the empty cake tins in a line near the ceiling. It became important to me that she stay and I tidy up the haircut. But my sister had fastened the makeshift rain hat onto her head as determinedly as any old lady. My sister was on the bolt from me again. I had called her that curious word.

Whereas Alana said Ann-Clare seemed like a little pixie with her short hair, when she saw mine, she shivered and said, oh, it's a hyena's cut.

On our morning swims, I try to ask my father why it was Alana didn't like me, but he can't answer.

He says, 'Oh, she loved you but she was always afraid.' My father pauses, thinking about his words.

'That's right, she was afraid of me.'

'Well. We were sometimes worried one of our girls might go a bit like my poor old mum. We sometimes worried about that, you know. Brrrrr,' he says, 'cold this morning, isn't it?'

'But she was afraid of me. And whatever I did was always the wrong thing. Anything. Don't you remember when I took her for that massage? When she was only just diagnosed? Anyway,' I say, turning the attention back to Betty though still thinking of Alana's look of fright when we arrived at the masseur's. 'What exactly was wrong with Betty? Really?

144

I mean she survived all those years on her own. She can't have been too bad.'

Alana had glared at me and the man, and in the end he had only massaged her toes. Afterwards her silence nearly withered me away. She leaned towards me but it was only to pull a loose hair from my head and to put it with great care into a street bin we were passing. I tried to take her arm. I was over thirty years old. Pretending not to notice, my mother swerved into the cafe for an icecream, more determined to deter any affection than to live. 'I'm a soul with a goal,' she said, asking for a double butterscotch.

'Well,' says my father, 'it's hard to explain. You ask such nitty-gritty questions. I've told you, haven't I, how Budge came to marry Betty in the first place?' And though yes, he has, goes on to tell it again. 'Betty had actually fallen in love with Tin, I think. That's what I always gathered?' Trevor Irwin Nevitt, Budge's father. But for Betty to marry him was out of the question. He was old and unsaucy with a cough that would turn to throat cancer in no time. 'He had just enough dash left in him I suppose to attract the attention of Betty. Her terriers were on a badger hunt with his in Kent. Oh dear. The cruellest blood sport. I think the dogs actually bite off the noses of the badgers. All rather awful.

'They came to this kind of compromise. Budge, who was already in Africa by then, would marry Betty but Tin would come to live with them, which he did, because I can remember him. There you go. Isn't that amazing? To think I can recall him so clearly.'

'Ann-Clare thought she looked like him.'

'Well I remember him as an old man with a big pipe and a terrible cough. Budge had a large rondavel for him. You know the family motto?'

'No, I don't.'

'That's terrible! Haven't I ever told you the family motto?'

'No.'

'*Virtus est vitam fugure.* Virtue is when vice flees, but Budge used to tell me that after you have worked through all your vice, then try virtue.'

'If only Ann-Clare—' I begin.

'Yes,' agrees my father. 'Before Jonathon Michaelhouse.'

'Alana used to say Mr Michaelhouse was like an old grey pasty. *Virtus est vitam,*' I test the family motto out.

'*Fugure,*' finishes my father for me.

My father considers his memory to be invincible, but the histories stay gapped and fragile. The dam water parts and folds before my fingers. It is numbingly cold but I put my face down into it anyway for the final overarm sprint to the side we call the jetty. When I look up Ally is looking down at me, laughing. 'Your lips are blue, Mummy.'

'Look, an *Onthophagus gazella,*' my father tells Ally, on the walk back to the house, rolling open a dung pat with a piece of gum branch. 'Now that is quite a rare dung roller for here.' And absent-mindedly puts one in his pocket. His profile is steep and old but from the front, if he is laughing, he is young again, his face the kind that doesn't easily age. His legs are very white from the knee down, from the wearing of long socks, then abruptly brown. To our right every ridge is exposed; the deeper the ridge the deeper the blue.

## CHAPTER EIGHT

'How many more letters, Able?' Lavinia is always asking. 'And how long before you are finished with them. How long before you can move?'

'Not much longer now, Lavinia,' I am always replying but even as I try to speed up, the letters slow me down as I read the correspondence which passed between Ann-Clare and the mouse man of the Faraway Group. His letters are huge, detailing as they do every mannerism of the marsupial mice he has been trapping for years in state forests and along dry riverbeds of the Lindley district; the dance of their tiny legs as he watches them mating at ten minutes after midnight.

'The thing is I don't want to miss anything, Lavinia. Lavinia?'

'I wish you'd begun to read them years ago.'

'Yesterday I found the letters from a writer who used to correspond with Ann-Clare from her sewing machine. I mean she used to use it as her desk. She was a doctor in a tiny country town.' I too once wrote the doctor a letter, indicating my relationship to Ann-Clare, shouldering in on my sister's correspondence.

I longed to receive the doctor's witty and erudite treatises on books and writing, her amusing descriptions of patients, but the effect of my letter was an abrupt halt of the doctor's letters to Ann-Clare. Although I sent several other pleading notes, the doctor never replied to me.

'It's clear to me, darling, that you must soon curtail your letter reading.'

'With every letter I read, I see another sprig of another story. I'll stop only when I've read every letter there is to read. If only you could meet Ann-Clare.'

'You know,' Lavinia says, 'there are plenty of people whose sisters are alive, who haven't seen them for decades. Who choose never to see them again. Who find it a nuisance to be phoned in the middle of the night with the information that their sister in England has just died.'

'I know. You told me that story. But Ann-Clare. I don't know if you can understand. We were inordinately close.'

'Able?'

'Iris still keeps in wonderful touch with all her sisters.'

My lover's arms encircle my middle. She changes tack. The skin on the inside of her forearms skims my navel. 'I remember this belly. Our first night.'

'I know. It was showing off. For you.'

My father suggests the mail I am reading become a bonfire. If not before it has been read then immediately afterwards. Without reading one letter, he tells me, he put a match to all his mother's correspondence with his childhood teddy bear on top of the pyre. He says all the idle paper is encouraging rodents and insects into the lining of the house. As if to underline his point, something rustles in the roof and small fibres arrive in a waterfall into the fruit bowl. I don't mention how I think he may be right about the bonfire. And has he noticed too how the house has begun to smell like the obscure library where I worked? That to slide open a drawer in my mother's desk is reminiscent of an old card catalogue, the entries handwritten on thick yellow cardboard you can't buy today, in handwriting so full of loops and flourishes they were like tiny works of art. When Ann-Clare used to visit me at the Romance Library she would sometimes come in disguise. So that for a moment I wouldn't recognise the old man with the moustache having trouble finding his way around the catalogue or the old lady weeping with laughter in front of the new detective titles.

Whenever Ann-Clare came to visit at the Romance Library, I'd feel sad when it came time for her to go back to the turkey farm, for some chore or other Mr Michaelhouse had left for her to do, or to put on the roast. He used to write my sister lists he expected her to complete in the single day she'd already set aside for me. The library would seem emptier without her presence at the reading chair to the left of the tall wooden windows. I would hurry little Mr Pocock along, encouraging him to vacate the chair early if Ann-Clare had written, alerting me in advance of the day she was coming. I would send Mr Pocock outside to paddle his feet in the sea or to fetch the newspapers. I would go into the office, close the door and climb on top of an empty bookshelf to see if my sister was anywhere in sight.

When it came time for my sister to leave the library, to catch a bus and then a train back to the turkey farm, she'd linger at the door, as if wanting to tell me something. She would hug me goodbye, tucking her face for a moment into my neck. After she left, I'd close the office door and again use the bookshelf as a kind of stepladder. I would watch her walking along the side of the building. She'd know I was watching. She would turn her head round on her long neck, knowing that I was crouched up near the ceiling. As she rounded the corner into the street where she waited for her bus I could see her body's final relief at having escaped my gaze. The last flick of her heels before the building cut her from sight. The bookshelf beneath my feet was very beautiful— the fine red grain of cedar or rosewood that may originally have been cut from the forests around Lindley. Then Marguerite Rawlings knocking on the office door; the smell of leaking gas suddenly more prevalent than the smell of the waves I could see breaking, the holiday feeling of having my sister at work fading fast.

Although I once worked in the Romance Library by the Sea, shelving or ordering or lending out books as I tried to be an artist after hours, I'm a rememberer now, if there's any such word.

Or I'm a preserver, Lavinia tells me, sitting in the

chair I've made for her back garden using railway sleepers and cedar left behind years ago by cutters in the forest. I insist she must be blindfolded before she's allowed to sit. I feel in advance my delight. For it is a chair for a giant, so that to sit in it is to find again that feeling of being a small girl, one's legs unable to reach the ground and an acre of space around your small bottom bones. The dangle of your feet over the edge.

If I attune myself to my sister's past, if I try to make myself as quiet as Ann-Clare used to be, as still, if I act as though no noisiness has ever propelled me, I am more able to understand my sister.

When I do this, I can hear the way my fingers move along the edges of thin paper, looking for the right words in Alana's old dictionaries. Remembrancer—isn't that the word I mean?—related to necromancer in more ways than syllable stresses.

Then I'm often waylaid by a word previously unknown so that I forget my original intention. My eyes fall upon archaisms that are lovely to utter because of their unfamiliarity. For instance the archaic word springal or springad, as in youngster or stripling.

'Hello, darling springal,' I will bend to my daughter putting my arms around her shoulders from behind.

As well as writing letters when she was married, my sister was secretly reading Mr Michaelhouse's old correspondences. Idleness or boredom or her inclination to seek out the secretive things and ways that run an invisible route behind every usual track brought her to the point of reading all her husband's letters. Or perhaps it was me, letter reader of the future, on one idle afternoon, whose drifting hand touched a letter that had fallen out of the top of a box and began as a joke, to read it aloud to Ann-Clare. Like Ann-Clare, Mr Michaelhouse kept copies of his replies, putting them into the same envelope, before tossing them into boxes.

After my visit was over Ann-Clare continued to read her husband's letters. She told me it was more like reading a history of a faraway time, about a person she didn't really know. My sister read on. She learned that many of the women who were still his friends had been, at least for a while, his visiting lovers. Also, there were the more hidden letters. Ann-Clare found these in smaller boxes, revealing a history of taking into his bed sixteen-year-old children whose faces held no wrinkles, into whose holes his small penis fitted tightly.

At first, Ann-Clare was surprised that the jealousy she experienced was so intense. At first, when my sister found photographs to match the names, she might weep if she perceived them to be more lovely. She would think about Mr Michaelhouse with Mary, Justine, Jane or John and of how he'd once taken them through the corridor tall with the shelves full of bottles, to his bedroom and persuaded them to let him take down their pants. These feelings ran strongly alongside the shame she felt to be married to a man so old and fat. Alone in the azalea-coloured light with illicit letters dangling from her fingers, she was half-afraid. She could see how the shingles of the window awnings were fringing and lifting and sometimes that would be enough. Or how old and dry the air smelt. Out on the edge of the garden, the shade line was changing all the time over near the turkey paddocks, with extravagant tree growth resulting from the use of pelleted turkey excreta.

'What I mean,' says my father, 'is that you've got to get going with your own life again. Setting out to read every letter, not only of Ann-Clare's but every letter in the house, seems rather unnecessary to me.'

'I want to find Mary Shore's address.'

'Haven't you found that yet?'

'I haven't really begun to look. I'm trying to be systematic about the way I'm reading.'

'Letters won't bring anyone back,' says Grandma, walking into the kitchen at that moment with my daughter. 'I always burn my letters the moment they're answered. I light them in the salad colander in the kitchen sink.' Another kind of sadness is imposed with the appearance of Patricia. Whenever she puts a finger to her hair to tuck it behind her ear, we can see the hobgoblin folds of flesh that lie behind, which are the remains of a fourth and largely failed facelift. Yet she moves as if still emerging from a Spanish sea, wearing a white bikini and moving her hips for the benefit of any man who might be watching. When we were growing up, she invariably sent resort snapshots of herself in white or cream bikinis.

For a school project which required us to bring a

photograph of our grandmothers, we were deeply per-plexed. We did not want to reveal our mad-inside-her-head grandmother's face, lest everyone detected the instability, the eventual suicide. Betty's face powder was too obvious, we thought, cracking across her face like a lunatic's would. Yet nor did we feel we could pull out the latest snap of Patrica lounging on a banana chair by a pool, her skin scorched brown. Instead we pretended that the grandmothers, as was really the case with the grandfathers, had died before we were born. And that all that unfortunately remained were their names in my own.

'Letters won't bring anyone back,' Patricia says again. 'You know your sister always did remind me of my sister Winnie, and it was nervousness that caused Winifred to kill herself.' She says this in a way that infers without doubt that Ann-Clare's dis-appearance was due to suicide.

'I thought you said Winnie died of excess iron,' says my father. 'Alana always used to speak very fondly of Winnie.'

I can hear my grandmother pouring herself a large glass of cheap wine.

Storm light from the west is moving closer. I notice how the vortex looks female: like a womb. There is an umbilical cord trailing for earth. As if the storm has thrown a statue down.

If there was a naked woman across the river, on that slope of land, would I see her? And what colours would I see? Or would I only just be able to make out a faint stencil of a figure, as difficult to sex as a baby mouse, its holes or protuberances hidden by the distance? If it was my sister, wouldn't some extra sense in my blood, in my bones, tell me she had begun to cross the land immediately in front of the hills and was on her way home? How far away would Lavinia have to be before she became invisible?

In the house, in a storm, you could almost be in an ocean-going vessel. Storms make it seem quite frail. I can feel the internal timbers of cheap yellow pine taking on a judder. The original farmhouse is stronger. Even though its timbers have popped out in places along the most exposed side and the roof in one section has begun to peel back, its shape gives the feeling that it will never fly apart; that its final passing will take place slowly, long after we are dead, the hardwood walls nailed when green, unclenching out of position only with severe reluctance.

I go back into the kitchen to find that the spinning top flight of a dung beetle has arrested my family's attention. Ally catches it. Its iridescent wing cases stay disarranged.

'A little *Onitis alexis*,' says my father. More than any pasture experiment or resulting publication over the years, it's the beetles' presence in Lindley that brings my father his greatest sense of pride. He speaks of dung burial as if of some mysterious, magical rite.

'Is it hygienic?' Patricia asks.

'Remember Ann-Clare kept the boxes the beetles came in?' I say, peering outside, trying to see any small clear passage through the view our mother, in her own paradoxical quests for invisibility and drama,

156

obscured by dense tree plantings. 'Even when she left Mr Michaelhouse, she still had them.'

My sister liked boxes from a very early age. They were part of a secretiveness which was already there when she came out of our mother, curled around her own thumb which she was sucking. She didn't talk for such a long time Alana took her to a doctor, who feared autism. Ann-Clare liked small perfume bottles; scents intensified within contained spaces. Alana began finding boxes for Ann-Clare's birthday and Mr Michaelhouse continued the tradition.

In my sister's room where Grandma has been sleeping, there are jack-in-the-boxes, and small wooden boxes and the tiny silver smelling salt container, shaped like a book, that had been Betty's. All the boxes I helped my sister pack up from Mr Michaelhouse's.

'Once upon a time,' Ally says, 'Aunt Ann-Clare and Onitis Alexis . . . ' She doesn't finish her story. There's a silence. There is the first thunder. I feel guilty in the knowledge that I've been telling too many Aunt Ann-Clare bedtime stories.

My father is describing to Grandma Patricia the beetle's ability to clean up pastures and help prevent soil erosion. He waxes lyrical about the sacred scarab of Egyptian mythology. 'A beetle of lapis lazuli is propelling the sun god, a ball of dung, across the sky from which new life will burst forth on the emergence of young beetles from the dung ball,' he says.

I tell Ally that to look at a cow pat where the beetles have been at work is to see what looks like a board for a game of Chinese chequers.

On his most recent trips, my father travels with 300 *Onitis alexis* he has washed out of dung and packed with care between layers of soil. He seals the boxes with squares of mosquito net and is careful not to stay parked too long outside western cafes where his beetles might cook to death. No one pays him for these services to Australian soil, and as far as I know no one else is aware of his task. As he always used to, he turns his car down unmarked roads in the hope that he will find without a map or tourist-pamphlet suggestion, a view of eerie magnificence or a scrub glade of unparalleled peacefulness.

He dreams of spreading the rarer beetles west; the hard to establish *Onitis caffer* and the shiny black *Hister nomas* that, although not a true dung beetle, nevertheless resembles a Turkish delight chocolate.

'How fascinating,' says Patricia, 'the Australian wildlife.'

'African,' says my father. '*Onitis alexis* is an African, not an Australian.'


In Africa, in the half-light of my imagination and memory, it is getting dark. Ben Jussab's ruby waistcoat gleams in the moonlight. It's almost impossible to tell that underneath the acres of blankets are sleeping mothers and children, brothers and uncles, all waiting for a bus that is presently eight hours late. I see how honed the muscles in Ann-Clare's legs have become, as if she's been walking in mountainous terrain for months.There are scratches all over her legs and her left big toenail is missing.

The night's easy to see through. Only the night-watchman across the road in front of a low, long building seems to notice us. He is hunched in front of his small fire, facing our way, a knobbly bit of wood in one hand. A maize worker goes by on a tractor with only one headlight. He is wearing a hat. I want to catch my sister's eye to say: 'As if the moon could burn him!' Or to ask her if she knows what makes the African air so spicy. Does it remind her of the cardamon lily over the back garden tap? And to what town is she hoping to reach on one of the rackety local buses? But at that moment my sister gets to her feet. She goes around the side of the building, behind a tree. Some African women are there and they laugh with their hands near their faces, because it is a white woman having a pee in the African way. Half-standing rather than squatting down.

Patricia taps the bottle. My father's broken nose has brightened with wine. Between us we are drinking three bottles a night and that doesn't count Patricia's own private cellar that she has in her bedroom. He is still explaining to little Alana about the magic of dung beetles; the legs that can roll such a round ball. Ally drapes herself over the kitchen counter and makes a joke about a beetle burrowing by mistake into Grandma Pat. Patricia is intent on draining her wine. I begin to make tomato sandwiches. My father bites into a tomato and a seed lands on my child's face like a shiny bead.

After my sister was born I arrived with our father

at the hospital carrying a wicker basket which carried its own small white doll and a very large Granny Smith apple. Because our parents had moved to Lindley from Africa, the nurses couldn't believe the baby wasn't at least a bit brown. I remember putting my baby doll near the woodpile and chopping its arms and legs off, but I don't remember the host of other small, jealous cruelties Alana said I inflicted upon Ann-Clare. I don't remember trying to spoon a bottle of cough medicine into her mouth or that when no one else was in the room I'd begin to pull Ann-Clare's hair out until Alana, fearing Ann-Clare had baby baldness, took her to the doctor.

When I came home from Africa to have Ben Jussab's child in Australia, nurses who might've been girls I went to school with came to stare at Alana Clare's mulberry eyes and to marvel at the way they matched her skin. I wanted to ask were they so-and-so or so-and-so, the sister of the girl in Ann-Clare's class, but they shifted their eyes away from mine and only half-normal pleasantries were exchanged.

Our father was present for Ann-Clare's and Ally's births. And if the presence of a father was considered odd for Alana's labour with Ann-Clare, a grandfather's presence during the birth of Ally was considered even stranger. Our father, as when we were children, has no grasp of how the Lindley district perceives things. He's such a proud grandfather that even now I'll overhear him telling an old farmer who has come to ask his advice about a noxious grass, all the details of his grand-daughter's birth, oblivious to the farmer's obvious discomfort with such a subject. Not even noticing, my father presses on more eloquently than ever. He wants to convey how close to life it made him feel, even though half his family has gone—Alana buried with the Catholics and Ann-Clare never home from Africa. It's also as if an old farmer who has rashly called in for some free advice about the Giant Rats Tail grasses invading his farm, who will never risk it again, might hold a hitherto unthought of answer. Or as if the very ordinariness of the old Australian man before him, on an ordinary autumn day, might bring order back into his own life.

When I begin to sprinkle salt onto some of the sandwiches, my father adopts a sorrowful voice. He says salt is white death. He says it's a crime to have Ally wanting salt on her sandwich.

'Not really true when you think about Iris,' I point out. 'She still drinks a spoonful in every cup of tea. She says it's an elixir not a killer.'

'Is that really right?' asks my father.

'Shall we have a record night?' Patricia asks.

'Pat, my knees are very sore.' He brushes his hair back with both hands and looks at his image in the beginning of the reflections appearing in the windows.

As the storm hits, Ally too is preening herself. Alana hid the view with trees at the same time as insisting there never be curtains in the new house. As if there was still a sweeping outlook. In truth, at this time of day, the only thing we see is a glass tableau of the family itself, diminished by Ann-Clare and Alana's lengthening absence.

I've stopped asking my father if he'd like a haircut. The last time I cut it he picked a piece up from the verandah floorboards and said it seemed like the fur of an Arctic rabbit. Now he often refers to himself in the third person by that name and that character becomes part of the Aunt Anne-Clare, Arctic Rabbit and Onitis Alexis type stories, which I tell to Ally to send her to sleep at night. Or I sing *The big ship sails on the illy ally oh.*

Moths the size of sparrows move between the kitchen and sitting room. Ally pretends to shoot them, turning her fingers into pistols. The thunder matches her thumb pulling the imaginary trigger.

My father switches on the wireless. The news is the same as this morning's. There is a radioactive cloud floating in Siberia, three kilometres above the ground. Also, the man who invented Scrabble died today.

'Oh,' I say, 'Lavinia's coming over tonight to play a commemorative game.'

'Good, good, good,' says Ally.

'You can only play for a while, darling.'

'Oh dear,' my father sighs. 'More street fighting in Durban. Two women killed right near the Royal.'

The night I spent with my father in Durban's Royal Hotel wasn't enjoyable. He thought it would be the terraced and beautiful building of his childhood visits there with Budge but in the intervening years, a forty-storey tower had been built in its place and the old building could only be found in black and white photos on the new hotel's walls. The numerous staff thought I was my father's new young wife and it was only with considerable difficulty that another room with single beds was found.

Mist begins to rise from the faraway river. It is growing into the shape of several horses' heads which move in majestic procession along the little valleys and up the ridges. Then their manes seem to catch fire. As is often the case, the power cuts out after the storm has passed. Ally goes to find some candles in preparation for the Scrabble game. I hear Patricia licking her lips. It will be uncannily still tomorrow morning, all the garrulous birds blown away. The galahs. The cockatoos.

With Ben Jussab, in the story inside my head, it is a different month. The sky is so pale it's almost as white as the dead lawn. Ann-Clare says she can better understand her own propensity to fall in love with dead people now that she's disappeared herself.

I want to turn to Ben Jussab to say how impossible it has been to believe that my little sister who usually followed me, who was so irresolute over almost every decision she had to make, hasn't written me a letter clarifying her whereabouts once and for all, or details of an address where someone could send on her letters. Ann-Clare, I want to ask, was it because of your old husband's treatment of you? Or that when you were little your umbilical hernia stitches kept exploding so they tied your hands in hospital, separating you from us for too long? Is it because Alana died? Is it something to do with me?

Without light, the edge of the dry vlei seen through the threadbare hedge turns drab and surburban looking and my grievances stay unspoken. Apart from house staff going to catch buses home, the vlei might as well be the garden of Mrs Watts, the Lindley librarian; its own edges burnt from the vacant block's last blady grass fire. I wonder at what place in the hedge Ben ties the arm of marijuana he collects wrapped in newspaper from a man at Queens Hotel.

My sister drapes herself over Ben Jussab's shoulders from behind. As casually as I can, I scrutinise her posture, searching for the truth. Soon, I imagine, Ben Jussab and Ann-Clare will move to his house, across the empty parquet floors to the room where all that is left is a large, low bed.

Sitting in the farm kitchen I can feel my desire for Lavinia to arrive, to break off this story which carries with it a continual shame. I can feel the silence. Not even Patricia is speaking. The house holds the silence of a shadow.

Through the rip in Ben Jussab's bedroom curtains I think I can see Alana's tooth. It is so heavy and Ann-Clare's been wearing it so long, it appears to have given her a false lobe. The curtains are crimson and his skin takes on a crimson hue. Ann-Clare turns to face his nipples which are frilled and of different colours. She licks the pink one.

In Ben Jussab's last letter, he described how it was the click from a toy gun which made the latest burglar of his house leap through the bedroom window, leaving a human-shaped space in the glass.

After a storm, the flow of water in the gutters.

'You're very quiet, Able,' says my father to me. I don't mention that when I have fallen so quiet I am really in Harare. He would only think his and Alana's old fears have again or at last come to fruition. That if one daughter went looking for a waterfall and never came back, then the other is also following in Betty's mad footsteps, whose name is half my own.

Before Scrabble, I walk with Lavinia around the Abandoned House. The building stays empty and untouched. Alana's plans to one day convert it into farm holiday accommodation, and Ann-Clare's and mine to fix it up and live there as farming sisters never come to fruition. As I stand there at sunset with my Majestic Artichoke, she takes my elbow in her hands. Her arm is shorter than mine and she is taller, but still, in an odd kind of way, we fit together. Where Rosemary and Ann-Clare performed the tumbling trick are only unflowering salvias and a few wild snow peas that squeak in the night if they are picked.

'The light is exceptionally beautiful after the storm, isn't it, Lavinia?' For still I only call her majestic in my own mind. It is a golden light, drifting from hill to hill into the stinging trees.

'What is it about an old building?' Lavinia wonders aloud.

'What?'

'Whenever we walk here I want to turn you against the wall and kiss you madly!'

'I think it's a kind of sexual charge. Like a dark street at night. What would Grandma think?'

'She might get a little charged feeling, herself.' Lavinia squeezes my elbow a little bit tighter.

'Can you really put up with Patricia tonight?'

'As long as I can have Ally as my Scrabble partner.'

'When the Kincaids left,' I tell Lavinia, 'taking Rosemary with them, do you know what they gave us?'

'However could I?'

'Wildebeest tails!'

'What tales? Who wrote them?'

'No. The tails of animals. We were to use them as fly whisks.'

'Well!' Lavinia is leading me gently now towards the house. I can smell her surprising sweat. I'm just debating whether to tell my majestic friend that she smells delicate, like a wild rabbit's eyes, when my daughter comes exploding out of the house. She runs full speed, causing Lavinia to comment not about the tails after all but about how very long in the leg Ally's father must've been.

'Quite a giraffe, Able.'

'Yes,' I sigh, wishing he hadn't come into an evening's conversation again. 'He was a tall man.'

## CHAPTER NINE

At Harare Airport, which wasn't much bigger than the nearest one to Lindley, my father chose to wear his pack rather than wheel it on a trolley. It shone with newness, making him look like other retired Australians arriving for an African safari package. My pack was similarly unused. Stewards holding hotel cards up with names paid special attention to us until Ben Jussab came forward.

I thought there would be government officials, policemen. I thought the man in the shabby wooden box checking my passport would notice my name and know me immediately as the sister of the missing Australian girl. But he stamped my passport without a word and there was only Ben Jussab; no special delegations or envoys, no old university friends of my father because he'd deliberately kept hazy our exact day of arrival. The arrangements for Ben Jussab to drive us to Mutare had been made from Australia. I had first heard his voice from thousands of miles away like a soft bubbling fish over a very bad telephone line.

'How on earth did you know us?' asked my father. 'How could you know we're Ann-Clare's family?'

'Avis,' said Ben Jussab. 'Avis is the spitting image of her sister.'

'Hello.' I put down my hand luggage to shake his hand. He smiled and said he wished the circumstances were happier. His voice, more English than Alana's, made me feel by contrast that I was speaking an exaggerated kind of Australian.

Letter writers are spies. From Ann-Clare's letters, I felt I knew all about Ben Jussab already. I knew his family was quite rich: traders in concrete in Europe and the UK, but with strands of the family still living in Zimbabwe running restaurants, or in poverty in India. I knew he'd floated around a variety of jobs since finishing a maths degree in London. That many failed relationships lay behind him. As Ann-Clare had written, his face looked sucked in and sad, as if an inner emptiness had pulled away all the flesh from his cheeks. His ears, she wrote, his slightly pokey-out teeth, were so similar to ours, he might have been our brother, alive and grown, except for the darker colour of his skin. He had spent all of Zimbabwe's War of Independence in London.

'Look!' my father pointed to the airport's oval map with yellow neon, lighting up the cities of the world.

Thinking my sister had also managed to be here for us, though that was impossible, the hair on my arms stood up on end.

'Isn't that amazing,' he said. 'Alana carried you in her arms past that when you were a tiny baby.'

Grief had affected my father's voice. 'I'm all right, though,' he kept saying to Ben Jussab who wanted to take his pack. 'Don't worry about this catch in my throat.' Not so much a catch in his throat, as a curl in his tongue; a kind of strain underneath every word uttered. I remember my father staggering with the weight of his badly-balanced pack but refusing all help.

I did not see much of Africa on my first night. I could not see any family resemblance in Ben Jussab. It was dark and he drove fast, talking with a quiet animation about the changes. I could see that Harare resembled any poor city I had been through, including the raggedy outskirts of some Australian towns.

Western Brisbane, I thought, all the shops barred, the straggly gum trees. I thought of a women's bookshop in Sydney where Ann-Clare had once taken me and of the shabby Lindley arcade jewellery shop.

Ben Jussab maintained the kind of polite monologue you might hear on a tourist coach, pointing out the Independence Arch, the signposts in the process of change, the new BMWs and Mercedes going past with well-dressed government officials inside, and then, having exhausted those topics, was quiet. 'You must both be jetlagged. It must be hard to take it all in.' And still no direct mention of my sister by us or by Ben Jussab. He began to list all the other unfortunate incidents which had occurred to travellers in Zimbabwe since Independence as if this would somehow console us, as if the loss might be more easily borne.

Only the sides of the road allowed me any feeling of being in Africa. The heavy black bicycles of a kind I'd never seen; African workers pedalling home. In the utility, no one was at ease until after a while Ben

Jussab put on a Miriam Makeba tape. 'This used to be Alana's favourite,' mentioned my father, tapping his hand on his knee. She used to clap your hands together to this when you were a baby.'

Inside Ben Jussab's house, the ransacked feel of it was instantly apparent. 'I'm afraid all my visitors must lean against the wall or find a nice place on the floor.' Was there more furniture when Ann-Clare had rented his spare room? He'd set up mattresses and showed us the bathroom, the kitchen. My father said that for all his years as a bachelor in Zimbabwe he had lived in similar, underfurnished pads. And that the very first time he invited Alana back for dinner, they'd sat on packing cases in front of a bale of straw covered in a tablecloth, drinking gin out of toothpick holders.

In the morning I could hear the murmuring voices of my father and Ben Jussab as I lay in the room where Ann-Clare had spent most of her nights in Africa. Apart from the mattress where I was lying, and an ironing board, the room was empty. Yet once my sister had lived here, her tall blue backpack in one of the corners. Before she took her boots off in front of a waterfall, it was to this room she had intended to return. She had left things here—some clothes. On the house tour, Ben Jussab had pointed them out hanging in his wardrobe, and a pair of sandals: her dark, night-walking clothes, but also some shirts of locally printed cloth.

'Why are they in your wardrobe?' I'd asked.

'It's the only wardrobe in the house,' he said.

I lay still in the spare bedroom, trying to breathe

evenly, trying to imagine Ann-Clare. It was in here that Ben Jussab's maid Memory had at first shamed her, bringing cups of tea or chicory coffee in the morning until it became so usual Ann-Clare wrote she could well understand how the habit of tea in bed had become so ingrained in our father. The only kind of decoration I could find in the room was the pattern of vines in the wrought-iron security bars over the window. I stood up from the mattress. Outside the garden was shabbier than Ann-Clare's descriptions. Though we were leaving for Mutare, I pulled the sheets off the mattress and remade it, smoothing out all the creases. I saw a period stain in the shape of a water drop, so faded and washed Ann-Clare might have left it there on her first month at Ben Jussab's. Still putting off the moment of having to go into the room where my father and Ben Jussab talked, I decided to iron a shirt. I unrolled a crimson blouse from my pack. The iron was a small triangle of heavy, tarnished metal. The only way of adjusting the heat was to push and pull the plug in and out of the socket. I burnt the shirt immediately and left the bedroom with scorch marks still fuming from the left shoulder.

The parquet flooring echoed.

My father and Ben Jussab stopped talking.

'Whatever have you done to your shirt?' asked my father, separating his teacup from its saucer and pouring slopped tea back into the cup. 'Ben was just telling me that he felt Ann-Clare was quite depressed. When they parted, which was at Ben's father's place past Rusape? That's right, isn't it?'

'At Umli. Yes. I was going to take her as far as Chimanimani.Then we were going to walk with her friend Rosemary. But in the end, after we'd spent a couple of days at Umli, Ann decided she wanted to travel by local transport,' Ben Jussab looked at me. 'I'm afraid Memory's away or she would've ironed your clothes for you. Bloody tricky little irons, aren't they?'

The echo in the floor. As if Ann-Clare were walking behind me as I went up the hallway to the bathroom. I kept walking until I reached the main bedroom and looked inside. There was a large bed with a black truncheon on the floor, a security measure against burglars, Ben Jussab had said. Crimson curtains beginning to pull free from their fixtures moved like skirts in a slight breeze. I looked again in his wardrobe at the way my sister's clothes had been hung. The wardrobe smelt of cigarettes and aftershave. I walked back to the bathroom. The toilet was in its own small room. I sat down, my imagination failing. I looked at my riding boots on the red cement floor and saw that I had come to Africa without polishing their scuffed toes. After the clutter of Mr Michaelhouse's and her bedroom at the farm, I hadn't pictured my sister living in a house so bare. 'The house I'm living in in Harare,' my sister had written, 'is so empty I seem able to think more clearly. Ben Jussab works long hours. I don't know what he is or what he does. Some kind of project manager? I keep meaning to ask. I do ask! But it's so boring I never properly listen.'

After I'd washed my face and come back down the

hallway, my father and Ben Jussab were still talking about Ann-Clare's decision to travel to the Chiman-imanis alone. As if it was his absence alone that had led her into a dangerous situation. Outside, a girl in a yellow dress was washing down the fibro wall with a long-spouted watering-can. It looked like a watering-can from a Beatrix Potter illustration.

'I think I can understand,' I said. 'It was a way of proving to herself she could manage. Without a man.' I looked at Ben Jussab, wishing he was not the type who left too many buttons of his shirt open. His shirt was red and white with black, hair-like spirals as if in a deliberate contrast to his hairlessness. I imagined my sister padding in on bare feet; her surprise at finding us sitting on the floor.

My father was watching the way the watering-can outside was slowly moving the dust from the walls. 'She probably still had quite a lot of grieving over Alana to do. And as you probably know her marriage had only fairly recently ended.' He tilted his head. 'Listen to the doves,' he said. 'Such an affectionate cooing.'

'I was disappointed not to go to the Chimanis,' said Ben Jussab. 'I've never been. I'd been looking forward to it.'

'Really?' my father looked back into the room. 'In all your years here?'

He looked at me then and I looked away. His eyes, I have never mentioned to Lavinia, were the most bloodshot I've ever seen and this effect of dissipation was heightened by the hollows under them. 'She had a kind of carelessness. She'd lost her malaria tablets and couldn't be persuaded to buy any more.'

'Well, that was very irresponsible. I nearly died of malaria when I was a child,' my father said shaking his head.

'I tried to tell her,' Ben Jussab sucked on his second cigarette of the morning. 'I think Avis has hit the nail on the head. She wanted to be independent. Those were the words she used. That that was why she'd come to Africa in the first place.' I wondered whether the look in his eyes had anything to do with the childhood trachoma Ann-Clare had written about. An Indian doctor in Blantyre had popped out Ben Jussab's eyeballs and had rubbed crystals of copper sulphate into their exposed backs while seven-year-old Ben Jussab screamed.

'Where's Memory gone?'

'Visiting her mother near Gweru.'

'Oh,' said my father. 'That's such a pity. Ann-Clare used to write about Memory.'

'Yes, they really were good friends. At first I used to think Ann would go down the back to find a chair! But no. It was a genuine friendship. She'd play with Memory's baby. Eat down there with them. Go with them into town. Can I get you a cup of tea?'

'Water would be fine.'

'Oh,' said my father, 'another cup of tea would be nice.'

'When I first met your sister, she was actually writing letters. She was in my father's restaurant, on her own, writing. Then she began to read a book.'

'What was she reading?' My father wanted to know.

'Oh, I've forgotten now. Something African. She couldn't believe that there were guards with truncheons in bookshops. But she was always reading. She used to take Memory's husband's bike to the archives. Reading old agricultural magazines or women's journals, reading, reading and scribbling little notes she'd later use as prompts for her letters. I used to ask her sometimes what was the point of her having come to a new country if all she was going to do was rent the spare room in my house, read and write letters, and talk to my housekeeper's baby.'

'She was always a bookworm,' my father answered.

'She went to the archives to understand how it was when our mother first arrived here from London.'

'She loves reading,' my father said.

The terrible uneasiness of tense.

'She told me she was Ann from Australia. No *e*. I'd no idea that a Clare came afterwards until she began to get mail.'

'So how did you get to talk to her?'

'When she was leaving the restaurant she asked my father if he knew of any accommodation. And of course my father knew I was looking for someone to share the costs on this house.'

'Why would she have given only half her name?' wondered my father. 'Doesn't that seem strange?'

'And letters!' Ben Jussab's voice rose. 'I used to love to see Ann get mail—such a look of smugness.'

His posture was so bad it reminded me of one of the squashed out cigarettes in the large glass ashtray on the floor.

'I have never known anyone to write or receive so many. I feel I know you,' he said, touching my elbow, a medicinal smell on his breath, 'you wrote so many letters.' When he went to get two of my letters that had arrived after Ann-Clare had left his house and also a bag of gifts she'd been buying, I dipped my finger into his teacup. Raw gin. It was nine o'clock in the morning. My father had his back to me, still watching the girl with the watering-can.

'Did you sleep much?' I asked my father.

'Not really. I nodded off just before it was light.'

In Africa my father's voice immediately had taken on more of the accent Ann-Clare and I had had to guard against picking up as children. If ever Lindley school children came out after school, we lied about the names of the calves, all of whom had the strange rolling Zulu names our father had chosen. Instead of saying this is Umfulozi, Xagete or Mfazi, we'd say feel the tongue of Betty, Blue or Blackie.

'That's Victoria,' said Ben Jussab coming back into the room and seeing the direction of my father's gaze. 'Memory's maid. She's a bit funny in her head.'

'Actually,' said my father, 'I was looking at the turtle doves.' And he tilted his head to the doves as if to a duet in an art gallery.' Are you feeling very jetlagged, Avis?'

If Ben Jussab had opened the letters to read, he'd done an excellent job in resealing the envelopes. They were the last part of the artillery of letters sent to my sister in Africa. I'd sent two or three letters a week, numbered in the corner, demanding news and descriptions and lovely-sounding African names that

I might use as titles for paintings of the future. In letters number 35 and 36 I sounded more excited than Ann-Clare about her being in Zimbabwe.

It's a hard thing, reading one's own old mail. No. 36, the last letter I wrote to Ann-Clare, described in some detail the failures of Maurice Smith—the grey haired, chain-smoking crime fiction reader. Our friendship, beginning as it did behind the shelves housing literary journals from the fifties, in opposition to Marguerite's continuing courtship, was at best a furtive affair and doomed of course to fail in the open air of the farm at Lindley following Alana's death. It was at the farm that he first spat on me. He didn't transfer the spit lovingly down on his fingers or with his mouth but actually slagged on my unopen opening as if clearing his throat in the early morning into a gutter.

Yet every now and then I still wear his dressing-gown. It is very plush, with small diamonds woven through prussian blue cloth. After our first night together I remember feeling very soft about him because he'd sewn his name onto the inside collar. An old habit, he confessed, which made me forgive him leaving my bed in the mornings in order to trim his nose hairs with a special implement he kept packed in his bathroom bag. After he'd left I'd blow the ginger hairs down the plughole and wash myself carefully, every fold and crease, with rose-scented glycerine soap. It would sting a little but I always felt immediately better. So clean-scented, I could dress for the library in a reasonably good mood. He wrote once, asking for me to return the dressing-gown. By then I had already unstitched the name tag.

'I think I need to go for a walk before we travel,' I said to Ben Jussab, putting my letter to Ann-Clare back into the envelope.

'Well have some breakfast first, darling.'

Ben Jussab leapt up from the floor. 'Breakfast, yes. I'm afraid I can only offer you toasted sandwiches.'

Walking around the block with my toasted cheese and tomato sandwich everything about Africa felt wrong. It was not how I had imagined. It was ordinary. It was very suburban. There were dogs and gardens. The tomato skin burnt my lips and only the approach of two African women stopped my tears. I didn't know whether to say hello or not. 'Good morning,' I said. They said nothing but when I looked back they too had swung around to look. I felt it was Ann-Clare's fault and went past the beer shop she had described to me in some detail with my eyes averted.

As Ben Jussab had driven Ann-Clare, he drove us east out of Harare. I sat in the middle seat of the light blue utility, between him and my father. Mostly Ben Jussab was quiet as my father detailed technical things about rock formations and grasses we were passing. He held onto his quietness. Ann-Clare had said he was like our brother but I couldn't see it. He chain smoked without much grace. Ann-Clare hadn't mentioned the morning drinking.

Although I don't smoke, I've always loved the habit in others. Not so much the smell or the taste, but what the physical act of smoking allows. My sister used to shake her head at my efforts to roll her tobacco, and do her own, using one hand as she drove. Although Lavinia limits herself to ten a day, it permits such a wonderful display of limbs—of wrists, elbows, arms, fingers—sometimes even the legs can be involved. So that in the very act of supposedly being still, of talking, Lavinia can be as physical as if she's dancing. The tiny interplay of arm muscles involved in the striking of a match. Or Iris' inimitable style, seizing her weekly cigarette in a pair of tweezers, her hands shaking as she takes a few puffs.

On the road to the Chimanimanis, the grasses were yellow with dove pink flowers. The grasses were tall. Then the land grew more female looking with giant blue rocks curving out from the grassland valleys.

'Giantesses,' I said as we drove towards larger, more precarious *dwala* outcrops. My father was looking straight ahead, unable to believe how little the road had changed since he and Alana were travelling on it in his old work jeep.

The registration details of the pick-up were etched into each window and cast perfect shadows onto Ben Jussab's forearm. He reminded me of no one. I could see no resemblance to us in his dark, finely featured face.

Four number fours formed a shadow on his arm— my sister's favourite combination, her lucky configuration. So that despite the cramped conditions of the front seat, I felt light and hopeful leaving the city. When I glanced back, Harare was disappearing underneath a sky the colour of a cheap blue sweet.

As he drove Ben Jussab frequently tipped drops

into his eyes. The drops seemed to make no notice-
able difference to their condition. He drove fast. I
could tell by the discomfort of my father that he
wanted us to swap places so that I'd be in a seatbelt.
Ben Jussab was telling us a little of his history. He
said he had the feeling that his greatest wish at the
moment was to be a game scout in Nyika National
Park in northern Malawi. 'I'd barely be paid but it's
beautiful country. Not much to do with
mathematics.'

'Neither of my girls would go to university,' my
father shook his head. 'Yet they were the funnest
years.'

The air was so dry, it felt like my lips were lifting
off, a layer at a time. My father said it was the altitude
and offered me some suntan lotion.

For a moment I slipped on the sunglasses Ann-
Clare had left behind on his dash. The colours in the
msasa trees and boulders were instantly more lus-
cious. The msasas looked exactly the way they used
to on the faded Christmas cards that would arrive in
Australia from almost forgotten friends of my
parents. If not for the roadsides full of people and the
fact that there were no yellow and black kangaroo
road signs, I could sometimes have believed we were
driving on a road west of Lindley; that somewhere
close by, Australian children were sitting watching
'Kimba the White Lion' after coming home on foot
from a cream weatherboard school with green trim.
Living some way out of Lindley, Ann-Clare and I
had had to run up the farm road from where the bus
dropped us if we wanted to watch animated African

game moving with the credits across a black and white cartoon plain.

The African women walked very smoothly, with trays of eggs or mealie meal sacks on their heads and sometimes they were crocheting as well, a contrast that couldn't be stronger to the constipated dairy farmers' sons, pushing cows along for the morning milking.

'Why didn't you drive to the Chimanimanis anyway, Ben?' I asked. 'Meeting Ann-Clare there after she'd done her Africa alone bit.'

'I think she wanted the time with Rosemary. I think that's what she'd decided.' He unpeeled a tablet from a roll of peppermints for indigestion and I saw that each nail bed on his left hand was ruined. 'I get away from Harare whenever I can. It's why anyone chooses to come back to Zimbabwe. To get out of Harare. I stayed on at Umli. My father drove all the way to tell me about Ann-Clare. I tried to join the search party but they didn't want me. Rosemary Kincaid was giving her assistance. They said they didn't want searchers getting lost as well.'

'That was very kind of your father,' said my father. 'I'd like to meet him.'

'Didn't Ann-Clare tell you Rose was a bit of a nutter?'

'She said Rosemary's parents were.'

'Oh, that's a bit harsh,' my father stopped looking out the window and looked at Ben Jussab. 'I've known Douglas since we were six. We'll have to see Douglas and Fairy. They've bought the farm where I first met Alana. Shan't we give these people a lift?'

said my father, as we passed a woman and two children by the side of the road.

Ben Jussab pulled over and reversed towards the running children.

'Thank you, thank you, *baas*.' The mother's smile engulfed her face. 'Oh,' said my father. 'No, I'm just Jack from Australia.'

When she leant towards the window, one vast brown feeding breast nearly slipped from her shift. She had a baby strapped to her back by a crocheted sarong. The baby was awake but quiet.

Could she and her children ride as far as the next stores? the woman wanted to know. She had a bundle of sugarcane and gave us each a piece to chew. My father decided that he too would ride in the back. For a while, I craned my neck to see my father talking in an animated fashion to the woman. The next time I turned around, he was playing games with the children. The presence of my father behind the glass altered the nature of the journey. It made me feel like I was in a pantomime or play and accordingly, I waited for some further development of story. I looked at Ben Jussab's forearm which had become coated in a fine pale dust.

I licked my own outer wrist and the dust absorbed all moisture in my mouth. When I turned to see if my father was watching us, his back was facing me.

'Is he all right?' Ben Jussab asked.

'He seems to be.'

'Your sister had a terrible hangover when she left.'

'A hangover?'

'Yes. A dook and diesel hangover.'

'What are dook and diesels?' I felt his mood too had become different and that in a different story to the one I tell Lavinia, some kind of dark flirtation had at that early point in our acquaintanceship already begun.

'Cane spirits and coke. White and black. I'll make you one before you go back to Australia.'

'And what exactly is Umli?'

'Three hundred acres of virgin Africa. A house, a few huts and land. An uncle set it up, building much of the house himself. All the stone is hand hewn. But when he went to England it became a kind of artists colony. The artists go to a bigger more organised place now in the south. I'm really the only person who goes there any more. Just for holidays. On the way back we could go there.'

'I'd like to. My father might not be so keen.'

My father began to tap at the glass.

The mother and children said goodbye to my father and he came back into the front of the pick-up.

'Hope and Redemption,' my father said.

'What, Dad?'

'Those were the names of the children!'

'Hope and Redemption,' I repeated, as if this was the first of many such lucky alignments we were going to encounter.

When we arrived at the Mutare magistrate's office there was a sign up on the door saying that it was closed for cockroach fumigation. Although the sign had been printed out from a computer, it was graphically illustrated with a skull and crossbones and numerous suffering insects. We were meant to have arrived in Mutare yesterday, explained Mr Dilley, a white official whose exact position was never made clear. He was like a firefly without its wings, with a luminously pale abdomen when his shirt untucked as he reached up to straighten the sign. He let us into the building and led us through a succession of beautiful old doors, all pasted with the same warnings about fumigation. The insect artist had become increasingly carried away with depicting the agony the cockroaches were going to suffer. Mr Dilley wore epaulettes and a pair of black rimmed glasses that added to his pallor. A cluster of secretaries looked up as we passed. They were examining a basket full of plastic gold hair ornaments. There was a slightly festive air, because due to the fumigation, everything was closing down.

No, Mr Dilley was telling my father, he hadn't actually been in the Chimanimanis but he had been responsible for the searches from the air which had gone out three times over the southern lakes section of the mountains. Of course it had been the ground party that had come across my sister's boots. That extraordinary friend of my sister's, Rosemary Kincaid, had accompanied the search. She had seen the boots first. She had encouraged the search party to scout for an extra two days along the Mozambique border when they were all for calling it off.

Although we weren't due to meet Rosemary until tomorrow I felt my hostility for her rising with every word of praise Mr Dilley uttered.

Ann-Clare's boots had been arranged on a table in

a shoes-on-the-wrong-foot position, in the middle of a room full of filing cabinets. A young man in uniform sat on a chair in the corner like an art gallery attendant. He stood up when Ben Jussab went over to him and they whispered something together.

In Australia, I worked out, counting back the hours, it would have been three o'clock in the morning. I felt the tiredness in my eyes yet paradoxically an acute kind of liveliness. I picked up the boots. Mr Dilley had taken my father away to meet Mrs Pluke who'd been in charge of the administration of the search. I had preferred to stay in the room where tangible evidence of my sister was present. I looked under the inner sole, looking for a letter. I couldn't believe my sister hadn't left me a letter. I turned my back to the young man and lifted the boot up to my nose. No smell really.

'Could you please not pick up the footwear,' said the young man.

'These boots were a present from me to my sister,' I said, swapping them over so that the boots sat neatly. 'We liked the laces. Red and green. I helped her pick them.'

'Please, please. Don't keep touching,' said the man in a tetchy voice. 'That is how they were found,' he said, standing up and rearranging them.

'We'll be taking these boots with us. They're my sister's.'

The attendant looked at me with sorrow and said that he knew how I was feeling because he'd lost two sisters and a brother in the war. I made a polite series of consoling noises, unable to tell him that my sister had often gone missing when we were children. That although her sense of direction was as poor as our mother's, a system of calls between us would always lead me to her eventually. 'We're going to go to the Chimanimanis,' I said. 'We'll need the boots.'

At this point I looked outside to where Ben Jussab had gone to smoke and saw him kick a chicken. I wish I could remember a nudge. I wish I could say Ben Jussab nudged the chicken with his soft running shoes. I wish I could tell my daughter something simple; that her father liked poultry. But it was a kick I watched. His shoe came out and hit the chicken squarely under its tail feathers. The young table attendant looked up at the sound of the chicken's outrage. The feathers floating along the paving were tan and white and Ben Jussab's shoes were blue.

Mr Dilley came back with my father and Mrs Pluke.

Mrs Pluke had a certificate for my father. Even though my father tried to say that the search had been far from conclusive, it was clear he was going to accept the piece of paper. I remembered holidays at the coast; our father's chronic lack of timing; in the old Heron how he'd yell, Ready About. But that before he'd said Lee-Ho he'd have changed tack and the boom would've hit Ann-Clare over the head.

Mrs Pluke held the certificate almost coyly, I felt, as if it was some other kind of certificate altogether. A certificate of merit or a highly commended. Mrs Pluke was wearing a huge white collar that made her collarbones take on a fine and delicate tinge. Her hair was braided in silver cotton to one side of her face and her extremely long fingernails were also painted silver. She looked away when my father accepted the piece of paper and then down to her watch which was gold, with a black, thin leather strap. Her skin was as flawless as a fresh blackberry.

'I am so sorry to have to give you this.'

My father also was apologising.

'I'm terribly sorry,' said my father, wiping his face with an Amnesty International handkerchief. 'I'll be all right in a minute.'

Mr Dilley was patting my father's elbow, saying 'there, there', as if to a child, and commiserating with my father that he too had two daughters. He was saying that we couldn't be in more capable hands in the Chimanimanis if we were walking in with Rose-mary Kincaid.

'Yes,' said my father. 'I was at school with her father.'

Rosemary had found my sister's boots, positioned as if to go on the wrong foot but with their laces in neat bows, the scuff marks freshly polished, as if she were putting them away in a wardrobe, not leaving them at the edge of a waterfall. I imagined Ann-Clare bending over to tie the laces, her finger holding each knot. I wondered did she remember, as she was doing this, a How-to-Tie-Shoelaces board I made for her when she was five years old. I made a cardboard sheet with laces put through holes, so that she could practise the technique. I would put my finger over her finger and they'd get stuck together underneath the lace.

My father folded the certificate and tucked it into his wallet.

'Ann-Clare's boots,' I said.

'Oh yes,' said my father. 'May we take these boots?'

'I'm afraid not. We'd like to keep the boots here as part of your daughter's file.'

'I helped buy those boots,'

'Please,' said Mr Dilley, pointing to a fumigation man coming in wearing blue overalls. 'You must vacate the building now.'

'Avis,' said my father, leading me out of the room. Then as I walked ahead of him down the corridor he remarked that my own shoes were not really suitable. 'Those shoes look very odd.'

'Odd? They're just riding boots. I even used to wear them to work.'

'Such an odd shape though. Not even polished. And couldn't you have worn just a little bit of makeup?'

'I don't have makeup.'

'You could've packed some of Alana's. Lipstick. A little bit of lipstick.'

'I don't like makeup,' I repeated, my riding boots slipping on the parquet-floor corridor past some cockroaches already with their legs in the air. 'I don't think it matters. It shouldn't matter Dad.' But he was crying again.


'They wouldn't give me Ann-Clare's boots,' I said to Ben Jussab.

'I think the attendant probably had his eyes on

them. Impossible to buy boots of that quality over here.'

For a moment, I was all for storming back inside to get them but in the end it was the image of the boots, their forlorn pose on the table, that stopped me. 'Mrs Pluke said they might be of use.' As if, like some different version of Cinderella, a Mutare official would travel the countryside with a heavy boot in his hand, seeking the foot that would slot, a perfect fit, into the boot with the prominent bend in its side from my sister's bunion.

Mr Dilley had called Rose Kincaid remarkable. I could feel something constricting in my diaphragm. Breathing was different, coming in shallow, difficult waves through the haze of my jealousy. Even though we were some hours away from meeting each other again I could feel all my old antipathy rising, and it was as strong as it had ever been. I wanted to tell Ben Jussab to stop exclaiming over the odd appearance of a chicken in the middle of town.

As my father queued at the post office phones, Rose Kincaid's phone number written in biro on his wrist, I had a vivid picture of Ann-Clare disappearing. Without her boots which had given her stride such a certainty and confidence, I saw her travelling on bare feet as if she had totally lost her way. I thought of my sister, deciding to go for a walk through grass so coarse and high, it would've covered a mounted rider's saddle. I thought of my sister disappearing into the grasses and continuing to walk, the grasses closing over her face.

## CHAPTER TEN

Rosemary Kincaid walked through the grasses with an elan I couldn't match. The awkwardness that as a child had made her move around our farm with the jerkiness of certain kinds of ceiling spiders had disappeared. Her backpack was enviably old. She walked with such spring in her step it was as if her pack, more loaded than anyone else's, was empty.

'You look so much more like Ann-Clare than when you were children,' she said, halfway up Bailey's Folly. She was barely sweating whereas I was in a lather. 'But you haven't got Ann-Clare's nose. Yours is thicker. I've been watching it.' As if my nose could shoot or injure her. For my part, I saw that she had grown to look like a picture of Debussy that Marguerite had framed for the library, the fanatical eyes and strange hair. I let my father walk with Rose underneath a sky that was full of mares' tails.

'Mares' tails?' Ben Jussab wanted to know. 'I haven't heard that expression.'

But in fact the clouds of the first day in the mountains looked more like fish bones; white vapour vertebrae. The mountains themselves were immense and

sharp but also soft in colour, a blue and pink chalk-
iness which bore as little resemblance to the ranges
seen from Lindley, as Rose to the skinny mad child
from the Kincaids' holiday in Australia. She'd
matured in a way which emphasised sinews and
muscles. I heard my father talking in his most animated voice about abseiling trips Rosemary had taken
in the Chimanis. I saw Ben Jussab watching her legs.
I put my hand on his hair, pretending to be testing
its temperature but really to avert his attention. In the
sun his hair was as hot as metal. 'Ouch,' I said and
for all of the first day avoided Rosemary as if I'd set
off up the Chimanimanis with the express desire to
discover nothing of Ann-Clare's last days.

'Uncontoured,' said my father, pointing out landmarks and naming the peaks. 'Alana and I would've
camped somewhere around here on our honeymoon.
That must be Turret Towers over there.'

I was conceived on a slab of Chimanimani granite.
The day Ann-Clare found a chart, covered in red dots
and old dates, recognition was immediate but still a
shock. We had after all heard the story so many
times, accompanied by our parents' sideways kind of
laughter which indicated the memory was at least
somewhat sexual. Each red dot indicated every time
Jack and Alana had made love as they travelled east
to the highlands, trying to make the baby who would
be me. Ann-Clare had found my conception chart. If
the chart was telling the truth, it was rather shocking,
I felt—the relentless way they went about it and
therefore even more inexplicable that Alana didn't
warm to me from the first. That she had given me

the middle names of their unloved mothers.

On the first night in the Chimanimani Mountains, I couldn't sleep. I couldn't stop thinking about things like my conception. I lay awake remembering the exact structure of conversations held one or more decades ago. In these, we were silent and our mother's voice smooth. She told us things we didn't want to know. 'After we'd made love . . . ' Our mother told us too much.

Alana said that though our father was the kindest man, and her kindest lover, he'd picked up some tropical diseases from his childhood in Africa. We turned our faces away. I held up my lemonade to see the beauty of the bubbles on the underside of a thinly-sliced lime. Our father was out in a paddock and although we couldn't see him we could hear the tractor moving up and around, closer and away, closer and away, as our mother described his smells and sensations. There was sweat in the crease of our elbows and the lemonade bubbles seemed to reach into the top of our thumbs for it was a hot June day.

'Conversations like this make me feel as blue as a vein,' I might have observed.

We longed to change the course of this marital narration. Tell us something else, we wanted to ask. Meaning tell us something normal, meaning tell us something not about sex. Tell us again about your startling lipstick and whorled dresses from London or about the refrigerator cake in a sunken garden in Africa, after all, if need be: the beautiful cold cake our father and mother ate slices of together the day after they met, the orange icecream streaked with crimson fruits. Details we'd known off by heart for years. But instead we found ourselves imagining the type of fungus our father might possibly have: its rainforest greens and where it would grow.

I don't think you should tell us things like that, Ann-Clare thought, without the words actually leaving her mouth. The silence, the politeness, was already settling inside her and already, though she sensed their danger, she felt powerless in the face of the next cautionary story about men. The overwhelmingly scatological backbone of the histories.

Alana and Jack had their funny little boasts and let it be known to us that there were certain spots on the farm where we must not go if they were out roaming. In warm rain, we knew, they'd set out hand in hand wearing only their raincoats.

If a stinging leaf fell in front of us as we tried to walk in the opposite direction from our parents, Ann-Clare would read it as a sign of impending pain. For a while we'd wait near the tree for another leaf to fall to cancel out the threat. Or Ann-Clare would pick it up between twigs or dock leaves to examine the holes as if they might be read for every question that needed an answer. Within seconds it might turn into late afternoon. We could tell time was passing by the way the fruit of the stinging trees seemed to have ripened in the deeper shadows to resemble purple lumps of pudding. Something would melt in our bellies if we thought we saw some bit of a parent's flesh like a white snake, or a naked ankle like an albino joey, moving behind the blackberries. But by the time I'd put the back of my finger to my eye to feel the lash tickling my knuckle, the ankle and foot, or illusion of such, had moved higher through the weeds. And if we heard our mother's telltale giggle we would pretend that no, it was a rainforest bird, chortling to the fantailed male at her back through the fast blue air. Ann-Clare's face would duck with embarrassment before we'd continue down the track, the danger over for that afternoon.

Was there anything we didn't know?

We never discussed it. It was a silent recognition between us that our knowledge was over-intricate.

Thinking about these things and remembering the kitten episode, I found that it was impossible to lie so close to Rose whose tent I was sharing. I didn't want to begin any exchange of whispered bedtime confidences.

'Still going on Australian time,' I said to Ben Jussab coming back out to the fire. 'Ann-Clare and I used to dream of walking here together. When we were children.' I looked up at the night sky. Ann-Clare's feet would be cold. Even in summer in Australia she needed woolly socks. 'I didn't think it would be so cold. I'm surprised there are crickets.'

'What's that other noise?' said Ben Jussab.

'My father beginning to snore. Rose should've pitched her tent at least another twenty feet away.'

'You're joking.'

'Just roll him over onto his side if it doesn't stop.'

'Why don't you have some of this?' he suggested passing a capful of whisky.

'Thank you very much,' I said, feeling that inside her tent, even though she'd said she was tired,

Rosemary Kincaid was listening. I could also feel the presence of the mountains, mile after mile of them, valleys and then mountains, grasslands and peaks, rolling east as I tipped caps of whisky down my throat.

Ben Jussab said my sister drank so much that the morning after a dance she'd find her hands and wrists covered with the telephone numbers of African men. Yet she could remember nothing. She couldn't remember the people she'd danced with or that she'd tried to give her shirt to the African prostitute in a red and blonde streaked wig who was always at Queens Hotel on Saturday nights.

'What would she drink?' I try to hide my disbelief at the stories he is telling me about my quiet sister.

'Anything.' Ben Jussab took some seeds from his pack and threw them at the fire. Marula tree seeds, he said. They burned brightly, like candles in the middle of the fire. He told me how the fruit of the marula tree is rich and delicious. 'Ann was reckless. She liked Castle beer or gin. She couldn't bear this,' he said, waving the whisky, 'but would drink it if that's all there was. I was always having to bat away the fingers of African men.'

'But Ann-Clare?'

'She'd let them put their fingers over her jeans.' He made a *v* with his fingers and indicated my groin, 'Like that'. He told me other stories about Ann-Clare, the alcohol threading him into a more talkative mode. Just little things, such as the day she was sick in the stomach from eating the cream of tartar fruit of the baobab tree. Or times at the Mbare markets buying food and hats made out of chewed msasa bark that she was going to take home as presents. He painted a picture of my sister defying the unspoken rules of Lake McIlwaine Sailing Club by sleeping off a hangover on the lawn in front of the restaurant.

When I showed him photos of my sister from Lindley, he looked not at Ann-Clare but at architecture. He noticed bricks and joists and the soulful expression of dogs trotting in the corner of a photograph. He laughed at the chimes I had made, with small wooden arms banging and tapping away at the tins. 'They sound like a spastic orchestra,' I said. 'Ann-Clare thought you could be our brother,' I said, 'but I can't actually see that.'

'You're so similar to Ann. It's quite strange, sitting here like this.' When his arm touched mine I refused to notice it as well as thinking it was an indication of something physical to come. I recognised the pressure in his fingers. I leaned a little more his way.

'Avis,' called out Rosemary. 'Please come to bed. We'll be up early in the morning.'

I pulled a face. 'I can't understand why Ann-Clare wanted to walk with her. All her childhood,' I whispered, 'she was in psychiatric places.'

'I know, your father said something about that,' he whispered back. 'Terrible parents.'

'Oh, I don't know. She was a very peculiar child. She tried to stab her mother.'

'The mother probably deserved a stabbing. If you could meet some of these farmers' wives. They're really awful people. If you meet her parents on their home turf then you'll really understand. Rosemary seems nice enough. Sometimes that happens. Some daughters escape. But most just turn into replicas. Ann was keen about walking with Rosemary because apparently she knows parts of the mountains inside out.'

'Well,' I said, tapping him on the shoulder, 'I'd better go.' To hide the dank nature of desire I felt had begun to float between us, I took the bottle from him and flooded my mouth with whisky. I looked with annoyance at my backpack, which even in the firelight, seemed to gleam with newness.

At dawn, when everyone else was still asleep, I found myself creeping out to the dead fire. The whisky bottle was nearly empty, sitting neatly on a rock, the cap back on. I began to dab at my pack with ashes, trying to make it look more like Rosemary's; more travelled, more mature. I worked from the top down, streaking it with pale soil as well as ash and using water to spread the colours.

'What *are* you doing?' Rosemary asked. She too had tiptoed from the tent to the fire. 'Listen, Avis,' she said. 'I want to talk to you. But alone. Not with your father or him.'

'One of Ann-Clare's boots was burnt,' I said to Rosemary. 'I noticed that when we were in Mutare.'

'That happened our first night up here,' Rosemary said. 'Her boot lace went into the fire when we were cooking. It was a really hilarious night. Remembering my visit to Australia. The fights between your mother and mine. Fairy came home, you know, and told everyone that Alana had turned into a raving communist.'

I wondered what else my sister and Rosemary Kincaid had discussed. Did Ann-Clare talk about me with pride or with a half-hearted kind of obligation? Had they laughed about the kitten incident? Had they mentioned me making Ann-Clare cry as I cut her hair as short as a Baldwin boy's? Or had those kinds of memories remained tucked away, each waiting for the other to mention such things first?

'Why do you think she took off her boots, Rosemary?'

'Blisters. The walk to southern lakes had given her two whoppers on each heel. It's quite a way. We went along the eastern side of the river which made it longer.'

I looked at Rose with naked dislike, hating her greater knowledge.

I brushed my pack down with my hand, attempting to convey that it had fallen over in the fire. 'You gave me a fright creeping out of the tent behind me.'

'Sorry.'

I tried to hide my hands. I tried not to look directly into Rosemary's orangey-coloured eyes, still small and watery with sleep, in case she said something. In case she mentioned how she'd paused for a moment at her tent flap, watching me trying to make my pack look more used than its brightness suggested.

My pack looked ridiculous, cut in exact half by its clean-dirty divide. To deflect our attention from it, I said something so unfair Rosemary Kincaid flinched and then crawled back into her tent. This is the kind of thing about myself that I will never be able to tell Lavinia. Tears well in Lavinia's eyes when she says

to me, 'Able! You're so absolutely adorable.' She
will take the whole of my lower left arm in her hands
and, supporting it gently, say there isn't a mean bone
in all of my body. 'My horse rider,' she will say. 'My
lover.'

Lavinia cares for me so much I bow my head. I
dip my face into her breasts or into the hairs underneath her arm which are so fine it's as if feathers
are brushing my face. For a moment I don't allow
my eyes to meet hers in case something in my own,
some flicker, some dark green spot, reveals that I
am not as I seem. That I don't deserve such uncon-
ditional love. That I am Avis Betty after all, who
so upset Rosemary Kincaid in the Chimanimani
highlands it has taken the whole lifespan of my
daughter for her to write to me with information she
once wanted to give so freely. Information that, had
I listened, would've meant I would have no daughter. So that I can't be regretful. 'I can't wish to turn
back the clock, Rosemary,' I write back in reply to
her letter, 'For here is little Alana Clare'; enclosing
two photos. 'Here is my daughter and Ben Jussab
is the father.'

*But thank you for offering an olive branch. It is very
kind of you because I remember that in the mountains
I was extremely unpleasant. Sorry. After all this time
it should've been me writing to you to apologise. My
behaviour was unforgivable.*

I write to Rose that I am fairly certain Ann-Clare's
last letter was written to a Mary Shore. I explain that

she was Ann-Clare's oldest friend and that in the absence of our mother, she is the only person I can think of.

*Mary Shore?* I write to Rosemary Kincaid, forming the letters of the name carefully. *Do you think that name rings any bells?*

Next to the waterfall where Rosemary had found my sister's boots, Rosemary came over. The water was so loud I kept clicking my ears open and shut. I thought of the Victoria Falls on the other side of the country that Ann-Clare had visited for a day; their vastness compared to the relative thinness of this one. Their upside-down rainbows. The small duiker whose nose Ann-Clare had almost touched. The smell of water in the dust, she had written.

I remembered sitting underneath the Lindley's Little Cascade with Ann-Clare. The roar of the water yet, paradoxically, the sense of cool space. Putting our noses into the water and feeling it whizz against our ears. The dark skinny wrigglers that would cling to our skin.

In the Chimanimanis, there were no rainbows hanging over the waterfall and the only animal was a persistent black crow, hoping to raid our backpacks for food. The river was as black as its wings, sliding more swiftly towards the waterfall's lip.

As Rosemary put out a hand of comfort, I imperceptibly sucked in my breath and my muscles so that her skin wouldn't meet mine. I could feel my jealousy spreading, its leaden tint. I was covetous not only of her role in the search for my sister but of her old friendship with Ann-Clare. I understood again how jealousy could really arrive as a physical sensation. A punch to the middle. A bitterness as strong as the local coffee in my guts.

I looked at the waterfall, thinking that it seemed not so much that the water was running down, but that the rocks alongside were groaning or creaking upwards and that the water was still, like candle wax that had cooled. Some bright crimson type of berry tree was bringing out all the blues in the mountains behind us.

'The search party spent almost a week from this point. As well as planes.'

'So it really was a very intensive search?' I asked.

'Yes, Avis. Really.' Rosemary gave an exasperated sigh. 'I wish I could make it clearer to you.'

My father had accepted Rosemary's assurances. He was sitting on a rock cutting everyone a piece of packet fruitcake. The pocket-knife wasn't up to the job. Ben Jussab accepted the handful of crumbs my father offered him with good humour. My father was taking out photos of Alana to show Rosemary and Rosemary was talking with her mouth full of fruit-cake, saying 'Shame, Jack, shame'. Saying her memories of Alana were very fond.

'There's some fairytale, isn't there, about boots? Oh, what's it called?' I threw my bit of cake over the waterfall and watched it until it disappeared in the spray. I could feel the threadbare nature of the civility I maintained with Rosemary when the others were present and felt everyone could see the holes. 'Elves who mend the boots for the poor, hardworking bootmaker and his wife in the middle of the night?'

'Avis,' said my father. I looked sideways at his legs bulging out over his knee guards.

The creases in the tall blue ranges to my left were too tight. As I walked away, grass blades sliced open the skin of my fingers. The grass was sharp and tall and my father hadn't mentioned its name. No change of weather had happened. The mountain ranges from this point looked sharp and unapproachable. If my sister could have seen us, from a peak looking down, we would've looked the size of matchsticks or thinner.

Rosemary Kincaid came after me. 'She took the boots off because of her blisters.'

'They were my present to her. When we bought them she said she'd have them forever. Now they're probably on some Mutare official's feet.'

'They might be, but the boots are not the point, Avis.'

'What *is* the fucking point?'

My sister never had my noise. She didn't swear. Whenever I made her cry, the tears came out silently, without sobbing. Like paper daisies, which our mother used to call Everlastings and which are dying off along all the Lindley roads at the moment, the quietness opens out in my sister forever and doesn't disintegrate.

I sit at my mother's desk, remembering like someone double my age. I don't like to think how my horrible behaviour towards Rosemary stopped her giving me Ann-Clare's letter. For the full five days we were in

the mountains, she carried Ann-Clare's letter for
Mary Shore. The letter lay at the bottom of her pack,
touching socks, flattening under the weight of food,
shut inside an airmail envelope. It lay there, unfinished in the same sense that a painting or a book stays
unfinished until it finds its audience. The letter waited
for its reader. Unknowingly, I followed it, seeing only
the well-worn canvas of Rosemary's pack. On the last
day, I jammed a jar of coffee upside down at the top
of Rosemary's pack. The jar wouldn't fit in my pack
or I didn't want its rim digging into my back. As we
began the walk down through Long Gully the lid
loosened and began to let out the coffee. The dark
grinds travelled through clothes, mingling to a paste
with Rosemary's sweat, found the letter and smudged
underneath the envelope flaps, so that the letter itself
grew stained.

Mary Shore reading the letter must have wondered
at the marks. She must have thought some African
mountain insect had made them or that Ann-Clare
had grubby hands from camping. Or she might have
held it up to her nose and caught the faded but still
rich smell of coffee.

When Rosemary Kincaid was hugging my father
goodbye, Mary Shore's letter was in the pack on the
floor of the tea room of the Chimanimani Hotel.
There was still time. Rosemary might've thought
about calling me aside and passing it over, or at least
discussing with me the ethics of opening the letter.
Or Avis, she might've said, here is Ann-Clare's letter
you could deliver when you get back to Australia.
But I was playing slug football. I was with Ben

Jussab in the bar. I gave her no opportunity. I said goodbye to Rosemary Kincaid with a grimace, shaking her hand so hard it must've hurt. I watched the way she hugged my father and thought it was the hug of a desperate little animal, wanting to bury into his neck.

I don't like to think of myself back then. I don't like to remember how I gloated at the time over Ann-Clare's last letter from Harare, so sure that of course my sister would've sent her final messages to me. I don't like to remember how much Ben Jussab drank the night Ally was conceived. He drank so much that, for nine months, I was certain my baby would be born with a look of damage, an alcoholic's goblin child I wouldn't be able to keep.

My father was reluctant from the first to go to Umli. He couldn't see the point.

'But it's where Ann-Clare stayed,' I insisted. I said it would hurt Ben Jussab's feelings not to make the visit, when he had been so kind and taken so much time off work.

The gate into Umli was a high and empty frame. Anybody or any animal could simply jump through. From here my sister had said goodbye to Ben Jussab and caught a local bus to the Eastern Highlands. She had forgotten her sunglasses, left them on the dash of Ben Jussab's truck. He had helped her board the bus. She had looked worried even though she was smiling. She was smiling at the children trying to vend her boiled eggs, and squashing herself and her pack into the seat where produce and luggage was being piled. She was eating a liquorice allsort, waving goodbye to Ben Jussab, a boiled egg suddenly in her hand, a headache stretching like a black rainbow around her head as the bus engine juddered to a start and three chickens escaped from a cage on top of the bus and formed a race line at the front.

Ben Jussab drove slowly for the first time on the Umli road, pointing out favourite trees and rocks. My father sat in a kind of daze, talking about the possibility of us visiting South Africa. I agreed it would be good to see the places of his childhood. 'I was thinking more of going to a few game parks,' said my father. 'When Avis was a girl,' my father told Ben Jussab, 'she was quite dotty about Africa. Didn't want to travel anywhere else. She had these Little Animal Gardens. They were rather good.'

My right thigh touched Ben Jussab's. He was wearing pale sports shorts. I was wearing a pair of jeans cut into shorts, the edges of which frayed upwards to where my thighs became rounder. I felt my skin against his all the way along a track made narrow by a sweep of smooth rocks. I felt like I used to feel if ever a parent walked into my bedroom when I was a young girl with my fingers over my underpants. I felt a sexual kind of hush had taken me in its hold.

I'd never seen such fluid rocks before. The rocks were dark, and dark blue shadows were cast down before our passage through them. When we emerged into a more open landscape, the sky was a mesmeric, fading blue. The road ran on, under low msasas. My thigh stayed against Ben Jussab's and when I attempted to ease it away I was sure he moved his enough to ensure that the skin contact wasn't lost.

'See over there?' he said.

We looked over at a rondavel. Numerous goat tracks spread out from it and ran away in all directions. 'That's Mission's house. He won't be far away. He's been caretaker here since before the artists and stayed on after they stopped coming.' Ben Jussab stopped the ute.

A man appeared from behind the rondavel. Ben Jussab went to greet him and for a while they stood talking together. Even the most basic words of Shona eluded me. As if in the circumstances, my mind couldn't hold two languages. Pieces of goat were barbecuing over a fire. The meat had been coated in bright orange peri-peri sauce. I could smell the kerosene oven heating up in preparation for some trays of scones. Everything around seemed very pale: the land, the colours of the children's clothes, the dough on which some of the children were sucking. One tatty flock of chickens kept passing back and forth near my feet. It seemed to be like the kind of scene I'd have liked my sister's letters from Africa to describe. Right down to the children tapping wire and tin toys along at high speed, to the goat's head lying on a plate, so little and black and young it had barely had time to grow a beard, the landscape felt like a letterly one.

For a moment my father and I stood next to the drum fire which heated the water for the house. He said it was exactly how the water had been heated when he was a child. Although the house was made from the strong stones of the area, something in its design made it look perished. Tussocks of grass grew all over the flat roof. The house sat dwarfed by the configuration of rocks it was built underneath. Some were the shape of gravestones, as if a bit of the Lindley farm had landed in Africa. In the late light, anything seemed possible. On the other side of the house was a procession of animals. An elephant, a rhinoceros and a giraffe made out of some kind of concrete.

Jussab smiled at them deprecatingly. An old relation, overzealous about concrete but trying to be an artist, had made those models years ago. They were something of an embarrassment to everyone which is why the bougainvilleas had been grown over them. 'Yet Mission insists on pruning the vines into the shape of umbrellas! Defeating their purpose altogether. He pretends it is because he was once a garden boy in Rusape but really it's so his children can keep on climbing up the elephant's trunk without getting thorns.'

We went inside through a stable door that led directly into the kitchen. Sugar ants with big heads were flocking around some syrup left on a slab stone table. There was a monastic feel to the cottage—all the bare stone, the stark edges of walls and, glimpsed deeper within, low stone beds built into the floor of the room with the fireplace. The curve of cornerstones didn't soften this sense of austerity.

Ally was conceived at some point during this evening, probably soon after my father had expressed a desire to go for a walk, and had followed Ben Jussab's directions to climb the *koppie* behind the house from where he would be able to look into a hidden valley.

Ben Jussab made the promised dook and diesel. He brushed the pinkish dust from my shirt. I drank mine fast and the alcohol almost immediately brought tears. I thought of my sister here at this house and I couldn't think where she might be or why it was we were in Africa at the same time but not together. The tears came up from out of a lump that seemed to have lodged in my throat. I tried to put my thumbs over my eyelids to shut them in but my lips had begun to thicken and I felt that if I didn't cry I'd be choked by the size of the obstruction in my throat.

I was standing at one of the large windows looking across to a view of a dam when Ben Jussab came up behind me. 'Let me cover your eyes for a moment.' He put his hands over my eyes.

'Oh,' he murmured. I could feel each callous on each finger's joint. He kissed the back of my ears. When he said, 'Lift up your shirt,' I did so, still with his hands blindfolding me, and my tears falling. I can never tell Lavinia.

I imagined my nipples were stalked eyes gazing into the foreign landscape. 'They're looking at Tit Rock.' He called me 'my friend', so that I felt genderless and almost afraid. He took his hands away and I pulled away from him. He told me my nipples were the size of the new Zimbabwean one cent coin.

I turned back to the view. Quite far away, in the

direction of the gate and road we'd come from, I could see the configuration of rocks he'd referred to and understood how it got its name. An apparently treeless, smooth stone mountain swelled out and up. One smaller rock, mauve in the evening, rose at the top.

Even as he was undoing my shorts, curving around me to reach them, I felt unequal to protest and also as if somehow, him having me without permission might unlock some hitherto untold information about Ann-Clare. There was silence. When my sister and I reached the age where the inside of our regulation school-blue pants grew sticky in the middle of each menstrual cycle, our mother said that it meant eggs. That we were ovulating. When I tasted it one day it tasted of lemons.

At Umli it was growing darker. I could feel the ovulation happening in my left side, which is always more painful. I was not particularly wet, I can truth-fully tell Lavinia, but in he pushed. I opened my mouth to swallow away the cool and thick sensations. I looked down. Mission walked past the window but gave no sign of having noticed anything untoward. I hoped my father's evening walk would be of its usual reasonable length. I stayed still. I watched the boots on my feet tilting slightly. Then a last slant of sun, so that the air wasn't dark, it was beautiful. I could imagine it was the kind of golden timeless air that would fossilise birds as they flew. I felt him moving in and out of me and wondered would he, in the way of many men, pull out at the last minute. I remem-bered the game of Rag Doll, wherein you flop all muscles and let someone else move you this way or that. He didn't pull out, I have told Lavinia. That is certain enough.

When my father was a while coming back and it was getting darker, Ben Jussab said he would also go for a walk. I saw how I'd dried on his skin, and realised my tears too were also tight and dry on my face. I watched him climb up the beginning of the *koppie*. The window frames and doors of the cottage were bright red. In the fireplace twigs and paper lay in a pattern that suggested one match could send a flame into the centre lengths of thicker wood. Even though there wasn't much chill to the air, I couldn't resist lighting the fire. In the reflection in the glass, the flames looked like long hair burning. I continued to walk through the red doorways until I reached the bathroom at the end of the house. The skin all over my bottom tingled and tightened. The bath was a roughly-tiled square set thigh-deep below the level of the floor. Discarded sculptures, carved from serpentine, crowded the corners of the room. When I tried to turn their faces to the wall, other faces materialised in the disfigurations of stone at the back of their skulls.

In the bath, the steam billowed around. I couldn't see my toes. As I twisted the taps, I became aware of a faint but definite smell of rust, rising in the heat. I looked around for a bottle of bubblebath or even shampoo but there was nothing apart from a disintegrating and empty packet of Lux Flakes that looked as if it had stepped right out of the sixties, the style of packaging was so old.

I heard my father and Ben Jussab come back inside. I stayed in the bath until my toes wrinkled and I smelt burning meat. I let the plug out for a moment to make my belly appear as a small brown island in the middle of the bath. I think I knew already that I was pregnant.

'No one's ever used that bath. I doubt it's ever been cleaned,' Ben Jussab said to me when I came out. Light from the fire sprang across his skin like black and white wings. Magpie, I thought. I didn't know anything about him. I averted my eyes. The *Saut de Pie*, I thought. The Magpie Jump. An irregular passage in the middle of an otherwise immaculate dressage test.

'You should've come for the walk, darling,' said my father. 'There's a hidden valley.'

'There are many of those,' said Ben Jussab. 'If you weren't in such a hurry.'

I promised them that tomorrow, in the early morning, I would have a look but that my father was right, we shouldn't stay too long in Africa. There was the farm. There were arrangements about Ann-Clare to be made.

Long after my father went to bed, I didn't sleep. My father slept in the corner bed about fifteen feet from the fire. Ben Jussab stayed up, drinking by the fire, looking over at me every now and then but I had my head buried into the bedding in such a way he couldn't have known I was awake. Eventually his snoring joined my father's and I could be awake without need for disguise.

I was still looking when the night began to fade at its edges. I tried to look for the resemblances Ann-Clare had often written of and still couldn't find them. Ben Jussab's skin was like that of an aubergine: no wrinkles, yet he didn't look like a young man any more. A thin sweat slid out from under his arms, across his chest. I got up to have a better look. I noticed the queer, alcoholic swell of his belly. But muscle not fat. If he were a horse you wouldn't buy him. Odd conformation of the legs. My own stomach when I lifted my shirt was mauve and fatless. I kept drinking water, filling an enamel cup. Drinking it down. I saw curious sculptures of ash as they grew up from the bottom of the nearly dead paraffin lamp. For so early in the morning there was quite a strong wind. A check curtain in a window above my father's bed was being sucked in and out. I moved between my father and the father of my child. I traced a hide-and-seek snake on Ben Jussab's sleeping body. Draw a snake on this man's back, dot two eyes and paint him black. I put my hand next to his, imagining the colour a baby would be.

Outside, the wind made a tunnel out of my thighs and blew my pee away. One grass tussock blew clear of the roof and landed with a slapping noise into the dam. The first sun picked out the crimson of the tree leaves and I began to follow what seemed to be a pathway of light. I came to a place where I could see not plains but uneven valleys, cut open by rocks. But within the miniature valleys, yellow grasslands and smaller rocks that were golden, not grey.

Eventually, if I'd kept walking, I'd have reached

Slit Rock, with its narrow dark lips of stone. Last night Ben Jussab had told me that pink quartzites were inside the cave which when rubbed on skin made a person sparkle and glitter, and on its eastern precipice, the digging and grinding tools of women from very long ago. I could see the Crusader he'd spoken of, a configuration of cobalt granite in the exact shape of a tall knight who'd died in a country far from England. And underneath the Crusader, the small spindle of grey rock pointing across the valley. Like a small boy's horn, Ben Jussab had mentioned, grinning and assuming too much.

There were footsteps behind me and with a sense of fright I turned, my arm up in a gesture of fending. But it was only my father, his hair like a fluffy silver halo, upset that when last in Zimbabwe, he and Alana had been forced awake by the strength of the bird-song, and now the bush was almost silent. Couldn't it just be the wind, I suggested. But no, my father said, it was the state of the country, the loss of so many native trees during the war and the subsequent years of steady deforestation for fuel. He scooped up a handful of dirt, saying that perhaps in South Africa we would find the birds of his boyhood, the masked weavers and grass-seed eating bishops, the hah de dah ibis or the go away birds. A memory of my father opening his fingers to let the crumbly soil fall back to the ground, putting a false cheeriness into his voice as if we were indeed in Africa solely to commence some kind of strange father–daughter bird safari.

## CHAPTER ELEVEN

'These should be your halcyon days. You need a lovely, local companion,' my father says, meaning a man. 'Someone to go with to the recitals'

'No one could be lovelier than Lavinia,' I say. 'I'm not a child any more.' Lavinia is fond of my father without being very aware of his more exasperating qualities. She likes his smile and his absent-minded ways. His womanliness. How he'd suit a dress.

'You're still my child.'

That I am glad to be a single mother, that I've always avoided marriage, that I knew when I was as little as six I didn't want that, is something he refuses to understand.

'Did you see in the paper, there's a Spinsters Ball to be followed by a mock wedding? That might be quite fun. You could go with Lavinia.'

'Dad!'

'Well it isn't much of a life, massaging old feet.'

'I only do Iris'. And if you knew what pleasure it gives.'

'You don't even get paid.'

'That's not the point.'

214

'What about your art or seeing about a job in the library?'

'But I'm making things all the time. Cards. Chairs. I've been doing quite a few sketches at Lavinia's.'

The conversations can go on like this. Soon I will be forty-one but my lack of grey hair makes people uncertain. I don't say to anyone how Lavinia has saved me. How after seven years of sleeping alone, I'd begun to sleep with my hands clenched. In the morning even the bones in my fingers would hurt. But now Lavinia has unfolded me. How this has made me a kinder person, actually willing to stroke an old foot for reasons that have nothing to do with money or art.

So I'm shocked when I realise that certain young men of the Lindley Plateau are still sometimes trying to attract my attention.

There is the man who wants to do our firewood for winter this year, who keeps on arriving with his utility's radio playing loud music. With a kind of horror, I realise it's for me the way he stands there talking from the back of his ute, with his hands on his hips and his groin nearly at my eye-level. And for me, over the past few days, the noise of wood being split, at no extra cost, into the different sizes needed for the two fires that warm the house.

'Do you know you're just far too lovely, Able,' says Lavinia. 'Honestly, you flash him that smile and he thinks he's in like Flynn.'

'But I find it hard not to smile.'

This young man looks like a tubby bullock with white eyelashes and enlarged cheekbones. He's living in the old timber cottage on his uncle's place, he says, which is the Merwinneys' farm and working as a peeler at the abattoir. When I make the mistake of asking him what that means, he says he strips off the faces of beasts. He keeps making reasons to come by, though the load isn't ready. 'I'm searching out the best dry stuff,' he says. I look at his fingernails which have been scrubbed white. I begin to see that Lavinia is perhaps right. That my tendency to smile frequently and to nod agreeably to jokes not remotely funny allows such bullock-like boys to think that I like them. Such old, ingrained habits are hard to break.

When the wood arrives, if it ever does, it will be the uneven shape of the sounds I have been hearing in the evenings and we'll need all the skills of a dry-stone waller to make a stable wood pile. 'We should've got our own,' I say to my father. 'What's wrong with our chainsaw and axe?'

'But he was so eager, wasn't he?' says my father. 'And you're immersed in those letters, aren't you? And if it isn't letters it's old Iris Michaelhouse's feet.'

'I love her stories,' I tell my father. 'Iris can remember the beginning of the century.'

'Have you ever asked her about the local Aborigines?'

'I tried once but she didn't want to talk.'

'How old is she exactly?'

'Ninety-six. She's quite amazing. And to have lived alone for so long. She's a letter writer too. I write them for her now because of the arthritis in her fingers.'

When I next see the bullocky boy I'm sitting in

the cafe in town. It is a cold day and my father has put on his kangaroo fur ankle-length coat. Grandma is in mink. The whole cafe smells of its mothballs. The boy mistakes Ally for one of the Aboriginal children being billeted out from Mungindi for the running carnival. When I say no, she's my own Ally, short for Alana Clare, his face becomes even more like that of a Hereford steer being pushed towards a gate it doesn't want to go through.

If Ann-Clare arrived back in Lindley now, she'd be excruciated by the outlandish look of us, maybe even walking past the cafe a few times. She would've squinted in past the annoying bullock-faced young man, trying to attract my attention.

You'd think that having lived under the same roof with my father since our journey to Africa we'd know all there is to know about each other, but in fact the opposite is true. Instead, his vague, kind presence makes me realise how much his character has always mirrored those to whom he was closest. I see Alana fading out of him as for a while he sees this woman or that, learns to say ta and tea instead of thank you and supper, and adopts sweet milk tea instead of strong and black with such enthusiasm you'd swear he'd liked those things forever. He even picks up school slang from Ally without seeming to realise.

But gradually, after initial enthusiasms on both sides, the interest of the widows always fades. They can't get him to cut his hair or cure the African tinea that makes them itch too, and in their absence my father will again be home at night to tell Ally stories and to remember afresh the absence of Alana.

In a fashion I recognise as my mother's, I fill any letter I write with jokes about his foibles, but my knowledge doesn't extend far beyond those.

Tlot, tlot. Tlot, tlot, tlot, tlot, goes my father, as if a bit of Noyes or Tennyson has been muddled in, telling my daughter any story that stars a horse. Some of my father's stories are not suitable but she loves them as much as we did. He tells *The Hound of the Baskervilles* in such a low, tense voice I remember exactly the way Ann-Clare and I would look out our bedroom window at night and see the hound baying through the mist with its green phosphorescent mouth and red lunatic eyes. And sometimes there really would be howling: in winter, when half-dingo dogs came over the river from the forests on the other side and hunted calves or sheep or anything weak in the steepest paddocks.

My father still leaves out paragraphs when reading stories aloud. With us this was to hasten the story to its end and to get us into bed quickly, but with Ally he is trying to leave out anything to do with fathers. So that the *Just So Stories* can become quite disoriented and half-lose their meaning. Ally who begins to check the words as he reads will remind him what a large chunk he has left out of 'The Elephant's Child'.

'Oh my best beloved,' he says with a rueful smile and backtracks accordingly. To the bits where Rudyard Kipling really goes on and on about daddies and their daughters. And my father stops for a moment to tell my daughter that her father is alive and well in Africa.

'But why? Why's he in Africa?'

'Because that's where he grew up.'

In a second-hand shop recently, two women were in a room behind the counter sighing over a particular photo when I heard one of them say, 'Ah yes, the little girls are always their fathers' favourites. They need their fathers.'

'Excuse me, that isn't really true,' I wanted to rebut, but continued instead to lurk in an aisle full of smelly old romances until I was lucky enough to pull from the bottom of a pile a beautiful hardcover of *Tess of the D'Urbervilles*, its dust jacket in fine condition. According to the inscription, it was a present to Dr Hall, from Reginald, his gentleman friend of Junee.

Lavinia laughs on reading this, finding double meanings. She is good at this and at making me examine certain things in a new way. For instance, addiction to sadness, says Lavinia, requires as much pruning as any weeping rose.

'Yes,' I agree, thinking that if ever I have had strong belief, it has been a belief in the power of abandonment. My father abandoned his mother, tearing himself away from her in an undignified tussle in a Cornish hotel. He had said he was going out to buy them some breakfast, but sensing his imminent disappearance, Betty grabbed his suitcase which was already outside in the corridor. She felt sure he wouldn't travel back to Africa without his clothes. She thought that if only she kept holding on to the suitcase handle, she would go back too. But my father arrived back in Africa with only the clothes he was wearing, black ski trousers and a red jumper, and although he eventually resumed a correspondence with Betty, the abandonment was, by any measure, thorough.

My father left his mother and suggests flippantly, that I must abandon him. 'Yes,' he urges, 'or else even a holiday to Zimbabwe or Malawi or wherever your Mr Jussab is now. Don't think I won't cope here.'

'He isn't my Mr Jussab. He just happened to father my daughter, that's all.'

'Well, doesn't Ally deserve to be shown her heritage?'

'Oh please,' I can't keep the note of exasperation out of my voice. 'Ally is more Australian than Ann-Clare or I ever could be. Ben Jussab writes to her sometimes. That's more than enough. I don't want Ally to meet him. He's only her father by accident.' Which makes my father fall quiet because in all this time he never has enquired how it was that Ben Jussab came to be the father of Ally. And then I feel mean. It seems a cheap trick with which to obtain silence. Following such conversations, I should mention that we are moving. That as soon as I have finished with the letters, Ally and I are going to move to Lavinia's. I don't even know what stalls me really. A feeling that he will be upset, that he will get all weepy.

It's the grass that turns pink in the late afternoon light that makes my father cry. Or when he reads certain passages about the rich and matted grasses of

Natal. Little Alana has nodded off to sleep but still he reads on, sentences full of the antelope and Limpopo grasses of his childhood. And then I think how lucky it is that Redclack isn't far away. That my abandonment, if he chooses to go with that definition, will not be total.

The grass that goes like pink feathers in the evenings has a long and lovely name but you can just call it Natal Top Red. He used to put it into the bunches of flowers he collected from other people's gardens to give to Alana. It has always grown in the cemeteries. It can make the roadsides look like a foreign land. Or silvery and sad, as if you are about to remember something so upsetting tears will blind your progress.

In South Africa together, travelling through the landscapes of his childhood, the sensation that he was waiting for one revelation, as I waited with equal patience and longing for another, was always prevalent. My father's idea that a holiday in South Africa might somehow alleviate our suffering didn't succeed. In the hire car taken from Durban, we were cocooned from the heat and from the political situation by the weight of personal grief. My father thought it would be comforting to pass through old territory but the land was so altered it had the opposite effect. Memory usually magnifies things, but more often than not my father's memory seemed to have flattened out the land or, as with his old school's layout, remembered things back to front, as if looking at a slide the wrong way around.

We travelled along the east coast following a list that my father composed on the connecting flight to Durban from Johannesburg. The list included game parks, old childhood friends and haunts. As each site was visited he crossed it off using paint, a duty completed or an awkward meeting over. Some of Betty and Budge's contemporaries were only barely alive, and in their senility thought that I was Betty. It was very dismaying.

'You know the most exciting colours are alizarin and rose madder,' said my father, trying to regain a sense of excitement. 'Like venous blood.' But I could tell the strain behind the effort to appear his old enthusiastic self, his absent-mindedness as he tried to sketch my portrait sitting on the bench outside the Hluhluwe National Park rondavel. He kept dipping his paintbrush into his tea, and instead of painting me he painted a young Alana which embarrassed us so much he left it accidentally on purpose underneath a carved monkey ashtray on the tin table. More often than not we stayed on our respective sides of the rondavel or hotel room trying to stifle the endless sense of marking time. My father would lie drinking his tea on his side. His knees curled up. Or he would flap his hands that the news coming on was in Afrikaans not English.

For his birthday, which coincided with our stay at the Royal Hotel, he went into the toy shop of his childhood and was seized with the desire to buy a tin boat from India. It cost a thousand rand, and when Ally makes it move through the dam water it makes a ppp, ppp, ppp noise.

Only when I think of my father's childhood, can I feel any real familiarity. Then I see him as clearly as an ink and pen drawing, in a literary classic for children. I draw him as a line boy on a line pony the colour of old cream paper. There, that is my father as a child. Definite edges. And if the paper is old enough to have turned a particular shade of yellow, the pony is a buckskin. From the folds in the boy's knapsack anyone looking at the illustration could see that he's carrying a book, a bottle of lemonade and a sandwich.

Why is it that I begin to see so clearly my father as the line boy, looking around or looking ahead with a vulnerable expression on his face? Lavinia thinks it's partly a hope that I can force the past into an explanation for the present. Several times I interrupt my letter reading to sketch him in pencil.

Sometimes you see a living, walking child with the line-boy look. It makes people say ahhhhh, there goes a boy or there goes a girl with an old-fashioned air. In their wistful voices, in the lingering nature of their gaze, is a chafing kind of longing, a second-hand sense of pride. Then after this comes the temptation to follow the child.

I sometimes can't help fearing that my own daughter, having this look to her, will one day be followed. That someone, seeing the old-fashioned translucence of her skull towards her ears, that smile like pale curds and whey even though her skin is almost as dark as her father's, will want to put their fingers on her face to check that she is real.

The day our father found out his mother was sick,

he was Ally's age exactly, with a round, smooth half-worried face, clicking up his pony, trying to keep pace with his father. In the mist, Budge rode ahead on a gelding with an injured stifle. The horse also had scarred ears from Budge's efforts to tentpeg lemons. Practising in the grove where no one would see him, Budge's pith helmet had slipped over his eyes and he'd nearly cut off the gelding's ears.

The mist became denser and my father could no longer see anything much. He could see his hands holding the reins, in independent position; the size of his thumbs against the gigantic Indian army reins; the purple ears of his mother's horse.

Budge explained it was only his silly old dad who had hurt Blazeaway's ears.

The boy could hear his own pony's nostrils. But how, exactly, had Blazeaway hurt his ears? Again the boy kicked up his pony, full of questions. His pony's nostrils cracked in time it seemed with the cold.

The mist gathered in such a way along the edges of things on the early morning rides he'd go on with his father, that when they'd eventually reach the higher ground, it looked like someone had snapped diamanté earrings onto their horses' ears.

In the oldest sections of the wattle plantation, the trees locked together high above the riders and then the mist arcing over the wattle arches. When they reached KwamaGwaza Stores my father held Blazeaway. He didn't really know why they rode all this way every morning that he was home from school, but Nan Meakley or Di Hobson always came out shouting that there was a sherbet fountain for him, and that alone was a good enough reason. He sucked the sherbet up through a liquorice straw, watching his father checking Blazeaway's hooves for stone bruises.

'In fact,' says my father, 'I think they might've been lesbians. Even though they lived there with George Rogers, who became Budge's good friend. And then later, I rather believe Betty developed an infatuation for Dianne.'

'Are you sure?' This has never been mentioned before.

'Well that's just the feeling I gathered. I know that for a time Betty was very keen on visiting there. And Budge didn't really mind because he liked George so much.'

'What would you do?'

'Oh, whatever litte boys do. I was probably most often away at school.'

Budge and the line boy rode back through the estate. Budge being too shortsighted to fight in 1942 carried an air of apology and shame about this. But greater even than that, he tried to hide his wife who it seemed was almost certainly not coping in Africa. Mist gathered on Jack's eyelashes. And then drops of mist fell into his sherbet. Their creaking saddles seemed to be creaking out *guti, guti, guti*, which was the local word for mist. Budge told his son that although they weren't able to be officers in the war, they were key workers. Just imagine, he said, if our wattles were not producing tannin.

Jack couldn't immediately think until Budge said 'Boots, boots, for the boys in Europe'.

Mist made my father so cold that when he touched his nose he couldn't feel any skin. He clicked his eardrums open and shut, trying to hear better. When he asked his father what it was he could hear, Budge said it was the sound of the early morning air.

The horses began to reef the reins. My father bent his head against the cold and its sound and tried to make his body into the same shape as Budge, as if a curve could hold a horse.

But the pony was already picking up speed into a determined bolt. My father felt like he was travelling as fast as one of the racehorses. Just when he was nearing home and he knew his pony would stop, he caught sight of movement up on the black tin roof. It was his mother. All the house staff were with her too. Still he travelled faster though it seemed clear that Betty must be clinging there because something at ground level was no longer safe. Toffee, the old man Budge picked up out of some back alley in Durban, who was meant to help with the horses but who preferred holding the wool out for Betty when she knitted, was up on the roof too. And Mrs Tookie, the old English lady employed by Betty to make sure Jack didn't pick up an Afrikaans accent. The air seemed to actually creak or ache with cold and the certainty of endings. He could hear this, underneath the gallop. But even so, he was aware of a great beauty amidst the incongruity; of wattle trees on rolling sandstone hills and flamboyantes peeping up from the deeper gorges; the red-hot pokers all in flower near the palm trees.

His mother was calling at the rondavel too, as if

Tin was still alive and also in danger. Yet Tin had died two years before, cancer of the throat, his horn-blower's pipe buried with him.

When the pony propped abruptly and my father fell off, he turned to see what his father was going to do. 'Go away,' said the Go Away bird. 'Go away,' copied Betty. On her head was a blue hat. Some furniture was on the roof, as if it too was endangered. It was some of the little and light-coloured cherry-wood pieces from England, most precious to Betty. Betty's desk, which became Alana's where I now sit each day with my sister's letters, was on the roof, its cabinet open.

Jack tugged at the Union Jack saddlecloth his mother had sewn. The saddlecloth had slewed sideways under the saddle. Budge looked at the sky. Budge tried to talk but this was quite difficult because at such times she firmly believed her husband to be an imposter and that the real Budge now lived against his will on Querboo Mountain.

'You see,' says my father. 'She believed a mole had moved on Budge's face. This convinced her he was someone else. That he'd been swapped by the Russians. And there was an incident with soldiers.'

'Soldiers?'

'One day when I must've been about fourteen, she told me that soldiers had seen her masturbating,' my father shakes his head. 'My poor old Mum. It was really very odd. To tell me that, at that age. But by then of course I knew she was sick. I've never known whether she meant she'd been fondling her breasts or lower down.'

'*Sakabono, imbegapazulu,*' called out the African staff to Budge as Betty walked backwards and forwards on the rooftop. Good morning, Man Who Looks at the Sky, because his gaze upwards was habitual. They gripped the steep sides of the tin roof with their bare feet as Betty put down a chair on the skillion roof and sat down at the desk, as if to write a letter home to England. But it was photo albums she had up on the roof with her, and scissors not a pen. Betty was easing photos from out of the corners and cutting out the faces of those people she could no longer trust. There are not many full photos left of Budge, only his bony knees beside a terrier sitting near his shoes. Over time, the only album that remained intact was the one Betty used to keep of sea passages. When I look at this, the photos are all pale seascapes or occasionally the odd other boat that must have passed Betty's.

She called her only son Muffin, as if he were warm and edible. She wanted to live with him forever and, when she couldn't, wrote to him incessantly. She favoured green, mist-coloured English cards of birds or bloodhorses in fields under oak trees. Although our father didn't keep his mother's letters, as a child I judged her cards beautiful enough to make a kind of collage on a masonite board which I propped for years at the end of my bed. When I unstick the cards I find that though whole words lift up with the glue, there are some written remains. In the cards Betty calls my father My Darling Muffin, writing to her thirty-year-old son as if to a young, estranged lover.

When I walked on the mountain at Querboo with

my father, I was thirty-three years old, and at first his childhood corner of Africa seemed much more prosaic than the stories he'd told us. Africa was like kissing someone I thought I knew only to discover my almost complete ignorance of them. Africa was a bit like finally meeting a lover I'd been writing fervent love letters to for weeks; first an awkward pause, then a certain boredom. But that feeling was as much influenced by the time in Zimbabwe as by the dullness of the land. The ordinary peculiarities that would arise for any daughter travelling with her father also played a part.

Around Melmoth the wattle industry was long dead; the Australian wattles that had been part of my father's childhood had been listed as an ecological green cancer, as an alien plant, to be exterminated in rigorous regional programs.

Gum trees had been planted right up the sides of Querboo so that you even lost the feeling of being up very high. But after a little bit of walking around, my father found the remnants of some wattle avenues and we were able to walk along these. The light underneath felt very old, and because the wattles were just finishing their old-age flowering, the light also smelt of honey. My father turned and said that although it did seem very ordinary, he had so many other feelings, vaguely defined, incomplete and mysterious. In his mind, he said, he would always see Budge and himself as a small boy, trotting to keep up, and the mist, sometimes cleaving or closing in until the road was lost. Then cantering down the hill to the store and seeing the tall and good-looking women, Nan and Di, who always shouted out the name of the yummy little treat they had for him.

That is how my father talks. He overuses the diminutive so that sometimes everything seems to be coming out in the archaic sentences of Alison Uttley—Little Grey Rabbit and Little Fuzzypeg in the fields of England. This is how he wrote the letter to Mr Michaelhouse from Africa. For almost an entire morning my father sat crouched over a little tin table in a rondavel at Hluhluwe National Park, writing to my sister's husband.

'Why, Dad? Why take so much time?'

'Because he is still Ann-Clare's husband. Because there's never been divorce. Because he asked, he specifically phoned me don't you remember, imploring me to write to him with any news.'

Sitting on my side of the rondavel I feverishly began to count up the number of game park slides my father had taken so far. I held them up to the light. Fifty-seven impala, twenty kudu, thirteen warthogs, one baby giraffe. In each slide the animals are so far away they might as well have been in my Little Animal Gardens. I wrote a scathing note to Marguerite on the back of an out-of-focus hippopotamus postcard. I described the mess strewing out in every direction from my father's side of the rondavel, the disappointing slides and the disappointing activity of my father. He was being overpolite to Mr Michaelhouse. I could tell by the way he was pausing so carefully between pages; by the way he looked up to study his appearance in the small mirror in front of the table. His words, I knew, were coming out at a pompous trot. Tlot, tlot, tlot.

The old-fashioned way my father writes and speaks can be endearing or irritating, especially when I re-read old letters of my own and discover that it is my voice too. Nearly every week, wintry winds or other old memories coming like a cold wind across the Lindley Plateau bring tears to my father's eyes.

The day will arrive when I cry again. If Ann-Clare were suddenly to appear. Or if something befell Ally, whose perfectly normal Australian voice never ceases to amaze me. Then I would cry. Or if our father died and I were to find him lying as if asleep in a yellow tunnel of lantana, then I imagine my tears would fall without thought, with feelings of grief and freedom. If Lavinia didn't exist.

My father was with Budge when he died an early but conventional death, on a wattle plantation near the town of Kranskopt. They hadn't even begun to discuss the different difficulties developing with Betty, when Budge, gesturing towards a curiosity in the landscape he most loved, fell backwards and died. The Grassman, as the formation was known, was a large knoll of stone that from certain angles resembled a face. According to the time of year and day and what grasses were in flower or in seed, the colours of the Grassman varied considerably. Budge had wanted to share the almost mauve sweep the Grassman's forehead had assumed in the spring. My father says it was one of those dewy and exquisite African mornings, the cloud only just beginning to disperse but then thickening unexpectedly to the left of the knoll in its exact shape. So that there was the real Grassman's head and then, almost adjoining it, one made of cloud. And in the clouds where the light was beginning to hit, colours such as one would normally expect to see in a wave.

When Budge died my father cried as he looked over the edge of the Tugela Valley where Budge had first stood as a young man. He could see all the African location areas, stretching out in the valleys and far beyond, to the north, Qudeni, the Mountain of the Cockerels, where as a child he used to go camping.

'You might say,' my father recalls apologetically, 'that the Europeans had all the best land and a cooler climate. And my Dad grew these wattles in what you'd call the Mist Valleys. There was mile after mile of these rolling hills and always a sort of misty haze. On the morning my Dad died I looked right across to the other side, to the Nkandhla Mountains, I suppose, which would've been two hundred miles away. But I couldn't bear to look at Budge's face properly, in case what I saw looked tortured. So I took off my jumper and put it over his face by feel.' My father sighs. For a moment he contemplates saying something about the possible nature of his own death but he falls silent instead. He brushes the hair out of his eyes. In a habitual gesture, he pulls an old rubber band off a door handle and ties back his hair.

One morning as I lie waiting for it to get a little bit lighter, I think I see my father racing a Red-necked Pademelon. My father's hair freed from its ponytail is streaming out behind. When he reaches the rows of furrows in the land that are all that remains of all his old efforts to cultivate South African proteas, he runs at them like they are hurdles on a track. He leaps over fallen tree trunks, moving the way he taught us, using his arms to make his feet carry him faster. The moon which is nearly full sends his shadow ahead of him across the land.

I lie back down. My skin is chilled from the air but in her sleep Lavinia reaches her arms over and under me and pulls me close. She kisses me ten times in a horizontal line between my shoulder-blades and goes to sleep twitching, all the little muscles relaxing themselves as if someone is actually untying them, loosening them.

There haven't been many Pademelons here since Ann-Clare and I occasionally galloped horses alongside them. Years since our mother would point out their small droppings to visitors with the African *kiri* stick.

On mornings of heavy mist, the treetops above the river are islands of tawny green that seem to be floating towards the first sun. Mist and memory are always connected, I think. Something that actually obscures vision on the day intensifies the memory years afterwards. And aren't memory and sickness also interlinked? Aren't some of the strongest memories we have of sickness, particularly family sickness, even of some generations before?

On mornings of heavy mist, I tell Lavinia, I sometimes have to remind myself that I'm not a child any more, and that my sister is also not here or down with our horses and won't be again.

Lavinia casts me a look of pity. 'I have to bolt over to air poor old Edna Love.'

The mist is as thick as cream in the valley but up here where we are standing, only the barest wisps lie around us.

'Isn't this your day for Iris?'

## CHAPTER TWELVE

By the time Ann-Clare was about fifteen and a half she was already a fledgling, a first-year member of the Faraway letter-writing group begun by Mrs Mary Shore before we were born. Knowing that Mary Shore owned racehorses and lived on a farm, Ann-Clare wrote letters about horses and dogs. Or about our love of dereliction which had taken us far beyond the boundaries of 'Jocund Day', across land that had fences so old the posts were rising out from the soil as if the trees above them were trying to reclaim the soft red wood put to such unsuitable purpose one hundred or more years before. Ann-Clare would send letters about trailing for miles into the valley, jumping the horses over the lowest parts of the fences, or tacking down steep gullies and then across where no fences were left and down still further until the shadiest valleys of all were reached.

After a few hours into the ride, we'd pass the dank and sunless garden of an abandoned worker's cottage. We'd proceed more cautiously, branches held out in front of our faces against the yellow webs of the St Anthony's Cross spiders which if unbroken would catch your neck as if on a nylon gyre rope. Or there might be no cottage left at all, only the towering guard trees, grown twice or three times beyond all expectation of the woman who once planted them, and a dark, opaque wedge of green against the sky.

On the day that we first met Iris and Mr Michaelhouse, we were up before it was light. I placed ice cubes down the front of Ann-Clare's pyjamas as was the usual way of making my sister wake up for an early morning ride. I sat on the edge of the bed as she found socks, underpants, jeans, shirt and jumper, all of which she'd wrapped in a bundle before going to bed but which had dispersed with her dreams throughout the night.

'I'll go and make us some toast,' I whispered. 'Are you sure you're awake?'

'Of course. I don't want anything to eat.'

When I came back, even though she muttered something semi-sensible, when I turned the beam of the torch on her face I saw her eyes were shut, her shoulders still bare and rising and falling in the rhythm of sleep.

'Wake up,' I said, shaking her. 'Ann-Clare.'

'It's freezing.' She tried to put her head under the pillow.

'No it's not.' In the kitchen the thermometer-barometer read minus five. On parent days at Michaelhouse our father could see the round bulge of this barometer in his mother's bag. She held her bag by both handles in front of her, using both hands so that in time Jack began to believe that if he could only have thought to measure her arms when he first began at Michaelhouse and then again when he was due to leave, he'd have found a considerable stretch had occurred. He felt that his mother believed that the barometer might in some way control the forces which were seeking to control her.

'Come on, we're late.' I said and put the ice back onto Ann-Clare's bare skin until at last she acquiesced to the inevitable and sat up.

Following the telegraph poles down and down, it was as if my sister still dozed, her knees gripped to the saddle in a kind of half-sleep, her boots on the wrong feet like a clown and even the stars, it seemed, falling with us in a higher arc than the hills. The telegraph poles themselves swung and trembled in the cold. Only as the first light began to run along the manes of our horses did Ann-Clare truly begin to stir and call out to wait. Old though the horses were, at the first hint of sun, when the temperature does the opposite of what you'd expect and plummets, our horses still tucked their heads towards their chests, cracked their nostrils and tried to move us three-quarter pace, the way they'd once moved their tiny riders on the track.

On this morning the mist blew into our horses' faces, and then instantly iced fast, sculpturing their forelocks as if with white gleaming paint, as if they were carousel horses. And then on each eyelid and each whisker, white frost. And on our jumpers, ice.

I rolled my eyes at the signs of other people: toilet paper trailing away from behind trees; a Coca-Cola bottle, a Fantail wrapper.

In the half-dark, horses move with more grace. We seemed to be gliding through currents of air of various temperatures—first warm, then freezing.

'Look,' said Ann-Clare, as we neared home again. 'A seedpod boat from a blackbutt tree. A boater from a blackbutt.'

'Blackbean tree. It's a blackbean tree,' I said, glad the ride was over. I was sick of my sister's botanical inaccuracies and was so sharp that for a moment it seemed impossible we'd ever happily sailed the pods together in the water troughs.

My sister didn't answer.

White cockatoos bowed over in the red soil of a fresh paddock, saying their devotions. There was silence when we almost expected chanting but then the sound of the birds' wings going *shusha, shusha, shusha,* over us. 'Look,' said my sister, pointing over to my cemetery. 'The Moondaisy and his mother. They're here early.'

'Who?' I said.

'You know, Alana's Moondaisy. And that's his mother, we think. Or his grandmother. I can never tell through the binoculars. She's very little.'

That name because the man was so white and long, and where he wasn't going bald, he had yellowish hair poking out from his skull.

'The old lady always wanders around outside your cemetery,' Ann-Clare said, 'but he's always inside.'

The Moondaisy was running towards us, making our horses prick their ears.

'Idiot,' I said, before he was close enough to hear. 'Doesn't know anything about horses.' Yet it was for our horses that the man was running.

'Would it be possible for my nan to have a ride? Would they be quiet enough?' he wanted to know. His grandmother, explained the man, had been a very good rider. She had once had long auburn hair and won all the jumping classes at the Lindley show. She'd broken the ladies high jump record, riding astride a locally bred horse called Hellfire. One of the first women of Lindley to give away using the side-saddle.

I have the photos. Iris has insisted, saying that Johnny has never appreciated anything to do with horses. Saying that she'd always meant them for Ann-Clare.

The little old lady who was Iris went over the cemetery fence, rather than through the gate.

'One of these days,' said Mr Michaelhouse, 'she'll have a terrible fall. She doesn't like to feel her age.'

'Well!' exclaimed Iris to us, 'I thought you were little lads. Aren't they good horses? Has my grandson explained my heart's desire?'

'An aunt of the husband,' Iris said after all our names had been exchanged, 'had your name. I've forgotten where they've put her. She died of niddle-noddle disease.' She crooked a finger into the air and gave a laugh more boisterous than her one of today.

I fought not to duck my head with the shame of what I had been called but didn't quite succeed. Already Mr Michaelhouse had my sister's attention. He was telling her how Iris liked to come to the cemetery whenever he was visiting.

'Yes,' my sister said, 'we've seen you both before.'

Alana always had a soft spot for the Moondaisy.

According to Alana the Moondaisy always seemed genuinely interested in the old lady. She'd seen that they laughed rather a lot together. Not many Australian men were so kind or patient.

Iris stood next to Ann-Clare's gelding. What's his name, she wanted to know. She burrowed one hand under her arm and then held it out to the horse. 'See if he likes me first. If he is a he?' Ducking almost underneath the horse's belly to check. Ann-Clare's horse stood taking deep breaths of Iris. 'He likes me! Well. If I'd known this was going to happen this morning I wouldn't have worn this dress. Could I take him for a canter? Would he double? Would you trust me with him?'

'Iris,' Mr Michaelhouse warned, 'if you fall off that'll be the end of living by yourself.'

'Oh, be quiet, Johnny. One of the girls could give me a leg up.'

'He'll be all right,' Ann-Clare said. 'He's as quiet as his name. Avis can ride next to you.'

'What is his name? Did you say?'

'Still Water, that was his racing name but we call him Stilly.'

'All right then, Stilly,' Iris gathered up her reins. 'Nan!'

'She'll be all right,' I heard Ann-Clare reassuring Mr Michaelhouse. 'He's truly as quiet as a lamb.'

Iris was a lovely rider. Sometimes when I'm doing her feet I will still comment. I will say how when she cantered from the cemetery up to the house she was as confident and light as a child who has been on a horse from the day dot. I will tell her how easy it was for us to imagine the colour of her hair when she was young.

Later Ann-Clare and I marvelled at the lines of muscles we had seen underneath fine wrinkles in the legs of the Moondaisy's grandmother. Iris had hitched up her dress and though it was winter she wasn't wearing stockings. Later in the day we'd pulled down our jeans and flexed our own muscles and found them wanting. Though our legs were young and brown our muscles couldn't compare.

Close up, and under the kitchen lights of the New House, Mr Michaelhouse wasn't white, but mottled in the manner of the bricks of the New House. Iris apologised about her grandson's skin, saying that worry about his birds, which he'd left solely in the care of a new manager, had brought on an attack of eczema. 'His turkeys,' said Iris. 'They're in a bit of trouble.'

Crooked breast had crept into his stock, Mr Michaelhouse explained. A disease that might prove hard to get rid of. 'Imagine,' he said, 'some breast-bones are so crooked they look like the letter *s*.'

I felt sorry for the birds and for the way Mr Michaelhouse tried to hide the worst of his skin, placing his fingers onto that cheek. Every now and then he put the other hand up to his face and pulled the itching skin sideways in a way that made his eyes turn into slits. But I also saw immediately that the eyes, which were small and grey, were too close together. He wore a white shirt under the greenish-mauve sleeveless vest.

As we made Iris tea, we thought she would look

much more at home in the Abandoned House, sitting in a sensible chair, instead of in Alana's expensive leather and hardwood seats in which no one could find comfort. I sliced up a fresh loaf of bishops bread from the North Lindley store.

'Made with all the bishops of Lindley,' laughed Iris. 'I've always been partial to a bishop or two. And salt in my tea. Would there be some salt?'

'Our father doesn't allow salt.'

Iris hooted with disbelief. She said she had salt with just about everything. Salted oranges. Toast with a bit of salt was all right too if there was nothing else in the house.

'I could get you some horse salt?' I offered.

'That'd do.'

When I came back with some salt cupped in my hand Mr Michaelhouse was asking Ann-Clare for information about the Abandoned House and she was giving it shyly.

'Do you know if there are any old wells or tips around the old house?' he asked.

My sister ummed and ahhed.

'Well, not really,' I said.

'Well . . . ' said Ann-Clare at the same time, about to spill the beans.

'Behind the stinging trees, are you thinking of?' I said, still trying to be vague. Iris' fingers scrabbled on my hand getting another pinch of salt.

'There would be sure to be at least one somewhere close by,' said Mr Michaelhouse. 'How would you feel if I were to come looking for bottles?'

'Bottles?'

'Yes, old bottles, thrown into wells or in the old house tip.'

'Ohhh, watch out. This Johnny, I can tell you,' said Iris, 'always mad about his old bottles. Even as a tiny little fella. His poor mother. The laundry. Clogged full of mud and grass roots. The bath. Sometimes we'd find him washing the bottles in his own bathwater. He's been saving your farm up.'

'Oh, Nanna,' said Mr Michaelhouse, as if he was still a boy.

'We've got heaps, haven't we?' said Ann-Clare.

'What?' I said.

'Over at the Abandoned House.' She avoided my eyes. 'I was thinking of the well,' she said in a high and chatty kind of voice. She was talking too much. She was telling him how after we'd been to England, after Betty died, there'd been two weeks in Greece after which we staked out the farm tip like a real excavation site with pegs and string.

By the time Alana came back from town, Iris and Mr Michaelhouse were making their way out past the laundry door.

'That was the Moondaisy and his mother, wasn't it,' said our mother, heaving in through the other door a box load of shopping. 'What on earth were they doing inside? I caught a horrible whiff of old towels as they went past. I remember that smell,' said Alana, 'from poor children at the orphanage. All we had as confectionery was toothpaste to eat.'

'It's his grandmother not his mother,' Ann-Clare said, assuming responsibility. 'She had a ride.'

'Her name's Iris and she drinks salty tea,' I said.

'Not a smell of old towels really,' said my sister. 'I think it was tonic. Iris has to take iron tonic.'

'*He* wants to look for old bottles on the farm,' I began to fish around in the top of the grocery bags. 'And *she* told him about our well.'

'Oh yum,' said Alana, seemingly not very interested in our visitors.

'What?' We thought something very delicious must be in the shopping bags.

'The smell of the air after last night's rain. So wet and waterfally.' Such excessiveness of description in those days made my lip curl. I couldn't help it though it is that very exuberance I now remember with affection. The matter of Mr Michaelhouse didn't arise again until he appeared the following day, without his grandmother this time, to ask permission of our parents to poke around for bottles and other remnants. He had brought a small basket of Easter eggs. From Iris, he said, who was so thankful for her ride. Ann-Clare, who at the time thought she wanted to be an archaeologist, said she would be very interested to help Mr Michaelhouse in his search for glass.

After Mr Michaelhouse's holiday at his grandmother's house in Lindley was over, and after he and Ann-Clare had unearthed two black whisky bottles, an 1860 French sword, and three small blue Lindley lemonade flasks of such thick glass not much drink could ever have been contained in them, he sent my sister a pen. It was made in another country but of modern design, with Ann-Clare's initials engraved on it. He said on the accompanying card how he hoped Ann-Clare would always be his friend. He hoped that she would write. He enclosed copies of the photos he had taken of Iris and Ann-Clare.

'Yuk,' I told Ann-Clare, 'what an ugly pen.' And said that a present as expensive as this could mean only one thing.

I handed the pen back to Ann-Clare. 'He's been painting his shower,' said Ann-Clare, looking up from the card.

'Send it back,' I suggested. 'Don't be obliged.' I watched her taking the lid off and screwing it back on. 'He'll come and pester you every time he comes to visit his grandmother.'

'He only visits Iris once or twice a year,' said Ann-Clare.

'That'll change.'

Ann-Clare was practising her name with it on top of the envelope.

'Does he sign off, ''love''?' I asked next.

'His letter's scented,' exclaimed my sister.

'Can I see the card? I mean just the picture.'

'Oh, all right.'

Ann-Clare hadn't bothered to look at what was pictured on the card but it was beautiful. It was a reproduction of Hans Heysen's 1921 watercolour *Bronzewings and Saplings*.

'Let me see.' Ann-Clare looked over my shoulder. 'Oh. Turkeys. Of course. Mr Michaelhouse and his turkeys,' she chuckled as if his interests were something that had been affectionately amusing her for years.

'But isn't it a beautiful painting?'

'It's all right.'

In this card, the turkeys are crowding through thin, silvery trees. Heysen said he'd treated the painting's composition in the manner of a mosaic—with brilliant bursts of colour and clear edges. When the turkey eggs sent by the Hahndorf mistress hatched, many were white, which from bronzewing stock is a rare occurrence. It was the combination of colours which provided Heysen with his inspiration.

Inside the card Mr Michaelhouse was a master of pathos from the start.

*Last night I felt rather sad smelling the wet, newly-painted concrete in the shower. It reminded me of the smell of Iris' back verandah with its faded rugs, glass-fronted cabinet, completely dark toilet, multi-coloured slat seat that's so hard to sit on, ornate budgie cage, the wireless with the hacksaw blade antenna, tins of oily nails on little lace doilies. Ann-Clare, I do hope you will keep going to visit Iris. Your visits would mean a lot to her. Do you know how much you energise me?*

As if right from the start, in the first paragraph, my sister was a pill to pop in his middle age.

During their unusual and fairly furtive courtship Ann-Clare laughed and shook her head that Mr Michaelhouse had so few memories left of his own childhood. He said that one thing he could remember being certain about when he was a small boy was that he was rather like an old man. He told my sister this with pride not regret. So although Ann-Clare wasn't seduced by the appearance of her long hand on his leg where he'd placed it, she was seduced by the way he gave his stories so willingly, with complete trust into her keeping, as well as little trinkets that more often than not accompanied the stories. From the earliest days she conceded to his desire that she wear neither shorts nor bright swimming costumes.

Mr Michaelhouse said that once they were married, Ann-Clare might like his dead second cousin's crop and her beautiful pigskin saddle from England. For following his first indiscretion, he had declared his desire for marriage. He told Ann-Clare how the cousin had tossed a silk scarf over her eyes at a long ago Lindley Show. His manner when describing his cousin betrayed the fact that when he was a young boy he'd loved her passionately. Such was Mr Michaelhouse's storytelling ability, Ann-Clare loved the cousin too. She loved a girl who'd been dead longer than we'd been alive; she loved the flare of her nostrils in the old photos and the pictures of her jumping her horse, wearing jodhpurs which billowed around her long thin thighs. Mr Michaelhouse's stories were so powerful, Ann-Clare was usually able to dismiss from her mind the natural abhorrence she felt when he asked her hand to move at a certain rhythm.

Significantly, many of the stories and gifts arrived via the post because of the distance of Lindley from Sydney. Our mother would collect the mail when Ann-Clare was at school and leave his letter on the pillow of her bed. Sometimes Mr Michaelhouse would include on the back of the envelope small messages for our mother or enclose plumage from the turkeys for my trout fishing flies. In this way he kind of wooed us all. His courtship was also powerful from the point of view of his Australianness. He was a real Australian, Alana wrote in the Christmas circular of that year, with a kind of horrified fascination in all her observations. His broad accent entertained our mother, at the same time as allowing her to mock it when he wasn't at the farm.

That his surname was the same name as the exclusive school our father had attended in South Africa was a coincidence which pleased my father—one of those kinds of arbitrary validations for an otherwise strange friendship. Often it's the peculiar similarities or alignments that bring the most reassurance. In the case of Ann-Clare and Mr Michaelhouse, he was a letter-writing turkey farmer who collected ephemera and bottles from out of the earth, who had a surname that reminded our father of his past. There were also Mr Michaelhouse's birds. Although you couldn't conceivably imagine poultry farming as romantic, he somehow managed to depict it as so to my sister. He said that he had always viewed his turkeys, with their outlandish appearance and noises, as more fable than bird. If he could own one Australian picture for his own wall, he would choose the Hans Heysen *Bronzewings and Saplings*. There was also something quite romantic and adventurous in his desire to revive the lost Crimson Dawn breed of turkey.

After a while, as he came to Lindley more and more frequently, Alana said he must feel free to come for meals and to sleep overnight; that even good grandsons deserved some respite from their grandmothers. On each visit, he and Ann-Clare would disappear for hours on end. They would return with cobwebs in their hair and excitement in their voices about a tip or a well which had unearthed its unusual glass or other treasures to them. Or my sister would have spent slow, quiet, mauve-tinted hours with Iris. Because Mr Michaelhouse would fall asleep having eaten too many sweet biscuits or Davies soft centres, my sister would read old horse magazines with Iris, drinking one hot cup of black tea after another from Iris' best china. Mr Michaelhouse's head on her lap was a weight she eventually would move, with his grandmother's laughing assistance, onto a cushion. Ann-Clare and Iris would leave him asleep to go out into the garden. Much of my sister's correspondence from this time is about Iris or about working in Iris' garden. It was as if she'd decided to marry Mr Michaelhouse because she couldn't bear to disappoint his grandmother.

*Happy Month*, begins every letter written on the first day of a fresh month, in imitation of this salutation which was Iris'. She is such a sweetheart, my sister never tired of telling me, and although Mr Michaelhouse had taken to calling Ann-Clare his Shining Treat it was Iris who belonged under that title.

'You could say no now,' I remember suggesting to Ann-Clare who was crocheting Iris a rug, a few weeks before the wedding day.

She didn't reply with anything positive in his defence.

'What about his beard?'

'I'll ask him to shave it off when we're married,' she replied. She explained that many of the Michael-house men, Iris' husband for instance, had had the tendency to let their chin hair grow if their head hair was failing and that in addition, a beard hid the fact that the Michaelhouse chin fell into the neck below.

I said he reminded me of something squeezed out of a deep blackhead.

'You're so juvenile,' said Ann-Clare, crocheting furiously.

I watched the way the crochet hook was moving in and out of each bobble before, like an embalmer's hook. The way Ann-Clare was crocheting, it would push through the bone at the back of the nose with no trouble at all. Crack, crack, crack. In out. In out.

I despised crocheting. At the old people's home there were two double wardrobes full of rugs stored in mothballs after their owners had died. Ann-Clare said that seeing her favourite old ladies wrapped in their rugs on the verandah in the sun reminded her of cocoons about to hatch a very colourful butterfly. Whereas I knew the weight of the wool little bit by little bit, through night and through day, the clash of incredible colours, ebbed the old people's strength as surely as the loneliness.

Pineapple design, river ripple pattern, rose stitch and catherine wheels. My sister knew all the knots.

When I asked had she forgotten our anti-marriage

pledge she said no, she remembered it very clearly, riding our horses past the cemeteries. It was winter and we were wearing matching jumpers that couldn't keep out the evening wind.

'That's right,' I said.

Some of this conversation might've taken place silently because we were staring in different directions. I was watching the cemeteries, Ann-Clare was looking over to the hills. If we so much as glanced at each other, I had the feeling tears would fall. If only we could have wrestled each other to the ground in a fight the way we used to when we were small.

I confided to Ann-Clare a belief that had already come to feel precious to me, that those hills, which she'd always called the Chimanimanis, were like another land, but not necessarily Africa. Seen from this distance, a place not connected to the scrub and dirt and hopper ants that would of course be there if you were walking the area by foot. But an imaginary land. Somehow magic and eternal.

When she still did not reply, I retreated into a favourite spot in the old orchard that flourished with pests. I said I was going in there to listen to the stink-bug shells rubbing together as they mated which was far preferable to hearing her talk about her wedding cake.

'My bride cake. The icing's all Iris' own work.'

I began to talk into the smelly old ear of her dog.

'What are you whispering?' It suddenly seemed essential for Ann-Clare to know and she too waded in under the branches. What an archaic and beautiful name for a cake, I was thinking. A groomcake, I whispered, would be black and old and burnt inside.

'That you should be married in your cemetery. It'll be like death.'

'A bit of an Odd Pod, she's picked,' confided Alana to Patricia who was out for the wedding. 'But we all rather like him.'

On the day, Iris wore a red woollen suit and passed out soon after lunchtime as Patricia filled up her glass as frequently as her own. Mr Michaelhouse had provided Black Chocolate turkeys, a French breed of bird for the wedding lunch. The soft white flesh melted in the mouth.

My sister was an attentive wife. She made Mr Michaelhouse perfect cups of tea into which she'd float the finest sliver of lemon she could cut. I'd see her kiss Mr Michaelhouse's forehead, lifting her lips from his skin to listen to the peculiar cry of a turkey hen about to lay, or his guard dog gobblers, who set up an ocean of noise at the approach of somebody strange. With the dedication of many new young wives, Ann-Clare wrote out recipes as if they were poems, decorating the borders and then preparing each meal with care. Her letters from this period are full of romantic interpretations of her life. She could find beauty in his ramshackle house, every room of which glinted and spoke to you of the past from the glass of old wine and fizzy drink bottles. She dusted the bottles using warm water and flannelette sheet, creeping around, trying not to disturb her husband. As the sun moved, different windows in different rooms reflected the green and yellow flickerings of plants on glass, or if it was spring and the azaleas were flowering, the bottles became pink and crimson.

Ann-Clare became a kind of secretary and Girl Friday to Mr Michaelhouse's business. In addition, one of Ann-Clare's main jobs was the sewing of small protective canvas coats for the hen birds to wear. In this way she prevented over the years hundreds of injuries normally sustained by hens, when mounted by a turkey. From a yard of canvas she used to make about one dozen hen saddles. She used a stout canvas with tucks, so that the gobblers could find firm footing.

At first, the turkey farm was still small enough for Mr Michaelhouse to tattoo the birds' wings himself, using a pen-knife blade dipped in Indian ink. But over the next twelve years, the turkey farm flourished to support its own licensed abattoir and freezing chambers. By the time Ann-Clare left Mr Michaelhouse the farm employed many people. Some were collectors, who had to go out at night to catch the turkeys on the roost while others were debeakers or stranglers. The unlucky last workers at the end of the process, the hangers, were the ones who tied the turkeys' feet and attached them to a conveyor belt which led to a machine that chopped off their heads. Mr Michaelhouse himself continued to hand kill any spraddle-legged poults himself. He favoured a narrow-bladed knife which he used to sever the jugular through the roof of each baby bird's mouth.

Ann-Clare wrote all her news to me on Mr Michaelhouse's beautiful paper. Mr Michaelhouse had a military cabinet full of expensive and odd papers which he encouraged Ann-Clare to use at her will. She must address her letters in a certain way, always use beautiful stamps which he'd buy from the philatelic section of the post office and enclose them in the envelopes which had inside a second layer of pale tissue paper.

Whenever I came to stay for weekends or some parts of my holidays, our favourite place to lie was on the louvred-in verandah of his house, along its western wing. The bottles belonging in this room were very fanciful indeed, curlicued and turreted and shot through with pale blue or green hues. There was a shadow man too, up against the ceiling. What configuration of struts and blinds cast him there we never worked out but in her letters Ann-Clare would often include mention of him. Or of a small shadow child wearing a smock who moved across the roof at night when cars went past.

'You look like plumage,' Mr Michaelhouse said to me on their wedding day, before he drove my sister away. I saw no plumage. I saw only my own moon-face, the strap of my bridesmaid's dress slipping sideways off my shoulder and wisps of clouds reflected from the sky drifting along to the end of the car. I saw my sister's uncertain shoulders and feet which didn't know how to walk in high white heels. I saw that she believed in very little and least of all herself.

## CHAPTER THIRTEEN

To meet Ally, my sister might need to find the power of a salmon. She would have to turn her broken-boned body into a fish; to breast through white water as if it were a wave not a waterfall; to turn her death-wish around.

Mr Michaelhouse's great-aunt Olive, Iris' sister, had apparently done just such a thing, killed herself, then come back, but there was always doubt as to how this had actually happened. And that perhaps she hadn't jumped into the sea in front of her family, but had made a little leap only, just enough to take her out of view and then crept away in order to live for the first time a life of freedom, risk and poverty, without the encumbrance of her family. But after a few days her family received a letter, saying that Olive was at a certain hotel close to the section of coast where she'd disappeared. Iris told this story to Ann-Clare and now tells it to me as if her sister had come back to life.

'The most extraordinary thing,' Iris says. 'Our dear Mama *saw* her land in the sea. Almost certainly on vicious rocks. But when Olive came to the hotel, she was totally dry and without scrapes. Even though it had been pouring rain for days. She came knocking at the glass door near the tea room and when the girl let her in Olive was as dry as a bone.' Iris takes off her glasses and blinks at me. I feel she is telling me this story for a reason. 'I thought she'd disappeared,' says Iris. 'Into the deep blue yonder,' moving her hands to describe that expression.

Don't give up hope, I feel Iris will say to me next, in the same wafty voice, her foal's beard quivering. Don't you think your sister is like my sister, she will suggest. Seven years instead of several days?

But without mentioning any of these thoughts, Iris says she'll get me Olive's clippings. Only the other day, tidying through some boxes under the bed, she'd come across them.

Iris smells of violet powder and underneath that, the unwashed, salt-meat smell of old people's skin. 'Oh dear,' she says, 'you look just like Ann-Clare this morning.'

'Oh dear,' I agree.

'You seem very thin.' She takes my hand and strokes it, looking at me with the devotion of a dog.

'The clippings, Iris,'

'That's right! I was on my way.'

The newspaper cuttings detail the search that ensued for Olive and then her remarkable reappearance. Some letters to the editor afterwards were convinced it had been an act of God, others that it was Olive's ploy to get more people to attend the local production of *The Tempest* she was at that time producing. Or some said she was lucky. She was born on St Patrick's Day and had had the luck of the Irish.

'Oh yes,' Iris leans over me to read the clippings. 'She was a mystery, my sister. The theatrical type. Cleverer than the rest of us put together. This is Olive,' Iris says, picking up a framed photo of a group of sisters. In the photo Iris wears her hair in pigtails but Olive's is in a more elaborate coil around her ears.

'Could learn anything off by heart. But that's not to say she couldn't cook the most beautiful pies. Apple or meat. Before she lost her mind. Her daughter put her in a home on Sunday. Did I tell you? I never did feel any of us ever got to the bottom of Olive. They say she cries all the day through. In the home. When I think how she loved to travel,' Iris shakes her head. 'Now Johnny would never do that to me. He'll be here for my birthday.'

When I say that I won't be able to visit at that time, Iris' face contorts.

'Iris. We'll have a little party before he gets here.'

Mr Michaelhouse is a shadow in the back of my mind I must somehow resolve. Could Iris bring assistance? Couldn't she, with nearly one hundred years of life behind her, cast some kind of light on the matter of her grandson?

I used to think her grandson Mr Michaelhouse was quite a kind husband. After Alana died he requested a Mozart chorus on the radio for two sisters of the Lindley Plateau. When my sister grimaced and turned it off, I didn't understand. I thought she was being childish. Wanting to hold on to a grudge even in the face of such a thoughtful gesture. Could I write to him. But what would I ask him?

When I think of Mr Michaelhouse's house west of Sydney, I think of the old garden. I think of its length and its narrowness; the smell of the turkey farm drifting all through the house as soon as the afternoon wind arrived. The old bottles strung together with webs, or their open tops which were home to a certain kind of black, thick legged spider. I think of how in my sister's correspondence with a few of the women who belonged to Faraway, she didn't acknowledge her proximity to a city at all, writing to some of them for years as if she was still a single farming daughter living with her parents on land they had bought at Lindley when we were children.

Country Boy, Country Girl, Early Rose, Henrietta All Cream. In a letter my sister wrote to Mr Michaelhouse before they were married, she said that the names of the potato breeds our father sometimes put in as a crop were as comforting to her as cows with big udders. So that if in the afternoon after being to Redclack I drive up behind the barefooted Merwinney boy following his cows up the road to be milked, it's now the names of potatoes more than any other thing that come swinging into my mind. I say this to Lavinia and she understands exactly what I mean. This, she says, is the nature of memories; to arrive piecemeal, to connect up with some image of the present.

For years our father used to tell us that time spent in reconnaissance is seldom wasted. He said it was his dear old Dad's favourite saying and one of which he'd always taken note. But for years my sister and I misinterpreted the maxim, believing it to be a more fanciful way of saying remembrance; that it suggested a dwelling in the past with an air of faint regret. The air of faint regret was an important part of the definition for Ann-Clare because even as a child it was how she'd approached life. When finally she did check the word one day, she made a special trip to the Romance Library to share her sense of shock. It was the saying of a tactician, someone with a military bent, somebody not like us, she said.

Although Iris is soon to be ninety-seven, she's possessed of a wiry, indomitable kind of strength. When she tells the story of Sarah, I think of the river's fine wrinkles on an afternoon of high wind.

I stand up to look at the photo of my sister in her wedding dress. She looks incredibly awkward, tilted forward at the hips and grinning. Mr Michaelhouse isn't in the photo but he is all around her, in smaller, older photo frames, at various stages of childhood, and then later, holding a turkey in his arms in front of his farm. Most recently there is a photograph, taken on self-timer, of Mr Michaelhouse with his new wife and children. 'Lovely looking children.'

Iris agrees. 'Maybe if Ann-Clare had've had a little babe ... Maybe then everything would have been different.'

When I go to take the picture of Iris' husband off the wall she waves her hand and says to leave him there. That it wouldn't hurt the bugger to hear what she wanted to tell today. 'Ooh, he was an angry man,' says Iris. Even in the smooth shadows of early

Australian photography, I see his bright red complexion, the whisky nose, the way his bulldog throat bulges and strains at the tight white collar.

As Iris talks, she sinks backwards on a long lounge chair and I sit at its end, beginning as always with her left foot, which having been broken three times aches more in the cold. The curtains form a dull background for her talking. Through the moth holes, I see the wind blowing leaves, and the way the fences of the street are joined together by diagonal grey lines.

Although Iris rises so early, at five or even before, and has a morning bath, I always find between her big and second toe, lint from her flannelette sheets. Her second toes are both much longer than her big ones and I can't remember if I used to condemn this as a sign of inbreeding or to praise it as an indication of genius. As I massage, Iris talks about her husband; the temper he had. How he threw a baked and seasoned fowl out of the window because she hadn't tied the drumsticks together. How hard he was on his horse, Ol' Hollaback. Static in that poor horse's tail, which might give Gus a shock on a windy day such as today, could be enough to earn the horse a whipping. How Iris would creep out when he was sleeping, to attend to Hollaback's torn and bleeding mouth and to soothe him with carrots from her garden. Or liquorice straps Iris kept specially because he was a horse with a sweet tooth.

As Iris speaks, she continuously adjusts the collar of a blouse, once fancy, that she wears underneath a variety of jumpers. From her drifts the not unpleasant odour of earth and old food. Her hands fly up to the collar then down to her lap. She lifts her foot through the patterns of sun. She says what a blessed relief the day Gus died. And how no one cried except for poor Sarah, who Iris could see at the burial, flitting between the trees on the perimeter of Ann-Clare's cemetery.

'Who was Sarah, Iris?'

'Ann-Clare knew. I thought your sister might have told you the story of poor Sarah. Ooohh she was black,' says Iris, lowering her voice, 'not a bit of white in her I always reckoned but not even her colour hid what he'd done. That lightning bolt was a blessing. God help me but I do believe that girl was crying with relief. That's my feeling. It crossed my mind to take her in. But I left it. She died not long after him. They never lived long the skinny types like that.'

I look at the photo portrait again.

'I only knew her name after she was dead. Michaelhouse's gin she was known as when alive, and Michaelhouse's gin is on that stone in the ground. Did Ann-Clare ever show you?'

I shake my head.

'Go on with you. You two were as thick as thieves.'

I shake my head again.

'This Sarah used to live in the forest not far from the wine shanty, not far from your farm. Only a skinny little thing. No more than a child really, I realised. When I think of the size of her. But I used to be grateful to her existence. Meant I didn't get what he gave out to her.'

I knead and rub Iris' feet. We are silent for now.

I am thinking of Ann-Clare coming into the library with a bruise. A piece of kindling, Ann-Clare said, had flown up into her face but she didn't look at me when she was telling me how she'd been axing the wood sideways. She was flicking anxiously through Marguerite's sixth romance, newly released. She wouldn't laugh over Mr Michaelhouse's list in her pocket that day, so I snatched it away and read it out loud. He wanted her to fetch a particular kind of coffee with a particular kind of caramel bean. In capitals he'd written which kind of way to have it ground. There were slides for her to pick up too from the American Express building. I told her the bruise leaking down from her brow through her eye and into the hollow, was quite beautiful. Like watercolours through a piece of lovely Arches paper. I was flirting with Marguerite.

'You don't think your sister has been hit, do you?' Maguerite asked after Ann-Clare had left the library.

'Of course not.'

'Why do you sit up here like this every time your sister leaves?' Marguerite was following me up, her weight making the bookshelf sway more dangerously than usual.

'I don't know really. Being up here reminds me that Ann-Clare once perched above a door before womping me in the legs with a log. When we were children.' I watched my sister with affection as she appeared at street level. 'I wonder what job she's going to do first?'

'She's going to see Mrs Shore.'

'She couldn't be?'

'She said so. You must've been fixing up Mrs Roper's books.'

'Mary Shore lives in the Pilliga scrub. Way way out west.'

'Not any more. Don't you ever listen to your sister?'

At times I hold my mother's pen like a cigarette and pretend to smoke it, only realising half a second too late that my daughter is behind the curtains, watching. Patricia has made Ally two autumn costumes out of the same material as she made the curtains. I am disconcerted, as if little Ally has caught me out. Even my small, slightly bored daughter makes me feel a bit like a criminal, as if the very act of lifting up a pen to write down a thought or to not write down a thought is something that should be performed furtively. Ally comes into my lap and sits for a while. Or she takes the next old letter out of its envelope. One day she left a stamp on her tongue and then flicked it out at me to make me laugh, but usually she is quiet on a chair pulled up at the old school desk behind me, making her own letters or drawing the Australian Chimanimanis with smiles and eyes, and calling them the Happy Hills.

When my daugher sees me with my pen dangling from my mouth, it is to Mr Michaelhouse that I'm thinking of writing. But about what exactly? About Sarah or the story of Olive? But I believe all Iris has told me. It must be Ann-Clare who I'm thinking of mentioning to Mr Michaelhouse.

Ally has a handful of blue Jerusalems for my

desk. I take the flowers and stop pretending to smoke my pen. The morning at Iris' has disturbed me more than I can say but writing to Mr Michael-house isn't the answer. I take out a wad of unanswered letters but they fill me with the same inertia. When writing to anyone whose letter I've let sit too long, I find the desire to write back has almost quite worn away. This is no indication that the letter was dull. In fact I've probably been saving the letter to answer it at length and in as fine a style if possible. But because I didn't follow my initial impulse to write back immediately, a letter in reply approaching the quality of the one received has almost certainly been lost. A letter written today won't be the version of events and feelings written tomorrow or several weeks from now. Much might be missed in letting the days go past though the opposite can occasionally be true.

Then when weeks have gone by and the wonderful letter which I've probably read many times is in front of me, I do anything to put off beginning my reply. I find I have a pin between my teeth. Or that I'm walking around aimlessly, whistling over a biro's lid. I eat a whole packet of Jatz crackers noticing the way the pen moves across the page writing one dull sentence after another. I scratch my fingers through my hair and as with any repetitive action get sore arms. Then I must get up to do something physical, which might turn into hours away from the desk and away from the letter I know anyway to be ruined before it has properly begun.

I could write to Ann-Clare mentioning Olive but

my nose is cold, my fingers are freezing and I screw up the paper before I've even begun.

'I am not ready,' I say to Lavinia later. And tell the Olive story as a kind of defence. 'I'll write this letter to my sister that you think is so essential some other time.'

'You're becoming unhealthy, Able,' she says. 'Obsessed. I'm sure not even Iris believes your sister is going to make a miraculous reappearance.'

'I think she does,' I say but I can hear the uncertainty in my voice. For it's true, never once has Iris given any indication that she believes Ann-Clare is alive. She talks about her in the same wistful way she talks about Olive's daughter who died, whose saddle Ann-Clare was given.

'Have you asked Iris?'

'No.'

'Well. Don't you see Able?'

'*Ungena ngenxeba njeng empetu*,' I reply in bad Zulu.

'Yes?'

'I enter by the sore like a maggot. Adding sorrow to sorrow.'

'Exactly. That's exactly right, Able. You're punishing yourself. It's grotesque. Where are you learning all these sayings, anyway?'

'Dad has been teaching Ally things his dumpy-level holder, Samuel, used to teach him.'

'This family is bloody nuts,' she says and storms back to Redclack.

When Lavinia leaves me to my letters and the dogs, I do sometimes feel as if we are members of our own little lunatic asylum. One dog licks air as the other does anti-itch twirls beneath the furniture, its tail just hitting the spot and tantalising it into further circles. Moanings come from their mouths while my father's old kelpie is sitting on the other side of the glass, trying to catch moths in its toothless gums.

As the weather grows colder, as I wade deeper into my sister's history, as Lavinia drops in more frequently or I go to stay almost every weekend at Redclack with Ally, I write fewer and fewer letters. Correspondents complain and I throw their plaintive notes into a box under my bed.

'Able,' says my father, 'Whatever do you hope to achieve by reading old mail? What about taking Ally along to the park one day?'

Mightn't it yet reveal something unthought of? I think.

From an early age Ann-Clare and I were taught that the greatest sin was to open or to read someone else's mail without permission. One of the most memorable scandals of our childhood was the discovery that the postmistress of that time had for many years been tampering with the mail. When Girlie Snow died they found stashes of other people's letters, her favourite bits circled or underlined with comments scrawled on the edges as if they had been texts she was studying at school. After the Morgan family took over the shop and the post, the first thing they did was to root out every blue hydrangea Girlie Snow had ever laboured over, as if removing her flowers would also remove the letter-stealing procedures which took place over years. Although certain Lindley residents watched the mattocks chopping into the heads of hydrangeas as if they were cutting into the head of Girlie herself, I can understand the loneliness that drove her to her first illicit opening of a letter that was not hers. Or perhaps she began to read a story through a thin papered envelope covered in the stamps of a faraway and exciting country, and so succumbed to the need to know that story's end. She kept love letters in a separate drawer by her bed, making the rightful recipients of the letters, who were no longer as young as they should be, cringe. People tried to say she had baked too many cakes in the aluminium tins the store sold and that this had contributed to her disease. Some letters were found to be annotated with biblical quotes warning of the damnation of humans who fall in love with their own sex.

Perhaps uninvited letter reading is itself a kind of disease. In some medical journal would it be listed as the compulsive reading of other people's mail? Yet I sense neither my mother nor sister would mind that I am reading the carbons they kept of their letters.

Whether I have as much licence to read mail written to my mother and sister is another matter, something neither right nor wrong but the only written history available. The best way to read it is to pretend that it was written to me and that I am rereading things I had forgotten. The moment I question this, the script becomes queer and impenetrable so that I have to put down the card or letter and begin again.

Although I am so intent on reading all the letters, it's also a relieving feeling to find that mice have found some of the old mail, so that what I attend to has been arbitrarily selected by rodents. I immediately set traps for the mice yet I am also grateful.

The confetti that mice have made out of some of Ann-Clare's African mail is colourful, for by then she wrote on anything. From Zimbabwe her letters came on the back of pudding packets, the flaps of paperbacks, local out-of-focus postcards, or even the back of my own letters.

'Why continue,' my father says, 'to hope for a letter that's never going to come?'

I repeat something Lavinia's said, about how she waits at her letterbox, hoping for the letter saying all is forgiven.

Missing what I mean, he says, 'You don't need anybody to forgive you anything.'

Though I think of letter writing all the time and read until my eyes are exhausted, I continue to feel that something obvious eludes me still. There is an echo of my dismay in the questions of my daughter.

'Tell me more about my father,' Ally says. 'Please.'

'Darling, you know now all I know to tell.' Except that isn't totally so. There are things I can't tell.

Cover your eyes, said Ben Jussab and I covered them. It was an October evening in Zimbabwe. He lifted my shirt. I could feel the chill coming off the glass. I could feel his excitement.

'Please?' my daughter pleads.

'Well,' I say. 'He was very bony when I knew him,

a twig, just like you. And funny. Wouldn't you say, Grandad?'

'Ohh,' my daughter is crestfallen.

'In fact he was lean in the way of a starving horse that shows its thinness around the withers.'

'I don't know if that's very suitable,' says my father.

Whatever I tell is never enough. I shrug my shoulders helplessly. I say to Ally she must write to him, asking her own questions. On any letter she writes to him she likes to put her dog's paw mark on the back of the envelope. He writes back to her sometimes with news of his old dog or new puppy.

'Go away now, Ally, I'm busy.' I am thinking of old letters. I can't help myself. I am remembering how great the effort was for my mother to hold a pen by the time she was composing her letter to us about burial. Ann-Clare and I had walked in as was usual at that time, with tea for our father and a grapefruit juice for our mother. She was writing with difficulty. The bean-shaped wool hat she wore had fallen to a jaunty angle. I thought she looked like an old king about to wear away altogether from the front of an English cathedral. This small letter combined with the memory of the labour involved to write it used to make me cry. The love it expressed was so camouflaged, the written word trying to pretend that nothing particularly untoward was going on. The specification for driftwood not masonry.

Even when the disease that began in our mother's breasts began to swell her hands, she kept up her letters. This sometimes made Ann-Clare and me wish we hadn't come home to help; that we lived far away instead on a farm on the other side of Australia. Or in another country, travelling already in Africa; to know for sure the pleasure she would gain from receiving our letters rather than to be present for her dying, where nothing could feel certain.

There are other ordinary kinds of letters too, of course. Polite letters of thanks; or my father's kitchen table letters. These are usually written in haste about some daily matter or another. Details about where he is headed with his dung beetles. Shopping lists signed off with love.

Usually when my father goes driving west beyond the plateau he'll leave a letter too, for the roadside flower stall. You cannot see the farm that has always sold flowers from the road, nor have we ever driven up the red gravel road, but he has been writing to them on and off for years. The flowers are in buckets, under the shade of an old dairy can shelter. He tucks his notes to the flower-seller under a tin pail and puts more coins than are necessary into the makeshift moneybox. His letters explain how the flower-grower could improve the vigour of some of the flowers she's selling by adding this or that fertiliser.

Letters were as important to Ann-Clare once she was married as they were to Betty, who travelled to Africa to marry a stranger. Yet proposed visits by women of the Faraway Group could make my sister unkind—a particular type of cruelty that comes of shyness, from the fear of being seen as dull. From experience, Ann-Clare knew that she and her visitor would skirt around each other in curious and ludicrous ways. She would be appalled and guilty about being married to a man such as Mr Michael-house. The visitor, from having spent so much time alone on a farm or in a forest, may also have forgotten how to regulate the volume and pace of a conversation so that it would be a relief all round when it came time for Ann-Clare to wave them goodbye.

It's also much better my correspondents don't come to stay. Even though this acknowledgement makes me remorseful—haven't my letters made them love me or feel sorry for me or tender, or something? At any rate they want to visit—it would be best if they didn't. A few days into their stay a silence falls. I resent that they are not who they seemed to be in their letters and they resent the differences in me. They tire of the triangles of tomato and cheese sandwiches or chicken and lettuce I cut them for lunch. I explain local paradoxes such as the hottest bushfire days can bring the coolest mornings due to the mist and they aren't remotely interested. Marguerite, on her only visit here ever, in front of my most favourite view, said that it was all rather jejune really. Too bleak, she said, punishing me for the other bleakness that had fallen between us.

I see my hapless visitors wading off in unsuitable shoes around the farm and know they will try to change their tickets home and that I should've offered them a spare pair of gumboots or advice about where the grass was so long they'd find themselves wet up to their groins.

Yet the very moment I've waved them goodbye

from Lindley's train station, I instantly soften. Funny things they've said or done will come back to me and after a few falters, the correspondence will resume.

I like to open all the little drawers in my mother's desk, my head on one side as I drain the dam water from the morning swims out of my ears. The timber of each partition is remarkably fine. I find, as I always find, my mother's sharpened pencils and stationery scraps and the feathers of various birds that fly over the farm. I accidentally find again the message I have found long ago which says in my mother's handwriting that a call she'd made to me had been utterly USELESS, so that I still feel an obscure failure over what, and in what year, I don't even know.

As I watch my pen moving over the page, I pause. I have promised Lavinia I will make a real effort, a beginning at least.

When I look down at my letter, the fountain pen has splotched a dark stain across its beginning. I screw the letter up. What am I doing anyway, writing a letter to a sister who, apart from in my imagination, has left me no indication whatsoever of her whereabouts? Who chose to write her last letter not to me but to Mary Shore. I look at my face in the small pocket mirror I keep in one of the desk's drawers. I see the semi-aged features of a forty-year-old Australian woman, and they look quite afraid. Alana would've called my face a wrinkled old prune. She'd always say that Australian women didn't know how to look after their skins.

After beginning a letter to my sister, a walk to the horse paddock brings me back to earth. Away from the desk and all letter-writing paraphernalia, the sound of the water reminds me that my little sister was last seen in the vicinity of a waterfall, in the Chimanimani Mountains where thirty years before her visit, I was conceived. The water comes out of the hose with swirls and an undersuck, causing bubbles to surge to the surface. We used to swim in the horse trough when we were small, and then in the river or dam.

When tadpoles hatched in the pond we'd channelled out from the dam for my herd of plastic mauve and pink hippos, we'd pretend the tadpoles were people paddling little oars. I made the plastic hippopotamus travel at high speed along the muddy bottom to tip over the tadpole tribe threatening the baby hippos. Ann-Clare said that the fresh frogs eggs were the nets the tadpole tribe would use. At some point in this game I turned the tadpoles into gum my sister had to chew. When she began to cry I felt such remorse I told her I would do anything she might suggest. As she seemed incapable of putting forward any suitable punishment, I said I'd eat a frog and its eggs. So that about ten years later, sharing a plate of frogs legs with Ann-Clare for the novelty, in the French restaurant at the coast, rumoured to be run by lesbian women from all over the world, tears of laughter began to run down our faces.

What was it we were laughing at, Mr Michaelhouse wanted to know, fearing it may have been sisterly laughter against himself. The bread waiter, who was a beautiful woman dressed to look like a beautiful youth, was laughing too. Though she couldn't possibly have known the joke, it was as if she did. Or maybe she was laughing at our appetites, which were so huge that night from helping our father dig fencepost holes all day, that we ate two loaves of the plaited honey bread she kept slicing.

At the restaurant Patricia, in Australia for Ann-Clare's wedding, was soon so tiddly she wanted to leave the table to sit on the platform in front of the black piano. According to Mr Michaelhouse, this was where the lesbians performed daring cabarets and naughty skits later in the night. That night Mr Michaelhouse appeared to be attentive to three generations. Alana and Patricia responded with all the gaps in their teeth. Only Ann-Clare was very quiet. Her breasts weren't quite big enough for the cups of Alana's dress. I wished she hadn't borrowed that particular dress. She looked like a child prostitute.


In Lindley people still whisper the word lesbian in a way that denotes a different race, with a language of its own. Or they would prefer not to whisper it at all.

'Lesbians,' says Patricia, 'are travesties against the menfolk of the world.' She tells one story over and over and like all her stories, the sentences she uses and the cadence with which she delivers them never seem to change.

'I had two young girl boarders just after the war who turned out to be Lesbians.' My grandmother comes half-drunk from around the kitchen corner to retell. 'The dirty creatures had been peeing on the mattresses.'

Upon discovering this, Grandma opened up their door one night, hauled them out of the bed they were both in and banged their heads together. Try as we might, Lavinia and I can't imagine my small, much made-up grandmother doing this, not even when she mimes the motion of the heads cracking together.

In bed, Lavinia holds me as if I am something fragile. 'Hush your mouth,' she says.

But I am restless and playful, wanting to talk.

'Tell me again. Oh please tell me again about your dancing teacher?'

'Rita Little?'

'Yes.'

'A real hoofer,' says Lavinia. 'She used to smoke while she tapped. She wore these little pointy shoes and stood only about as high as my waist. But she had this incredibly growly voice.'

'A growly voice.'

'And whenever we'd tapped *Happy Days are Here Again*, she'd want to help me undress. She'd give me a sip of whisky. Against the cold, she said. She was incredibly passionate.'

'Not as passionate as me?'

'No one able, Able, could ever be.'

'Marguerite Rawlings,' I offer in exchange, 'looked like a black and angry chook.'

Shiver me timbers, my Majestic Artichoke likes to say, and it is as if the past is shivering up behind me. If only it could be confined, I think, like the grasses our father used to grow for experiments in small outside grids or in trays inside his glasshouses at the station. If I don't finish reading all the old mail soon, I begin to fear the shivering will increase. Yet even as I make haste, I seem to slow down. Farm work distracts me from my task and Lavinia and Ally want to go camping.

My father always seems to be away when the year-ling weaners get into the Catholic cemetery through the saggiest spots in the barbed-wire fences. They rub against headstones and eat the agapanthus growing in the grandest enclosure. Slender Panic grass, Hairy Panic, Shivery grass, the Briza minor species from Africa. I learn a few more names and their appearances until I have them off by heart. The fence strainers are old and difficult to get going. Red paint sticks to sweat in the palms of my hands. I find myself making the most makeshift of repairs, scurrying through foot massages barely listening to Iris' rambling stories, in order to return as quickly as possible to Alana's desk.

I am going to write to my sister, I tell Lavinia. I'm going to say how certain bends occurring on roads anywhere in the world have, without warning, reminded me of a place where we once had to stop when we were children, because Rosemary Kincaid was feeling carsick. Our mother urged her to eat a bit of dry breadroll and then suddenly the calls of bell-birds made us all look up.

On days when I believe you're alive and well, I will write, I'd think that maybe you too, holding on tightly to a bus seat as it took a mountain corner, as land presented itself like a bend in memory, remembered that day and thought it was time, like Iris' sister Olive, to reappear. To say hoax is over. Ha, ha.

I'll ask Ann-Clare doesn't she also think as I do, that in the end, much must be linked back to Mr Michaelhouse? That it is time I read the Mary Shore letters? One day too, I feel, I must open the three boxes of slides. I have resisted up until this point, Ann-Clare. Ann-Clare?

## CHAPTER FOURTEEN

My sister only ever falls in love with people who write good letters.

I always use the present tense as if from out of an autumn mist or summer haze of Old Lachlanstone Road, the mail van will emerge carrying a letter from my sister. Or maybe Ann-Clare only really loved the images or stories people gave to her in their correspondence. Sometimes the image that touched my sister's heart wouldn't occur until the last sentence before the salutation, or until the scrawled post-script—the writer of the letter deciding at the very last moment to tell her how she had heard bird wings like old hinges in the back garden; of the warm, sweet smell of sandstone in the sun; or of an old lady like a cobweb under a tree, sitting in her wheelchair sucking a mango.

Some correspondents had been sending Ann-Clare their ordinary and beautiful letters ever since she first became a letter writer; a time she marked as really beginning after she was married, when I was trying to be an artist and working in the Romance Library by the Sea, when she learnt that letters could fill many gaps in a life, even if they were one thin white page or a few sentences on the back of a postcard.

After Ann-Clare's wedding, habits of secrecy half-learned from Alana confirmed themselves. When Mr Michaelhouse came up behind her shoulder to read a letter she was completing, Ann-Clare turned the page over quickly. But her husband had such quick grey eyes that he would read something anyway and be appalled. 'You're telling that. About me,' he'd say, his voice full of grievance. 'To your sister.' This intrusive habit only caused Ann-Clare to hunch closer to the page and to buy a three-drawer filing cabinet where she could lock the answers she received. She never left any letters in the hand cut and rolled tin letter holder Mr Michaelhouse had procured for Ann-Clare from a great-aunt who said it had been made in 1842 using tin snips and kerosene containers.

Following early advice offered by Mary Shore, Ann-Clare learned not how to notice things, for the quietness of our childhood had fostered that anyway, but how to turn the dark-heartedness of her married life at that time into beautiful sentences.

As a girl Ann-Clare used to keep her diary on the middle cake-cooking shelf, in a small toolbox that wasn't always locked, of the old range oven in the Abandoned House. One day when I walked in I became aware of her presence up above the door.

When I asked my sister what she was doing perched up there, she drew back her melaleuca log and leapt, clubbing me on the knees.

'Why did you do that?' I shouted.

'You know,' my sister shouted back.

I could see silver stars as if I was in a cartoon, and

through them, the figure of my angry sister. She hit my knee and charged again as if she had every idea at the age of twelve of the way I would still be snooping through her life years later.

It is early in the morning when my father and daughter walk past the window. I look at them expecting them to look through the glass at me but Ally's smiling up at her grandfather and I feel I've suddenly become invisible. Half my face floats in the window's glass. I move and the face disappears. I wish my father would tap the window with his signet ring and call me to come with them. Here is the boat-shaped carpet grass, he has stooped to show Ally. And this is the spear-headed paspalum. Though it hasn't rained they'd be going to check the gauge, a granddaughterly ritual, and for a moment I leave the boxes of slides on the desk to watch their progress through the grove of dead wattle trees. The mist increases the resemblance of the trees to a dock full of dark, abandoned ships.

Our mother used to sit where I sit, her face full of angles from the desk lamp she had on even if it was daytime. Her pen was a wand in her long fingers. In autumn she liked to press leaves from the maple tree avenue under the dictionaries. Then she'd pin leaves along the wall next to her desk or cut oblongs out of them, before pasting them carefully onto paper. Some retained their elusive and poignant colours for years whereas those left pinned to the wall quickly lost their lovely loops and spikes, crinkled and faded, became the nests of spiders and finally dust.

I use the expression my mother's desk not in order to elicit any kind of pitying response but because I genuinely think of it as her writing place not mine. When it arrived from England with everything else, it was the only piece of furniture Alana liked enough to claim ownership over. All the rest of Jack's inheritance from Betty she tended to view as a terrible chore or a security nuisance. In the New House, with its mottled brick interiors and architect-designed half-walls, the old furniture looked, and still looks, peculiar. The oak is so dark it's purple-black and clashes with the pale table and leather chairs Alana chose.

Ann-Clare and I were always stubbing our toes on oak corners which poked out too far from the wall or losing toenails on the sharp, shredding corner of the grandfather clock. Alana's desk is of a different, beautiful wood. It's tall and slender, with a book cabinet above and intricate compartments in front of the writing section that folds out to rest on longer drawers beneath. It's hard to imagine how Betty organised her house staff to carry such a desk onto a roof.

'What was wrong with Betty?' I feel I will be asking forever.

'Oh she was tortured.'

'Tortured?'

'By these ridiculous thoughts and attitudes.'

I look out of the window again and the hills to the west of our farm are bellying out through the mist.

By the end of autumn the daisy petals will be flung right back from their centres and they'll never be as bright as Windsor and Newton yellow Indian ink again. Patricia will go back to England, I'll have read all the letters there are to read and it will be a good time to move to Redclack. Before we go I'll put in a good effort against the bracken and the muscat weed. The mist will come up higher and higher until eventually it'll stay all day lapped over the rim of the plateau.

New cottonwool, one of us will say, trying to find the right description.

Just like the mists of Africa, my father will seek a further definition. Don't you remember the cold mists of Hluhluwe?'

In the sitting room my father will light roaring fires so big, the new grate will be destroyed. He is good at making fires. When we come over from Redclack to visit, he'll teach Ally what he taught us, how the secret lies in turning a double sheet of newspaper into a knot around which air and flame can travel. Lavinia will make bakers-sized trays of coconut cookies which we'll eat until we feel quite glutted.

My father suggests that we get a small wood burner. Equally keenly, he also wonders couldn't we find the garden mattocks and long-nosed shovels, and get the wattles out of the ground once and for all? We won't, but we agree it wouldn't be a long job, they are now so fragile. Just some twigs left at the top edges of a couple of trees that still carry a few blossoms. I always snap off kindling sticks from the tree closest, so that that poor one is the only armless dancer moving in the circle. They were Sally Wattles, a name so bright and cheery it seems to have nothing to do with what is left. In between the trunks, beneath the unkempt grass, it's easy to trip over remnants of older trees long gone. I tell Ally not to go there, scared that she'll be scared or that she might somehow glimpse my sister and me at her age and wonder why it isn't noisy like that in the wattle arbour any more. Or she might see us boiling up wattle bark the way our father showed us, trying to tan great sheepskins and ending up with the air around them so rotten we and our horses took fright.

The wattles will have to wait until the wind pulls their frail roots out of the ground once and for all or until an afternoon when my mother's desk is driving me crazy and only some violent gardening will be a kind of cure. And even then the chances are I will go looking for a mattock only to find it missing from its place in the shed, its whereabouts unknown.

The Frenchman who originally cleared the land hoping for vineyards and formal gardens would be shocked. Even the Abandoned House has begun to feel more insecure than usual, perched on the plateau, as if like a wattle tree or the tent once pitched for Christmas in the garden, it could blow into the valley, unanchored at last by the force of the afternoon southerlies. At certain angles I'm sure its pointy roofline, which is echoed in the blue point of Gaungan Peak, has begun to slip sideways, or that the valley itself has begun to slide away from the fence. My father says it could also be a feeling exaggerated by the crazy angle of ploughing favoured by the new farmer next door. He might as well be from another century, for all the land sense he has—ploughing straight up and down the hills without a contour ridge in sight. My father imagines already the deaths of hundreds of dung beetles because the neighbour will almost certainly be careless in his use of chemicals and cow drenches. The neighbour has new fencelines which he is in the middle of painting white.

'What a silly bugger,' says my father.

And Ally says, 'What a silly bugger,' in the same kind of voice. She often talks in the frail, androgynous way of a grandfather.

My father sees the arrival of the neighbour's peacocks as the final indignity; as if the new farmer has chosen to have them in his garden knowing that my father finds them hateful. I quite like their weird call in the early morning and want to take Ally across one day so she can get some feathers for her collection. As a young man on his new black motorbike my father tried to run down white peacocks. If he'd been a political young man, one could read all sorts of symbolism into such a deliberate action along the Garden Route from Natal to Cape Town in 1954, but he was just a twenty-year-old agriculture student on his new Christmas present, about to start holiday work on some vineyards in the Cape.

The slide boxes sit on Alana's desk. Sick of myself and all this waiting, I pick up the scissors and snip away the tape holding the boxes shut.

I don't know what year it was Ann-Clare first suggested to Mr Michaelhouse that he begin to make love to her only once she was asleep. This is what the first slide I hold up seems to suggest is happening.

Small blooms of pink mildew are creeping along one side of the transparency. Perhaps it was the year they travelled? The room where my sister is lying looks English. There are low oak beams and the wallpaper behind the bed is covered in English flowers.

Pretending exhaustion from the day (touring stud turkey farms, looking for new blood for Mr Michaelhouse's flocks, in probably about their eighth year of marriage) my sister lies tensely but pretending to be relaxed on her side of the bed, waiting for the moment when he'll leave the small writing bureau of the hotel or guesthouse and come to bed. Sometimes my sister is aware of Mr Michaelhouse checking her face before he undresses. Ann-Clare has to keep her breathing even and clean as she hears the camera coming out of its case. She doesn't move as he manoeuvres across the sheets. At first what surprises her in England is his incredible roughness. The mandatory parting of her legs. Sometimes a knee gets hurt because it's in his way.

As if a solution has been found to this inconvenience, a run of slides in which my sister's feet are tied apart.

One morning when he has gone to Westminster Cathedral, Ann-Clare shaves off her pubic hair. I hold this slide quickly up to the light and put it down quickly, relieved that I didn't set up the projector. I don't think I could look at sheet-sized images.

The slide makes me remember a game I used to play with Ann-Clare with flowers. After drinking the nectar from the bottom of the flowers, we'd then force-furl them, so they appeared again as young and unopened. My sister would place them into her nests made of grass. Then, holding a nest in each hand, she'd implore me to climb with her up the tallest stinging tree to place them one at a time in forks along the way. This was invariably a hazardous task, before Ann-Clare's adolescent vertigo set in, requiring dexterity to stay out of the way of stray or falling leaves. We didn't know who had carved the crucifix cross into this tree or who'd hammered the struts of timber into its trunk, but to climb up what was effectively a ladder into the sky never failed to have an exhilarating effect. We might see a real nest, the shape of a beautiful wine glass made of thistle down. Even the Boer War bell hit by our mother calling us in sounded more like a peal of bells. Ann-Clare would put her nests in place. Look, we'd say, there's Alana walking over to the edge of the valley to see our possible whereabouts. From that height she looked safer, like a miniature, neatly painted mother from a farm animal set we could manoeuvre this way or that. We could see a trickle of smoke down a range or impending new weather, or closer up a tree orchid about to flower. Or Alana at the washing line taking down the clothes which were always hung with the colours of the pegs matching the colours of the washing. She did this to prevent boredom and each year dipped her wooden pegs into paints to keep their colours fresh.

This was before my sister's quietness had set in for good, before the Western pleasure man in an embroidered shirt and long Cuban-heeled boots asked my sister to go on the ferris wheel with him at the Lindley show. He had thistle-coloured eyes and a tongue that didn't work properly. His deformed mouth made it sound like he was saying, 'Come on the feral sweel. Come on the feral sweel with me. For the fireworks,' he said. When Ann-Clare wouldn't go on the ferris wheel he took her arm and said they could make their own fireworks. My sister tried to yell at the man but no sound came from her throat. What Ann-Clare realised was how keen she was not to make a disturbance. So intent was she upon that one thought, that she stopped resisting and walked into the stable of her own free will, for she didn't want anybody to notice her, or what was happening to her at the Lindley show on fireworks night. She didn't want to make a fuss. She wanted whatever was going to happen to hurry up because she knew in the older row of stables running away at a right angle, I was waiting for her to help control the stirred-up horses.

Once in the stable Ann-Clare felt he was at least a horse length away. She could smell the creosote painted on the stable. But then, even though his breathing made Ann-Clare believe he was standing far away, his tongue unlatched itself. Telling me about the incident years later, Ann-Clare said he then gave her a two dollar note and said in his spitty, imbecile's voice, to buy a doll on a stick.

'Ann-Clare!' I said. 'You didn't say a word to me at the time.'

Ann-Clare looked away. She leafed through a paperback romance I was repairing. She said that the horses were being too silly with the fireworks for her to find a moment to speak.

My sister was too quiet.

I think of how some people see a quiet face and talk at it until a kind of froth gathers at the corners of their lips.

The confidences of the vigorous, pleasant young woman who came to buy the runt of the puppy litter took me by surprise. She said that the last time she and her husband had tried getting their old dog into a young bitch, she'd felt so pent up she said to her husband, 'Blow this Mark, you attend to me.'

'I wish the bitch came on heat more often,' her husband had said taking off his jeans. Upon telling me this the young woman screeched with laughter. 'Dirty little moll, aren't I?' she said and made pelvic motions at me with her hips.

It was hard not to stop the frozen look crossing over my face and I can feel a similar impulse of coldness as I keep looking at slides.

Was it something to do with the quality of my sister's skin? Was it its velvet feel, its mauveness along stretches where the sun rarely reached that made Mr Michaelhouse begin to hurt her and the bones underneath her skin? Still in the next slide, Ann-Clare pretends to sleep. She pretends her husband is a stranger assaulting the body of a sleeping young child who has forgotten to put on her nightie. She has made herself go limp. She has allowed her mouth to open, to swallow in all the tall-ceilinged shadows, as if she deserved some kind of punishment. In this slide she reminds me of our old technique of tricking Rosemary Kincaid into thinking we were asleep. How to let your spit gather in your mouth, to not swallow, to keep your eyes very still.

I imagine things so vividly I might as well have been there. This slide is upside down. No it's not, it is just the position of my sister's face.

On the first morning after the night Ann-Clare pretended to be dead, not just asleep, she and Mr Michaelhouse found themselves sitting opposite each other as usual at the lovely sunny corner of the hotel breakfast room. She ate her boiled eggs with excruciating care, noting how the sun shone through the empty egg shells. Mr Michaelhouse thought he might go to the local museum to see if they had any etchings illustrating old turkey breeds. Ann-Clare buried her nose in one of my letters. 'Was Mr Michaelhouse growing a bit more of a tummy from all the stodgy food?' I probably wanted to know, or some other detail equally naive.

I open the window to see the whereabouts of my father and daughter but they have vanished in the mist.

Ann-Clare's poses are those you could find in any number of certain magazines which are still kept at the back of the Lindley newsagency, but it is the expression on Ann-Clare's face that pangs me. She looks so sad but also absent. Her eyes are dark and stare right at the camera lens, right through to me, through the passage of years. Her mouth is slewed, as if she has had a lot to drink. Or as if the shock has affected her face like a punch. Some of the slides are not of my sister at all but of rooms. In one I recognise the main bedroom. But mostly the pictures are from the enclosed verandahs. The slides bring sadness. The sadness feels blue. It is the colour of the horse meat Mr Michaelhouse ate at the first lesbian-run restaurant on the coast, which he ordered rare. It is the look on my sister's face as she leaves the Romance Library before five in order to pick up the slides from the photographer in the American Express building. She is so quiet handing over the money and receiving them, sure that the man at the counter has looked and knows. Waiting for him to say something or to unbutton his fly but he only ever watches her face as he holds the first slide up to the light coming in from the door, asking if they are the correct batch.

One slide makes me rush to the window, nauseous.

He could ask her anything and she would shrug. He would stand knock-kneed facing slightly away with the camera as she watched the light through the old louvres and the shadow man who flew or was flailed to the roof. For a while she called the shadow Angel Gluck because that was the music most often played by Mr Michaelhouse at that time. Sometimes she'd think it was to disturb the quality of the darkness and quiet in and outside his house that made the turkey farmer's skin so angry or that she received so many letters—and nothing to do with her own quietness after all.

Once, when his anger went right out of control, she felt it disappearing into her. Because she actually juddered, he mistook it for pleasure. Afterwards, he opened the windows. He still had on his jumper and a pen and notepad in the shirt underneath pushed the top left-hand pocket out like a breast. There was a storm coming. Ann-Clare could hear the dead leaves being whipped in circles and the falling berries. She thought of the gaudy pink and purple kewpie doll she didn't buy at the show when she was fourteen or fifteen years old. Or of a feral sweel. On the verandah the pink light of the azaleas was springing out from old branches shaped like hoops, landing in a line of beautiful glass bottles like a blessing.

'Avis.'

I look up and it is my grandmother, in a turban towel headdress, leaning around the wall. Her pyjamas are yellow and scarlet and she holds the electrical cord that keeps the power going into her heated slippers as if it is the train to a very elaborate gown.

'You're not planning a slide night, are you?'

I shake my head, tapping the slides back into neat piles, covering them over with the yellow plastic lids.

'Thank goodness. I really have never had any patience for slide nights.'

Soon Patricia will be back in her small London life, in her small basement flat in Hampstead. She will again travel to the pub next door, twice a day, where if she touches anything metal, an electric shock is created from the pyjamas she wears underneath her fur coat.

Grandma weaves her way over to me. She says she has something I might be interested in since I seem to have become the family archivist. It is a list on the back of an enlarged photograph from one of her Spanish holidays of the sixties, of all the countries she has toured by coach. Some countries she has toured fifteen or twenty times. Rhodesia is listed once.

'I didn't know you'd been there,' I said.

'I came over to help your mother after you were born.'

'She never once said. Or you.'

'I stayed at the Meikles Hotel. A seven star hotel.'

'And what was I like?'

'Oh, like any fat little baby. Alana wouldn't let me do much for you at all. I wasn't allowed to hold you. No. She was very protective.'

'Really?'

'Well, you were very, very wanted, wasn't she, Jack?' At the appearance of my father, her eyelashes flutter.

I feel a terrible distaste and pity, love and dislike. In the absence of any other men, my grandmother flirts with her dead daughter's husband.

My father says Ally wants him to read her a book and hastens away.

'My son Edward,' Patricia says. 'Do you think he'd want to see me? He hasn't wanted to for forty years. He married a Rhodesian woman called Jasper,' she says. 'Such a strange name for a girl.'

'We had two dogs called Jasper.' I mention 'That was their registered kennel prefix.' I learnt to do this working in the Romance Library with all the old people. It is a kind of conversational strategy but not really, because its ultimate aim is silence. You brush aside what you really think, with some silly and inane piece of information. Or you tell a dog story. But still, you have made a response, keeping hidden what you really think, and that is like permission to then return to shelving books fast so that in every hour I could also afford to spend at least fifteen minutes reading the book I carried in the pocket of my dust smock or sketching Ethel Commerford's face who came to the library every Wednesday afternoon for a doze in the sunny chair.

Jasper Salamander Skipper and Jasper Salamander Lady were a handsome pair of boxer dogs with a dangerous tendency to roam far beyond the house and farm. They had to wear boots against the allergy they developed to the stinging leaves. Our parents could call them back with what they called the mist whistle. This went on for a long time, alternating between two notes, until breath ran low and they took their fingers down from their mouths. Then Ann-Clare and I would call for the dogs too, sometimes imitating the rise and fall of our father's recommenced whistling with our voices, until we were old enough to have learnt the secret of the whistle. After a long time doing this, the dogs would eventually appear, loping in out of the mist that hangs for the longest time inside the rainforest remnant at the back of the house and inside the deep valleys that fall away from the front of the garden.

I look out to the lip of the paddock, as if the long gone boxers might roam into view on their spindly English legs instead of being shot dead fifteen years ago after all by a farmer's son who mistook them for wild dogs. Our mother said maybe the Jasper Salamanders became wild dogs and had deserved to die. As soon as they went into the mist how did we know if they became wild and feckless rather than the gentle, ugly Jaspers we knew?

'I wonder how my parlour palm is getting along,' says Grandma, and pours herself a small whisky.

If ever I join Grandma for a morning drink, pretending I have it to flush my blood with an illusion of warmth, everything is easier: letter writing and letter reading and the ache leaves my knees, arms and back, yet when I put my hands up to my flushed cheeks, they are icy, front and back, not warm at all.

Sitting at my mother's desk, a whisky poured but unsipped, I think even the air smells quiet. And it is that lovely cool autumnal quiet that might only be broken tonight by a wind that will release the stars from any clouds and make the dogs bark. Or the sudden light from the moon might wake them.

Some of the everlasting daisies, the longer-stalked ones at the back of the vase, are losing their petals faster than the other everlastings: I can hear them pulling back; a sound like small wings. Their seeds drift out and get caught by the spider webs. Brushed against the face, they leave a lovely yellow powder. Indian yellow pigment was first made using the urine of cows fed on mangoes. Cochineal, the scarlet dye that is Ally's favourite, is made using the dried bodies of female insects reared on cactus in northern Mexico.

The cessation of aberrations between Ann-Clare and her husband reminded her of the first frost arriving.

I want to believe there was a cessation. Some

imperceptible change in the air that alerted you to its coming: the skin on the top of your hands slightly older and drier. Alana's sadder singing. The Boer bell in winter, its freezing metal pressed to your cheek at breakfast. Or how in the middle of the night, in our childhood, when a cold stream of air would wake up the dog at the end of your bed and the dog would wake you, snuggling in closer to the bend in your legs.

At exactly the same moment Ann-Clare would also be wide awake and telling the dog not to bark. 'Do you think it's a frost?' one of us would whisper and the clarity of the air holding our question would assure us that it was. The sense of expansion that came before the crack, crack, crack under our early morning boots once it was light. I'd sometimes pull my quilt and dog off my bed and transfer us into Ann-Clare's supposedly to keep warm but more to make the moment last and to talk in a way that was so different from day talk. It meant autumn and all the high hopes and fears gathering together in clean flannelette sheets. And when one of us looked out the window, a frost in front of the cemeteries like a lake or a stretch of moonlit river. Or in the coldest winters of all, fine plateau snow, never thick enough for snowmen, but enough to mean a few icy snowballs to throw at each other's ankles.

My sister held Mr Michaelhouse's hand in the dark. I want to believe that nothing stirred, nothing. She told him, in the dark, things such as how much she'd always liked his fingers and the sounds his house made in the rain. And would then be able to drift off to sleep feeling quite glad, as if that had resolved everything, only to always reach a dream in which he killed her. She dreamt he hung her on a hook through her throat in the freezing room. She bowed her neck to the knife.

In order to leave Mr Michaelhouse Ann-Clare had to break all twelve of his anniversary presents. These English enamel boxes, hand painted, cost around the equivalent price of fifty prime Christmas turkeys. The one in the shape of the Victoria and Albert Hall, which when opened played *Rule Britannia*, was worth double the number of turkeys again. Later she'd come back with me for her beetle boxes and other ones.

I remember that my sister drove not to my place but to Mary Shore's. She counted the trunks of trees that she passed. Christmas time. The Christmas organ in a cathedral. And going past a pub, a man on a microphone calling out the winner of the giant raffle stocking. Down at a boat ramp on the harbour from where Ann-Clare could see the lights were still on at Mary Shore's house, there was a boy next to a small leaf-shaped boat. 'What are you doing?' asked Ann-Clare, because she could see he was having some kind of difficulty.

He said that he'd had a fight with his brother who normally held the light when they went fishing for mullet. So he was tying his carbide-run bike lantern to the side of the boat. The fish, he said, would be attracted to the light and leap into the hull. Ann-Clare helped him with the bike light, wished him good luck and pushed him out onto the dark water.

'Where are you going?' the boy called, as his boat slid out on to the water.

'To Mary Shore's house,' replied my sister.

'Good luck to you,' said the boy, as if he knew something was afoot in Ann-Clare's life.

## CHAPTER FIFTEEN

Sometimes the desk is so silent I can hear the paper daisies in the vase opening out little by little. Or it might be the sounds of Mary Shore's onion-skinned airmail paper unwrinkling further after I've removed a letter from its envelope. Not paper daisies at all.

Although I love Lavinia so easily, I'm shocked by some of the letters. I try to be casual about what I'm reading but in reality I think of my sister abroad in some girl bar of any city in the world, wearing black lesbian costumes and contracting dangerous infections which will render her infertile forever.

'Ann-Clare had a sort of girlfriend,' I say to Lavinia. 'As old as Alana or even older perhaps. I had no idea. It's come as a complete surprise.'

'Are you sure, Able?'

'There are photos.'

Mary Shore is not the gentle-looking reader and letter writer of my imagination. She is old. The hair above above her ears is streaked white so evenly in places I think of nothing so much as zebra. I look over Lavinia's shoulder as she skims through the photos. I remember Ann-Clare's nervous energy before her visits to Mary Shore's.

In one picture Mary Shore is wearing fancy black boots and rests one of these on my sister's bottom as if Ann-Clare is a bit of conquered game. The photos are all studio quality black and white with pinking-sheared edges. The look in Ann-Clare's eyes is the look in her eyes in the Mr Michaelhouse slides.

'My God,' says Lavinia when I show her, 'it's like lesbian porn from the 1920s.'

Although I have no idea what lesbian porn from the 1920s might look like I think I can see what Lavinia means. It is the staginess of the backdrops; the bookshelves and a grey harbour out the window. It is Mary Shore's horsy outfits and black leather riding crop; the suggestion of a pith helmet in the way she's lacquered her hair.

'My God,' says Lavinia, 'how on earth did Ann-Clare become her play pal?'

'I don't know. Letters. They used to write each other letters.' In opposition to the posed nature, the uneasiness of the photographs, the letters I'm reading are full of romantic sentiments.

'Yes,' says Lavinia, holding a photo of Mary Shore away from her. You wouldn't want to mess with her, would you? Looks like she'd eat you alive. Is she still in Sydney?'

'No. She ended up going back to a farm. Somewhere north of Lindley. Didn't really like the city after all. Sold the house on the harbour she'd bought.'

'She must be rich. Dare I ask—have you written your letter yet?'

'No. But I've found an address.'

'Not to Mary Shore, darling. I meant the letter to your sister.'

'Oh. That. Not exactly. But soon.'

After Lavinia goes to work I keep reading. There are probably few things as excruciating as letters a sister once wrote, seeking assurances. Certain letters written after Alana's funeral try to use the death of our mother as an emotional leverage to persuade Mary Shore to join Ann-Clare in Africa. These letters are mushy with emotions. If I run my fingers across that page I feel the old dimples left by my sister's tears. The letters annoy me rather than move me towards sympathy. The phoniness of the voice which Ann-Clare consciously or unconsciously assumed to woo Mary Shore, to make her want to abandon everything and write back instantly, reminds me of Alana's Christmas circulars. I have to stifle my irritation. I have to rein in my disbelief that not once did Ann-Clare confide in me about Mary Shore or Mr Michaelhouse.

The frankness of Ann-Clare's infatuation unnerves me, the freshness, though the letters are yellowing now. I find that as when riding a horse I think is about to shy at something ahead, I'm not breathing. I have to make myself breathe.

'Before it was light,' Ann-Clare wrote to her friend, when she was still Mrs Michaelhouse, 'I woke up thinking whelks.' My sister's handwriting, normally so neat and small is now wild and bright and green. I am not reading carbon copies but original love letters, filed between Mary Shore's. At some stage Ann-Clare must have requested back, or Mary Shore must have returned, every letter Ann-Clare ever posted.

*I woke up thinking of how a finger pressing open their door is like a finger slipping inside yourself or inside a friend when you are first in love and she is still asleep. The rich slippery feel of a woman's fingers.*

I read and I read. I open a window and lean out towards the hills undulating in mist. The grass smells womanly, the way it sometimes does, of pee or as if cows in milk have recently passed. I think of the wind at Umli and how it blew my pee away.

The damp air bends the piece of letter in my hand. I read about things you cannot tell a big sister who used to be your main bully. Things which are easier to tell on paper. I read of how my sister's years with Mr Michaelhouse had left Ann-Clare feeling like some kind of gap through which anything had trickled and might trickle again.

Out of Mary Shore's surprisingly crooning replies on the onion skinned airmail fall bits of tobacco. Or sometimes the smelly crumb of a scented cheroot.

After Mary Shore moved to the city, the friendship quickened. Ann-Clare continuing to send Mary Shore little notes or mementoes in the post, as well as making frequent visits. I began to see less of my sister. For years, even though Marguerite Rawlings didn't stock a particularly exciting repertoire of books, my sister had done all her borrowing from the

301

Romance Library. New libraries daunted her, she said. Their silence. Not knowing the procedures. Would someone come and dump the tomes where you sat or was there a special spot to pick them up from? In the company of Mary Shore there seemed to be no library my sister didn't visit.

'Why don't you bring Mysterious Mary to the Romance Library?' Marguerite would suggest.

'I will. I will,' my sister would promise, only for her own visits to dwindle to almost nothing. She would send little notes of apology. I feared I was becoming the Avis Betty file—areas of interest strictly childhood memories, ongoing vague horse concerns and turkey farm and farmer anecdotes. If ever Mr Michaelhouse phoned, I was to say that my sister had only just left the Romance Library. According to Ann-Clare, Mary Shore's house was like an immense library. One day she had seen her friend through one of the large glass windows, standing on a stepladder, stroking a leather-bound book as if it was the pelt of a rare animal.

'Come for afternoon tea one day with Mary,' I'd suggest to Ann-Clare. 'I'd really like to meet her. We could give her free membership.'

'Oh no,' said Ann-Clare. 'She doesn't read anything popular. She's been lending me the most obscure women poets.'

'Well bring her in so she can have a laugh.'

'I'll ask her,' Ann-Clare would agree, only for the promised meeting never to happen.

Mary Shore did come once to our farm. This was on the weekend Alana had sent my father and me off on a mission to the coast to find a piece of driftwood for her grave. Not a cross, Alana said, but an attractive wave of wood. Nor did she want us fussing over the grave. We were to plant a bush and that would do. Nothing tissy. Something tough and local that wouldn't need mollycoddling.

When Mary Shore wrote saying she'd be passing close to Lindley, my sister had written back begging her to call in, to stay a few nights.

'Won't it be terribly inappropriate?' Mary Shore wrote back. 'A stranger in the house? With your mother so sick?'

'Oh no,' fibbed Ann-Clare in reply. 'Distractions. You'd be a wonderful distraction for Alana. And you'll get to meet my sister!' As if, though Mary Shore never did visit the Romance Library, I was a kind of a lure. As if Ann-Clare must have told Mary Shore I was wonderful.

Mary Shore arrived a little later than the sunset. My sister turned away, waiting, while Mary parked her truck under the Port Jackson figtree. The nervousness was deep in Ann-Clare, under her wishbones. When they hugged, my sister had to tilt her body forward in order to avoid treading on the small Cuban-heeled boots her friend was wearing. The dogs were going into their normal frenzy of welcome and scratched the high black polish anyway.

The map Ann-Clare had drawn had been damaged by rain in the post and because of this Mary Shore had ended up in Redclack before noticing Ann-Clare's tiny writing on the map advising she'd come Far Too Far should she reach that little town.

Ann-Clare didn't like women who wore Cuban heels. In our childhood, in Lindley, girls who wore Cuban heels used to lie in the soiled straw of horse trucks with old or young men, or sometimes thirteen-year-old boys, also in boots. When we were girls, that was all that mattered—the walking into the back of the truck with the booted man or sideshow boy behind you; who couldn't speak in shapely sentences; who spoke in grunts not words.

But this night, although Ann-Clare was disappointed her friend hadn't seen the best of the dusk, her eyes alighted on the boots. The boots made the letter-writing woman stand tall and brought many memories back in a rush. It made Ann-Clare remember the nature of her desire.

This desire, Ann-Clare thought, was the same colour as the wattle leaves blown upside down by the summer winds. It cut across gender. It was the colour of a nail burnt out of an old fencepost and found in the ashes of the potbelly stove.

Although Ann-Clare was taller than Mary in an ordinary pair of black shoes, Mary hugged my sister in such a way that Ann-Clare's face fell into the hollow between her shoulder and neck. Ann-Clare thought it would only take one fast movement away from the embrace, to have the skin tear back from Mary Shore's bones in the way exquisite brocades eventually do from fine old furniture.

'Oh your dark Brahmany eyes,' Mary said and that she'd forgotten them. She let go of my sister to ask where was Gaungan Peak? Gaungan, which Ann-Clare more often than not mentioned in her letters because of its remarkable similarity to a woman's breast, looked quite ugly on this night. The timber mill was burning refuse and smoke hung in front of my sister's favourite blue peak. In addition, the abandoned dairy, which Ann-Clare was prone to describing in letters as castle-like and golden on a curve of ridge, was nothing more than a dark huddle of long buildings.

'Is that her?' Mary asked, pointing straight at Gaungan.

Ann-Clare said no, it wasn't. She said that it was only Mt Elizabeth. My sister immediately panicked, sure that she'd written to Mary Shore already with the information that Gaungan Peak had once been known as Mt Elizabeth and that many established families of the Lindley district still liked to use the older name-form.

Ann-Clare was glad then of the dogs' neurotic welcoming behaviour and even encouraged it slyly by praising them up in an excited voice. Perhaps Mary didn't hear her lie at all, Ann-Clare hoped, so intent was she upon the dogs. Rather than fend them off, she crouched down to be at their height. She spoke the sort of nonsense people do when meeting unfamiliar pets. She said the dogs were like otters and held my sister's gaze.

As they walked towards the house ablaze with the party lights our mother loved to have on each night during the last months of her life, Mary Shore said that the dogs made the same noise as the old diesel pumps of her childhood on her family's farm in western New South Wales. This made Ann-Clare clearly recall how much her love for Mary first centred around the way she'd used words and images.

From Mary Shore's left earlobe hung an empty cross. For once the jewellery Mary Shore was wearing wasn't made of any particularly precious metal, yet it held its own beauty. The beauty lay in the shadow the earring cast onto her neck. The shadow cross was dark and long, and framed two neck moles so that they seemed part of some deliberate decorative effect.

'These dogs run like old diesel engines,' repeated my sister aloud, in order to replicate the pleasure of a perfect description.


'That's a good likeness,' said Mary, who had never met our mother, standing in front of the larger-than-life enlargement Alana had had framed before the swelling began to take over her body. If anything, the glass, the fairy lights, the being outside the house, seemed to magnify the photographs.

Ann-Clare went on to tell how we loved the worn pictures best, in the falling-apart photo albums from when our mother was closer to our own age. Or else we loved the beauty that showed more clearly now that the illness was further advanced. We'd prefer, Ann-Clare told Mary, a photo of our mother in the long dove-coloured dressing-gown that made her seem ephemeral but elegant. It was an illness so pale it slid around as smoothly as light. If ever Ann-Clare tried to visualise the colour of our mother's pain, it was always as a turkey egg rolling bigger in her palm;

creamy, with speckles and twice the size of chicken eggs.

Our mother had fallen asleep and didn't move when they came inside and stood by the massage table. The dogs grew calmer. They lay on their mats in front of the fire. A pint bottle of morphine on the mantelpiece glowed the same ruby shade of red as every third party light strung along the verandah.

'Sometimes,' my sister said, 'I think she looks like she's died already. Wee Willie Winkie who died in the night.'

'She looks straight out of a Chekhov play,' replied Mary Shore.

This made Ann-Clare look at her friend in a way she'd hoped she didn't need to any more. She wanted to take Mary Shore immediately from the room of illness into her bedroom which she'd made suitable for a small child really, with flower posies of pansies and early blooming violets. Ann-Clare had tried to make the room seem like a child's to increase the delusion they were going to innocently sleep there.

Ann-Clare picked up the bottle of morphine to suggest that it looked like raspberry syrup. For ice-cream sundaes.

'Keep it away from me,' Mary Shore said, making a stagey gesture with her arm. 'You know how addictive I am.'

'I'm afraid,' said Alana, after she'd woken up and after introductions, 'that I've just had a strange dream. I dreamt I'd been at a wedding, inside a foam cathedral. The walls were foam and when the bride and her father came to the door, they were also all wrapped up in thick foam. Only as the bride left her father's side did the foam begin to unfurl. The bride was you, darling,' Alana said, looking straight at Ann-Clare.

'But I was married at the farm,' said Ann-Clare.

'To a turkey farmer,' said Alana, raising her eyebrows.

'I know,' said Mary Shore, 'Ann-Clare's told me lots about him.'

'He used to call me Little Turkey.'

'And,' said Mary Shore, 'I have comforted her that Chekhov used to call Olga Knipper by that same endearment.'

'But believe you me,' our mother grimaced, 'that man was no Chekhov. We never properly knew why Ann-Clare married him in the first place.'

From the very first, Ann-Clare was ashamed to be marrying a man so much older. She used to remove the wedding ring almost every day for twelve years, whenever she was away from him. Even if she was going to the nearest corner shop for bread, she'd wriggle it into her pocket. She was married on the farm on a fine July day to the turkey farmer. He wore boots and moleskins, a tweed coat and tie. Mr Michaelhouse was not dissimilar to one of the turkeys he reared to kill. His back was round and white with fat, but possibly I've exaggerated the likeness of man to turkey over time. Adult turkeys are twice the size of their hens and he never reached those proportions.

The ring, which was of old thin gold, and that had been Iris' was inscribed with the word *mizpah*. Years passed before one day, Mary Shore, seeing my sister putting the ring back on her finger after their fourth or fifth lunch together, recognised the word. *Mizpah*, she said, was a Hebrew word meaning watchtower. As well as describing several high-lying places in Babylon, the most famous being where Jacob and Caban made a compact with the words: 'The Lord watch over me and thee when we are absent from one another', it also described the bond of love that is meant to grow between a husband and wife over time. That night, on the train home to Mr Michaelhouse, my sister let the ring drop down into an ashtray, not wanting any bond to grow between herself and the turkey farmer. Or for any god to be watching over her when absent from his side.

I imagine much of the talk after supper was to Mary Shore about Ann-Clare's planned holiday to Africa. How she intended to travel all through eastern Africa, slowly spending her time living in this town or that. The way Ann-Clare spoke was, however, so tentative, so much of a whisper, that Mary Shore seemed to doubt she would really go. Mary Shore said the word Chimanimani made her think of a knobbled limb. That of an old man. 'It has two men in it, doesn't it?' she said. 'Two mans.'

'Oohh, isn't she clever?' said Alana. 'I've never thought of that.' She turned to Mary Shore. 'Ann-Clare's always urged me to join the Faraway Group. Now I've met you, oh, I wish I had. Too late now.'

It emerged that Mary Shore loved Jane Austen as much as Alana. *Pride and Prejudice* and *Emma* were their favourites. And it wasn't until late in the night that Ann-Clare was able to get Alana into bed and show Mary Shore the bedroom. Ann-Clare made Mary laugh telling her how they were going to sleep in the very bedroom where she'd once thought she was turning into a boy, all her girl parts elongating and swelling. Then my sister showed Mary the copy of Lesley May's *Showjumping*, stolen from the library and never returned and significant not only for its knowledge about showjumpers but also for the beautiful 1920s woman who had written it, who appeared with her showjumping horses in the black and white plates wearing jodhpur boots and whipcord jodhpurs with extravagant billows. But Mary barely looked at the long thoroughbred faces of either the woman or her horses.

Mary Shore was taking from her bag a picture of the American writer Carson McCullers. The picture showed McCullers at the New York premiere of *Member of the Wedding*. In the picture, Carson looked very young and very sad, her head resting on the comforting bosom of the black actress who played one-eyed Berenice of the crazy kitchen. Then Mary flipped over the card so Ann-Clare could read the writing on the back. The handwriting, noted my sister, was curly and relaxed and beautiful in the way of writing from another era. It was a small love letter.

Mary Shore was showing my sister the card as a way of reminding her that it was coincidence only which had aligned Alana's dying with Mary purchasing another old farm, two hundred miles north of Lindley. On this farm Mary Shore was going to live again with her companion of many decades. They had

had, as Ann-Clare already knew from Mary Shore's letters, a blissful reunion. Mary Shore said she and her companion were going to live happily ever after. She had mentioned my sister to her companion. Ann-Clare might be pleased to know, she said, that her companion had found Ann-Clare's photographs both amusing and exciting. Nor would Mary Shore's companion mind too much the occasional visit from Ann-Clare to their new farm.

'This is lovely,' Ann-Clare said, referring to the card and the message, but really wanting to take it from Mary's hand and throw it into the long grass outside the bedroom. She examined the black and white photo again. She remembered that the first book Mr Michaelhouse ever gave her was Carson McCullers' novella, *The Ballad of the Sad Cafe*.

Mary Shore began to undress. 'Why are you looking so hard?' she asked my sister.

Because our mother's breasts, which were the only ones she ever saw these days, had become old dillybags, said Ann-Clare, with curious seashell patterns formed by the loss of body fat. Mary Shore put her mouth over my sister's ear.

I read everything, feeling I should not. Letters and their replies. I read on from where the last letter turns into a kind of confession, never to be sent. As I read, I try to imagine my sister's voice and find it is lost. Whereas up until now, I have been able to imagine the words unpeeling from the pages in the soft sounds of my sister's voice, now there is a sense of impending silence.

In the morning my sister burnt her fingers on the ice on the old car, scratching down her messages of devotion to Mary Shore before scratching them out again. For quite a while my sister stood on the frost as some kind of self-punishment as well as a chance to search the hills for a substitute peak. Poor Ann-Clare's toes ached, turned red, but still she stood scanning the distances, as if she didn't already know there were only two little teat hills far, far away which would simply have to do. No other breastal line of hills existed in the view from the farm. She picked an early iris. It had three buds and one bloom. Its juice coated Ann-Clare's teeth with something strange when she carried it back into the bedroom in her mouth. Mt Gaungan was looking perfect; a thread of mist lay where the night before's smoke had been.

'This is how I love you,' my sister said and sat down in the curve of Mary's legs and examined the flower. As well as the obvious anatomical likeness, my sister thought the flower resembled a bit of torn silk garment Mary or her companion of that night might have left lying on Mary's bedroom floor, following some wild night.

Sometimes in Sydney my sister would arrive at Mary Shore's house to find her in bed with a hangover. Ann-Clare would take to her bedroom hot tea and Disprin laid out in flower patterns. Although Mary would protest that she was not a hypochondriac in the way of Mr Michaelhouse, she'd eat the Disprin delicately. Ann-Clare would pretend that she also had had something of a wild night with women in old mauve silk and groan over her imaginary stiff dancing muscles.

One day, through the branches of the plum tree outside the kitchen window, Ann-Clare glimpsed a much older woman sitting with Mary Shore. My sister knew instinctively, by the way they touched each other, that this was Mary Shore's lifelong companion.

My sister tried to give the iris from the garden to Mary Shore, who said she couldn't take any more flowers from Ann-Clare.

'We have to massage our mother everywhere,' Ann-Clare said pointedly and mentioned how she'd asked Alana could she still feel any desire.

'Your own mother?!'

Yes, said Ann-Clare, in our family we talked about most things and that our mother had told us yes. How she put it was to say that she still had squiggles every now and then.

Lines fell in fan shapes from their eyes as they laughed. 'Desire like writing in your belly!' Mary Shore shook her head.

But it was the sudden intrusion of our mother's body into the morning that brought to a halt Ann-Clare's desire. A vision of our mother's poor beleaguered body crept between them. Ann-Clare thought suddenly of Alana's dried out shin bones that already had appeared to have died some weeks before. And she thought of how when our mother had to part her legs in the heated room for massages, the unmistakeable scent, so that against our will, we could smell how our mother must once have smelt

313

when she was young and fresh and her belly aswarm with incoherent words.

Mary Shore never mentioned Gaungan Peak that Ann-Clare had told the fib about. And did it really matter as much as Ann-Clare seemed to think it did? Maybe Mary Shore knew Ann-Clare was lying or maybe she didn't particularly care about the female landscapes that surround the farm that was once a vineyard and long before that a place where tribes hunted along the plateau or found fish in its deep river valleys.

'Thank you for having me,' said Mary Shore—as though she was a child leaving a birthday party.

Ann-Clare tried to hug Mary but later wrote that it felt as distant and impossible as trying to hug a portrait.

The fireweed was out of all control in one of the bottom paddocks. It rippled like a yellow ocean. The writing woman mistook the weed for real flowers and said it could've been any flower field in Europe. A Liberty of London's bonnet trembled in turn on our mother's head as she laughed.

'I'd like to be able to draw hugs,' said my sister as our father and I drove up moments later. 'You only just missed her, Avis.'

'Has your friend already gone?' asked our father.

'She could only afford to stay one night,' said Ann-Clare. 'I'd like to draw hugs,' she repeated, 'in all their grace and clumsiness.'

Alana couldn't have been asleep the night before

after all. She must have heard Mary Shore's compliments and in response, stuffed wads of cottonwool into the corners of the bonnet to increase the Chekhovian effect.

'She made me laugh,' said our mother pulling off the bonnet and passing it to Ann-Clare to hold. 'Goodbye, Gardenia,' she said, waving her arm in the direction of the road and naming Mary after that flower that's still so beautiful even when it is going yellow. 'Did you find a stump?'

The purple iris that had come trembling inside on Ann-Clare's lips died fairly fast. All three other blooms opened. We lit big log fires. The iris flowers bloomed in the fire's warmth, became slightly sticky, gleamed, then tore in Ann-Clare's fingers with a minimum of fuss.

Our mother died about a month after Mary Shore's visit. At this time, the mailbox had begun to fill with letters of farewell. People saying goodbye to the Alana they had known decades before. The letters of farewell often used a high, romantic kind of style which made you cry in the way that operas do.

By contrast Mary Shore's letters became increasingly stunted.

Though the envelopes are fat, because of all the accompanying photographs, there is little substance to the letters. Her handwriting weaves out from the margin as if at the time she was permanently intoxicated. The photographs, often taken on self-timer, are of two women together, you would almost think elderly sisters, calmly pottering around an elegant garden. But when my sister received a handmade postcard written on the back of two women's faces kissing, Ann-Clare lay down on her bed and pretended to die as she hadn't done since she was married. 'Above the height of your heart is no sound,' wrote my sister, 'only bone.'

Ann-Clare didn't have time to write to Mary until after the funeral and the correspondence took a long time to recover its momentum. She had trouble resuming her letterly voice. The obvious explanation was that she was motherless. Or that Mary had, in effect, remarried her old wife. Yet in fact part of my sister's reticence was more to do with being robbed of her old method of starting a letter. Once Ann-Clare had come back to live on the farm, she'd begin all her letters to Mary with elaborate or simple descriptions of Gaungan. She'd describe the peak in the way other people might describe the weather. Gaungan invisible; cloud over Gaungan. But since lying about the whereabouts of Gaungan when Mary visited, she no longer felt entitled to describe the lovely lights and dimples of the peak. This seemed to reinforce their sense of estrangement. She felt herself fading too. She felt she had the wrong colour eyes, that she wrote too many letters, that she had too much fervour, that her youth had killed their friendship, until at last each wrote their last letter to the other, and there are no more for me to read.

The pigeon grasses were rising over our mother in the Catholic cemetery when Ann-Clare left Lindley, wearing Alana's tooth as her charm.

Such was the brightness of the day, the eastern rosellas looked black and tiny and although I knew Ann-Clare would be home within a year, I couldn't stop the tears that began to fall down my face, as if I'd never see my sister again.

I've heard of the occurrence of daughters suddenly finding out more about each other after their mother has died; a release of previously censored information; as if everything so carefully avoided could be disturbed. But Ann-Clare went away to Africa so fast.

Maybe she did try to tell me something more specific. I remember my sister trying to bring up some topic. Had I ever considered, Ann-Clare was curious to know, how many beautiful, flawless bodies lay under the frumpy clothes and ravaged throats of the farm women of Lindley.

I said no, it wasn't something I'd given much thought to at all and in my discomfort put a bowl of soup on the ground for the dogs.

Had I truly never thought this though, Ann-Clare pressed me, not even when we worked in the holidays at Lindley's old people's home?

'I only went a few times, compared to your dedication.' But without saying so to Ann-Clare I knew I did remember the breasts of our afternoon lady, Beatrice Lily Day, who didn't like to wear her nightie; we were always having to struggle it back over her head; their white perfection was hard to ignore or the strength and remarkable blackness of hairs that ringed her right nipple.

And perhaps in exchange, I offered some hint of Marguerite Rawlings? Or perhaps our father came into the room at that point in the conversation, to show us his partial success at having washed clean the lymph stains of Alana out of their bedding; staring bemusedly at the faint, tide-mark colours, deeper in the threads of cotton.

All the way to Sydney we sang songs. We sang *Isak a zumbq, zumba, zumba. Isak a zumba, zumba zay.* We bought Ann-Clare's boots and hopped our way to the Romance Library, laughing wildly. *Hold him down, you Zulu warrior. Hold him down, you Zulu chief, chief, chief.*

We didn't mention that we weren't going to Africa together. At the airport I said, 'Look after yourself, Splinter,' choosing one of the nicknames that hadn't been in use for years but was still appropriate. The length of her limbs, their fineness, the way her new walking boots tilted her forward even as she was swinging her neck back to mouth goodbye. Her arm unfolding into a loose and final wave.

Around lunchtime I often meet my father in the kitchen which hangs with early childhood handicraft efforts. We walk so quietly we should wear cat bells or boots. But barefooted or in socks, he stands at the pantry eating the sultanas out of the breakfast cereal. Some movement of his hand might set a mousetrap off.

'We must set some rat traps too, you know,' my father says. 'They're eating the new season apples.'

'I know. Another half an apple was gone from the fruit bowl this morning. It's a cheeky bugger.'

I eye the ugliness of an oven mat Ann-Clare

crocheted and the spice rack I burnt a cactus design into. I should get around to throwing these things out. I'm sure Ann-Clare wouldn't really like that pair of very tarnished and very ugly copper enamel earrings to stay hanging on the wall in the back bathroom forever.

My father is getting old in small slow ways. I see it in how he never turns the taps off any more, and in how he asks me to turn on taps I've turned off. In how he scratches like an old dog.

'I think I hear Patricia.'

'Oooh, well, we'd better make a proper snack then.'

I feel full of information I can't tell my father. He is being nice to Grandma, saying how wonderful it has been for me to have at least one grandparent in my life. If ever I criticise Patricia, my father is likely to say that the same characteristics which made kikuyu such a desirable pasture grass also make it a weed.

'My poor old Mum,' he says. 'I did think, you know, of bringing her out here but I really worried. She would've been such a difficult handful to look after. I sort of worried she—I mean, I could never have left you girls in her charge. I would never know. She might have left you somewhere. I don't think she'd ever have hurt you. She wouldn't have hurt either of you but she might've just wandered away in a shop and left you.'

I murmur a noise in reply.

'Is Lavinia coming again tonight?' asks my father, quite eagerly, I think.

'I'm not sure. Probably.' Lavinia would be in her garden at Redclack. I think of her shadow, large and smooth, moving across and back to the washing line. Her cats would be watching. Always on Lavinia's washing line you can see her uniforms and dresses, drying in the wind. Every time a car goes by, the cats on her fence put up their faces. Lavinia's house is at a bend in a road following a deep descent, so there is not much chance of any visitor to the district seeing it before they're past.

'I don't think you take Ally to the park very much, you know,' my father says suddenly.

'Dad. I don't think we ever went to the park. No one's ever there, are they?' I defend myself.

'But my darling,' he says, 'you had your sister.'

After my father has made this comment about Ally and the day wears on, I feel the panic drifting in me. Maybe Ann-Clare turned out the way she was precisely because, even from that young age, sitting listening to the machines of housekeeping and to our mother's humming, she was learning to enjoy too fully the feeling of being invisible. Upon thinking this, I abandon all thoughts of further letter reading for the day and immediately put Ally's red going-out sandals on her feet.

At the park next to the North Lindley store, we do not have a happy time. Perhaps my sense of being watched conveys itself to Ally? Or is it simply that it's too barren for fun? The park is fenced in to the left of the store and some kind of deficiency in the soil keeps the grass white and dead. And although it's quite a large park, I follow—or do I lead?—Ally to the furtherest corner under its one tree, where we just stand for a while. Ally turns a few somersaults climbing up my legs and flicking over but I worry, as I always worry, that I don't quite get the timing of the flick right and that I will dislocate something. Then we look over to the slippery-dip and swings. There are green ants but neither of us get bitten.

'You'll come to Iris' birthday party, won't you, Ally?' I say.

Ally squats down next to a piece of concrete and pokes at the ants with a piece of grass and doesn't answer. Whenever Ally has come with me to Iris' place, Iris and Ally seem equally fascinated by each other.

'What are you going to get her for her birthday?' Ally asks.

I shrug. 'I don't know. Something to eat I think.' I don't want to look at the houses across the road too much in case I find someone looking back at me out of one of the windows. The houses are as motionless and bland as a bad painting: their utter banality echoed in the local artwork sometimes hanging on fencing hooks inside the store or in chunks of old rainforest timber forced to assume shapes that mock the immensity or beauty of the original tree. One such local craftsman made wooden boots. He died a few years ago yet the store still stocks the remaining boots. The girl at the counter tells tourists passing through that though the best of them are long sold, those that are left make excellent doorstops.

The red and green roundabout over in the other

corner of the park looks like the best fun but it turns out to be an old paddock irrigator.

I buy Ally a pale pink icecream on two sticks instead.

'What do you think a little old ninety-six-year-old lady would like for her birthday?' I ask my daughter.

'Something red?'

'That might be nice. These little jams? Here. You post my letter for me.'

Ally shoots my letter to Mary Shore into the old red slot in the side of the shop.

'We used to think that was the mailman's mouth,' I tell her, 'smiling for our letters.'

## CHAPTER SIXTEEN

Patricia leaves with my father the day of Iris' birthday party. No amount of cajoling from Ally has made Patricia change her ticket.

My grandmother is wearing a fur coat and white knee boots. 'In Saint Jean de Luz,' she says, 'a gypsy dancer kissed the toes of these. I had to pull him up from the floor. He was very charming. You know Avis you'll catch arthritis of the throat if you wrap your wet hair around like that.'

'It's not really very wet.'

'You'll get a terribly wrinkly old neck.' Then my grandmother's and Ally's farewell tears began to fall. I avert my eyes. I wish I wore glasses that would hide my own lack of them. My father has dressed as if for agriculture, in a faded safari suit. He says the car has warmed up. His beetles and Grandma's luggage are packed.

Patricia stretches up to hug me. I probably will never see her again. She's being more optimistic; telling me to bring Lavinia and Ally to London soon. Then she gives me another kiss and says it's for the lovely Lavinia.

'She was going to be here, Grandma. I don't know what the delay could be.'

'I think we'll have to go,' my father says. 'We'll drop in at Lavinia's on our way through Redclack.'

'I'm sure you'll see her on the road.'

Grandma says, 'I'll give good character to Australian nurses when I get back to the Tavern.'

The New House feels empty without Grandma. I go into Ann-Clare's bedroom to find Grandma has left all her whisky bottles in a line with a note around the neck of one suggesting that I might be able to use them for my art.

I try to phone Lavinia but the signal rings out. I've already posted a letter to London, with some photos of Ally, so Patricia has at least one personal letter at her flat when she arrives home. I scrunch up an everlasting flower.

Ally's face bears the remains of tears. 'I want to teach you something,' she says.

I'm turning aerial somersaults without using my hands, on the spare bed—an act of faith in my daughter's tumbling advice, when Lavinia arrives.

'Hello, Able,' Lavinia is out of uniform. I leap onto her hips monkey fashion. She snuffles her nose into my neck and I yelp it's so cold. Ally is leaping around too.

'I can't believe you missed saying goodbye to Patricia. I tried to make them wait but Jack was impatient. He's going to make a dung beetle drop somewhere along the way. Can't you imagine Patricia helping him release them?'

'I really did want to say goodbye.'

'Write to her. She'd like that. She'll take your letter into the Tavern with her and read it out to everyone.'

'She gave me this,' said Ally, holding up Grandma's bracelet of golden charms.

'Able,' says Lavinia.

'Yes?'

'Ally, you go to my truck and you'll find some iced buns still warm from the bakers.'

Ally takes off for the truck.

'Darling, I've just been over to Iris.'

'Were you taking some things over for the party? That reminds me, Iris wanted me to fill a few bags of manure for her garden.'

'I was. But she's not answering her door. And I can't see her through any of the windows.'

'She's probably sleeping in. I've noticed she is getting much sleepier. We can be talking away like anything and then suddenly she's out like a light.'

'No. I checked the bedroom window. I'm scared she might've had an accident in the bathroom. Do you want to come back with me?'

'What about Ally?'

'She could play in Iris' willow.'

Whenever people die it seems to be very late at night: Alana at midnight, her arms like little wings; two of Lavinia's ladies, both with the names of birds. Lavinia told me of their passing after waking me from deep middle-of-the-night sleep so that in the morning when I woke up I had no memory of their deaths. I had to be told all over again about Miss Finch who died when Lavinia was passing a soft bristled brush over her downy scalp or of Mrs Wren, the secret midnight smoker, smouldering to death in the cottage between the new shopping centre and the motor registry office.

Leaving Ally in Iris' back garden I climb in through the broken back window and then open the door for Lavinia. The house is dark and quiet. The pale green floribunda smothering the back verandah has only just been cut back but Iris' efforts are too late. A wilder kind of vine, more brown than green, has swallowed the trellis on the other side. A nightie hangs by one peg from a baling twine washing line. It might have been yellow but the shade has made green mosses grow in streaks down its length.

'I'm a mean, mean woman,' I can hear Ally singing Lavinia's song of the moment as we tiptoe down the corridor.

'Iris,' I call, 'Iris.'

The table is all set for the party. Every coaster and salt and pepper shaker Iris has ever owned have been put out and three vases full of vine flowers. On the magazine table is a pot of nail polish. The smell of it is fresh in the room. 'She must be in the bathroom,' says Lavinia and goes past.

I see Iris' toes first. She had been painting her toe-nails when something, some pain or particular joy, made her put down the bottle of pink polish and get onto her hands and knees.

Iris had curled up under the sitting room table to die. 'Like a little dog would do,' I say as Lavinia crouches down next to me.

'Under the table must have felt safe.'

'I think she wanted to get out of sight of her husband's portrait.' I look up at the face on the wall but as usual his eyes seem to be staring at corners.

Alf Little used to arrive at the cemeteries balancing his pick and spade over bicycle handlebars, but for Iris' grave he's behind the wheel of a backhoe. He was more proficient with his hand tools.

'Ooohhh,' he says, when the backhoe stalls. 'You little, you little ... wretch.'

I look over to my mother's Chimanimanis and there is a brown, still sky immediately over them, as if someone has mixed a bad wash and let it lie. When Lavinia swats a horse fly on my leg, she wants me to smell it. As always, from the bruised abdomen of a big ugly fly, comes the smell of honey.

'Iris was going to find all Ann-Clare's letters for me. I'll never see them now. Mr Michaelhouse will get them.'

'Well, you could ask him. You could tell him that Iris intended them for you.'

'It probably doesn't really matter. I'm going to give Alf a hand. He'll have dug up old Gus in a moment if he's not careful.'

When I see Mr Michaelhouse again, I know for sure, for a split instant, that Ann-Clare hasn't disappeared in Africa but has disappeared into me.

He reacts violently to the sisterly resemblance. Lavinia has been to the service in town and arrives in advance of the hearse. She's wearing an old mourning ring she bought for the alluring hair plaited under glass behind the black stone.

This isn't Mr Michaelhouse's first visit to the cemeteries since the marriage to Ann-Clare ended. Once or twice, during Alana's illness, Ann-Clare or I spotted him taking an uneasy walk through the graves. But never with Iris; her outings to the cemeteries never resumed after the end of her grandson's marriage.

Remembering Ann-Clare's old habit of warding off bad luck by touching her own wishbone, which she imagined lay underneath the human heart, I feel for my own. Above the height of your heart is no sound, only bone, although Lavinia assures me that the sternum vibrates to music.

Mr Michaelhouse tries to hug me anyway but I stand stiffly away from his arms as the feeling continues that he knew me when I was fifteen-and-a-half years old, before I bought my first small bra with the faded pink velvet padders.

When he undid the zip that ran underneath the left arm of my sister's school uniform to just above the left hip bone, he silently listed all the relevant dates leading up to World War I. As a strategy to curb his excitement, this always failed. Even as Archduke Ferdinand of Austria was assassinated in Sarajevo by the unstable Serbian youth, Mr Michaelhouse's hand was over my sister's, showing it what to do.

At this moment of seeing Mr Michaelhouse, and after all the letters I've read, it feels like *my* memory. Not something Ann-Clare once recounted to Mary Shore. I see he has had a partially successful hair transplant which makes him look like an old doll. An extraordinary patch of eczema has also bloomed, half-crossing his face. His self-consciousness about his hair manifests itself immediately in a series of small hand gestures.

'Please,' he says, a plastic bag rattling in his hand, 'Avis, stand with us.'

I see his small sons waiting. I know their faces from all the photographs on Iris' dresser. They are staring at Ally. The woman isn't really facing our way but still I can gather that she's totally different from my sister. She has a hand on each well-dressed boy's shoulder, as if to replicate a royal photo. I wonder what she does and doesn't know. Is she a letter writer too? Does he tie her up and take photos?

'For all flesh is as grass, and all the glory of man as the flower of grass. The grass withereth, and the flower thereof falleth away,' says the religious man.

Apart from the Michaelhouse family we are the only others at the burial. *Ryncheletrum repens*. A day after you pick a piece of that grass and leave it to mark your place in a book or letter, the flowers turn white-mauve. The grass stays as soft as plumage but the deep crimsony pinks have vanished.

The coffin is so small they could be burying a child. Iris has ended up being in an aisle grave.

'Hold on to your hat, Iris,' says Lavinia, as the coffin bearers slip.

I look into the heart of a very pretty weed. It's dark green with mauve and gold radiations. About a fortnight after my sister's memorial service, someone left a figtree at the gate by the letterbox. Ann-Clare's name had been written in marker pen onto a triangular piece of plastic embedded in the potting mix. The tag explained that a special process had contorted the trunk of the sapling into the circle and that with normal care, the tree would continue to grow like this forever to remind you of your absent loved one. The Forget-Me-Knot fig died as it was always destined to die. Neither my father nor I deliberately killed it, but one day I saw all its leaves were gone and when I hooked my finger into the remembrance knot, the whole plant came out of the soil with dusty little roots.

Mr Michaelhouse is crying.

His letters asking my sister to still be his wife—I have read them all. They were glued over with flowers that served as messages: a bit of wattle next to Wattle I do if you never return. Or Forget-Me-Not flowers of the rich blue variety, without the sticky seeds, which Ann-Clare had propagated in drifts around the office at the turkey farm. The flowers next to Iris' grave are her namesake ones, unopened and as pointed as sharpened pencils.

'I must admit,' Lavinia whispers once it is over, 'he doesn't look like an ogre.'

'Exactly,' I say. 'The monster husbands are often plump and innocent and romantic about flowers. I'm going to ask him where Sarah, the Aboriginal woman was buried. I still haven't found the spot.'

Mr Michaelhouse has left the grave and is running after me. He moves with the long, awkward style of a lank moondaisy. The plastic bag rustles as he runs.

'Here,' he says. 'Ann-Clare's letters. Lavinia said you'd like them. They were on Iris' bed.'

'Will you show us where Sarah's grave is?'

'Didn't Ann-Clare ever show you?'

I shake my head. 'Over here.' He dives through the barbed-wire fence and gets caught on a spoke. Lavinia frees him.

As he walks in front of me I watch his neck. It is thin in diameter yet folds with at least four creases of fat. He pulls at some tough grasses and kicks at the soil underneath. 'Nanna used to bring a flower for her. For all those years, until your sister left me. Then she'd never visit again.'

As he shifts the ground with his boot, I begin to see a compass made of local stone, carved with the initials north, south, east and west. Michaelhouse's gin, I read.

'My grandfather apparently used to keep her out in the forest. Used to take her provisions. Nanna always wished she could have been buried under the stone compass, instead of next to Gus.'

'Who are you writing to?' asks Ally. 'It's raining outside.'

'Past your bedtime,' I say.

'Lavinia's reading me a book.'

'All right then.'

'Who are you writing to?'

'Someone I've been meaning to write to for ages,' *All our lives*, I write, to my sister,

... *drawn to people who reminded us of each other:*

*towards skin that could keep its scars for years which in my experience, goes with women whose memories are sharp and unremitting, who can for instance recall the exact pattern of shade cast by silky oaks in their childhood garden though they are now stumps on which grand nieces play King of the Castle.*

The ticking of the water hammer in the house. Lavinia must be having a shower. The house shudders the way a ship does. You hear how people respond to certain pieces of music by describing the tears that form in their eyes, as if grief is the most significant response of all to life. It is and it isn't like this with Lavinia. And she both does and doesn't remind me of Ann-Clare.

Mary Shore's reply has told me nothing except that I have been looking to the wrong correspondent for answers. The letter is written on the familiar airmail paper. The handwriting moves steadily away from the left-hand edge, forming its own slanting margin. 'I'm sorry not to be able to throw any light at all, but I never received any letters from Ann-Clare in Africa. I haven't any of her letters to pass on to you because at one stage she asked me to send them back, which I duly did.'

No hidden meanings in this bare, neatly printed script.

My sister wrote her last letter to Iris. The little letter in Iris' pillow case. When I find it among all the others Mr Michaelhouse has given me, I recognise it immediately by the coffee stains on the envelope.

If I laid out every page of every letter I've read

across windless land, they would cover acres of ground. Then if a wind came up that would selectively blow away all the pages I've already forgotten, I'd be left staring at a piebald stretch of ground, more paddock than words, which the grasses would quickly fill. The tall Australian grasses of the Lindley Plateau and the introduced grasses from east Africa; corridors of *Rynchelytrum repens*, their smell slightly spicy on a hot day and horse flies the size of my thumbnail drifting through them, hoping to find a creature to bite.

I sit at my mother's desk and all the read letters sit in the shadows to the left. I've tried to fasten each lid but some boxes are frail and letters or envelopes with exotic stamps gape out.

I finger the cloth of my shirt underneath the dressing-gown. The shirt is blue viyella, its cuffs soft, frayed. The pattern features fish and palm trees. I can still smell faintly an old clothes shop, as if that second-hand scent can never be washed out of a piece of clothing that has been abandoned. It is the same smell that used to line the pockets of the Romance Library smock.

The smocks were commissioned by Marguerite for reasons of dust and thrift, from Mrs Love, one of the borrowers who'd been a seamstress. Mrs Love preferred crime to romance and would scoot around the shelves, tugging behind her a small tin barrow of the kind usually for gardening refuse, into which she'd throw her books. The smock was unbearably itchy in summer but Marguerite insisted we wear them on Mrs Love's days. Mrs Love was a speed reader which meant the smocks were inescapable on Mondays and Fridays. If ever I'd run into her as I went up and down the rows reshelving, she'd start with fright, the purple polyester swirls and red pockets too much in the afternoon light, even for their creator.

The satisfying crackle of some of the letters! As if my fingers have been fire. I remember the sensation of some of Alana's old mail—all her energies and anxieties on roller-coasters of blue ink. The lightness of an individual letter, I think. The weight of them when they are all gathered together.

I hear Lavinia switch out the bedside light, but still I write. Even when we're sleeping in different houses, my arms are apart and soft as if they're enfolding Lavinia.

Every now and then I notice something around me. I notice I'm curved over my pen in Maurice Smith's old diamond-patterned dressing-gown. I screw up my face to calculate the depth my wrinkles will one day reach. My handwriting is neat—how can it contain so many cluttered images? But they begin to reach the page nonetheless and once read back feel rather precise and cold.

I look at a photo of Alana behind glass my father still likes to have on the wall. She looks alive and poised and for a while we stare at each other. I look at Lotho, draped by Lavinia and Ally in hats and scarves in unusual and witty places. I quite like Lotho these days. Lavinia's equally enamoured. Lotho, she says, must definitely make the move to Redclack too.

Viyella and flannelette fold an instant warmth

around your skin and seem able pull tenderness from out of your bones. They are generous and homely cloths, in the way of a pudding. In all the local church shops, the run on flannelette shirts and pyjamas has begun, but more come in with the first wave of winter deaths.

When I leave the letter for a moment to get something from the kitchen, I sometimes see, leaping from behind the graves, what must be the light from trucks on a highway, as if the sun is gulping up three hours too early, only to subside.

I tell my sister little things and big things. The order isn't important. How whenever I try to imagine the waterfall she reached, it never resembles the one I walked to with Ben Jussab, Rosemary and my father. The waterfall that continues in my mind to be Ann-Clare's is one that couldn't exist: the water flowing over the top of a totally smooth rock and turning a sharp corner. Ann-Clare is sitting on the wet ledge, overlooking the strange waters. I tell her the songs of the magpies are altered. There's something different I'm sure about magpies calling when it's cold. It's why Lavinia likes to sing out there: the air is thinner and all sounds that pass through it must grow purer.

Ally, I write, tells me to make the air in the shower warmer and I do, holding my arms out around her. I write four pages about Ally alone, describing how she was years before. How even as a baby she used to creep, first in circles then in a line. As a five year old she had her last sip of my milk. That her ankles are twigs.

For so long my need was to have my little sister as my audience but now I confess, I have become hers, unwittingly, reading everything, even though her need to stay hidden was always so strong.

I can feel how strong my desire to end the watching is now. It's late, Ann-Clare, and Lavinia's waiting. I'm trying to find the right moment to go. I say how high is my general anticipation. At Lavinia's cottage in Redclack, instead of our father listening for the fifth time for the news to come on the radio, there will be Lavinia, listening to bits of *Rigoletto*. The house at Redclack is old and loved. It has mild dark air. In summer jumbo jet hornets mesmerise her cats, flying from the goose pond to the eaves of the back shed.

I tell my sister that something unexpected has happened. That Mr Michaelhouse has given me her letters to Iris. That they are here with me. That I have found Ann-Clare's last letter from the Chimanimani Mountains, posted by Rosemary Kincaid to Mrs Iris Michaelhouse after all. Not Mary Shore.

At first it is a letter about glass. The letter is stained in places with the coffee. Iris must have kept it under her pillow as she told me, for here is a fine wispy hair.

In the letter Ann-Clare is telling Iris about a garden birdbath she has thought of making. During Ann-Clare's early years of marriage to Mr Michaelhouse, when she still went on expeditions with him in search of old house wells and bottles, she used to put fragments of glass into her pocket. She collected them almost absent-mindedly, for no reason at first except to put them on a pile on her desk or in arrangements on the window sill; liking to see the morning sun reproducing the indigo-coloured light that may once have spun across some long ago room. In the letter to Iris, though, she describes how she planned to turn all the bits of glass into a birdbath or a garden fountain, its cavity an intricate mosaic of female faces. Although she would've made the mosaic along classical lines, the faces she planned were invariably those of interesting but old Australian women, their faces a wreckage from the assault of the sun.

In my sister's sunbath, when visitors bent to wash their faces, they'd watch with mixed feelings the water settling back to reveal a face that rather than the anticipated angels could easily have been that of their Australian nanna or auntie or ancient second cousin removed. In her sunbath, wrote my sister, she'd planned to put the faces of Iris and Olive. Sarah.

*But it was only a dream. The fountain won't get made. I tried but I couldn't. I'm not coming back from Africa, Iris. I am not coming home. It's hard to explain the reasons for this. I wish we could still write to each other but tomorrow I'm going to walk to a waterfall. It isn't very far away and I should reach it in half a day. Not like your sister Olive, but like my grandmother. Like Betty. I'm not coming back.*

The hush of mail arrived and read years before. I try to explain now to my sister, my mistakes. I try to find the words, under my moving pen.

In choosing to reject her masochistic tendencies, in choosing to die, I realise how unwittingly my sister then became the person inflicting pain. Every time I pull my boots on and off. Every time I tie Ally's laces. And my acceptance of the pain.

Less concrete feelings too. How difficult it is to have discovered that for all the stories I've told Lavinia about our sisterly love, that there were things it was easier for Ann-Clare to tell other kinds of people, even an old lady like Iris.

I can hear the waterfall clapping at the bottom of the farm. The waterfall at night sounds like applause, Alana used to say, a whole river of applause coming up from the valley after a spectacle so lavish the listeners didn't want the evening to end. There are only a few letters left, like the last scattered claps still heard as some people are leaving. I don't expect them to take long. There is Rosemary's spiral letter, to read properly.

*There were things Ann-Clare told me about Benjamin Jussab. Sad things. If only he hadn't come with your father and you into the mountains. If only I'd been braver. Ann-Clare reminded me of certain women I met when I was in the South African hospital system. The kind of young woman who could die because she doesn't like herself enough, so she sets out seeking a situation or a man who will treat her badly, who will act in her life like a terminator. Ben Jussab was like that in Ann-Clare's life. Drinking was something of their link. When they were drunk, he used to hurt her.*

*She was so calm, Avis, the day she told me that. She asked him to hurt her.*

I turn the letter around and around in my hands.

What I wish to know is at what point a piece of paper smells old. Really, I'd like an explanation for the sweetness of certain old papers, the sour scent of others. Is it dust, dead paper mites, dried tears of pleasure or sadness—or more to do with the colour and kind of ink and paper used? Ann-Clare used to hoard old paper. She had a blank piece from Betty's writing case that she loved for its age. Rosemary's letter has been scattered with rose oil, as if the scent could help convey the hard truth.

I remember watching my sister showing Rosemary how a black kitten would automatically go into suckle mode. The kitten they had taken was my one, with the white whiskers and three white paws. They sat companionably outside the Abandoned House with their backs against the cool chimney, making my kitten purr. It hadn't taken much for my sister to suggest to Rosemary Kincaid that the kitten was hungry. It was December and they were both wearing summer dresses. My kitten was kneading my sister's leg with its small claws. The father cat must've had quite a lot of Persian in it because my kitten was of the rather fluffy type. After Ann-Clare had demonstrated the trick, and Rose had agreed how nice it felt, they fed the kitten real milk, using a toy baby bottle. First Ann-Clare held the kitten, then Rosemary Kincaid. When Rosemary lifted up her dress again, Ann-Clare said that the colour of her hair growing there was like the straw in *Rumpelstiltskin* which could be spun into gold.

I crept round to the other side of the house then and called out. The kitten was back with her mother when Ann-Clare and Rosemary answered me. They must have run fast. Then we all did, as if there was a wind behind us, into the first small valley together, past old bits of cow skulls, the wanderer butterflies of late afternoon and the red and yellow milkweeds they liked to hover over. We leant over the last water trough on our land, looking for snails and our own reflections. The sense of Ann-Clare's betrayal burned deeply, even as I swished my hand gently through the water. It burned for years, preventing communication with Rosemary Kincaid, hastening my desire for Ben Jussab.

When I realise I'm going to cry, I try at first to stop myself. I blink, seeking distractions. I feel how an old lady must, crying in public with nobody left in the world to care whether she stops, dies or sleeps. The tears spring out of the ducts in the corner of my eyes as if out of a fountain which has been dry for centuries. If I were to dip a brush in them, I'd paint with rusty salt water. I cry for the thought of Iris crawling under her table and for Poor Sarah, between cemeteries, her surname already lost. I am crying for my sister who thought she had to hide everything from me, even her death.

I pick up my pen to sign off the last letter to Ann-Clare with love and Lavinia's nickname for me. Though there's nowhere to post my letter, I put it in an envelope and cover it with airmail stickers. I think I'll put it in a book of fairytales. I think I'll burn it. I think it doesn't matter, death and disappearance receding in my mind, after all, the way grasses do in winter. Probably the letters should go over to the old house, where the mist will bend the papers first up and then down; the mildew will grow, making strange new words between the old ones before obliterating in time, all the words, sticking the pages together as surely as glue. At the Romance Library, Marguerite used to move through the makeshift archives with a can of insect spray twice a year as if that could halt the deterioration.

The coals in the fire tinkle like fine glass as I hold out my letter.

After sitting in front of the fire a while, I decide that it is time I bring out my Little Animal Gardens. Ally will be very excited. It is as if they are brand new. I set them out in pairs until they are wending their way almost around the entire room, through the legs of chairs; a whole herd of baby elephants and up on the mantelpiece every black gorilla with red eyes and lips I ever collected.

I can hear it's going to keep raining as the sound of the early morning air creeps up the valleys. The sound is as smooth as the river mist above small waterfalls of the Lindley River. It's as strange and silent as millipedes curling from under stone. The rain's getting into the Abandoned House much more than it used to. The gutters and water pipes are full of dirt. Ann-Clare would be surprised. We thought it would last forever.

As I walk around the old house, I sometimes see her surprise. In the reflections of shrubs and shadows held in certain broken windows, my sister's face is framed by the two bunches of hair she wore before I cut them off. The bunches are always an uneven thickness and the parting down the middle deviates and winds. Or one bunch has come undone, hiding most of her face, while the other has a starved waist where it is held by a perished rubber band. The bunches hang by the side of my sister's face like thin curtains tied back from the window on a nail. I can never see her eyes. I walk towards the windows, wanting to touch her long neck to feel for tears, and it is only my face I find or the shape of a tree root in glass, grown into the figure of a woman hiding her head. The window begins to glow as the sky changes colour and everything shifts. I look through that part of a window missing glass and it serves as a jagged, unromantic frame to the farm.

There are many broken windows but it's the roofing iron letting in shadows of the stinging tree forest and bigger creatures than before, who carry with them bigger seeds. The mattress that once grew grasses grows three trees now, the kapok fibres turning mysteriously to soil, the roof above the seedlings peeling back to allow the light to reach right into their small stinging leaves.